THE SCOT'S SECRET LOVE

Sisters of Ember Hall
Book 1

Elizabeth Heights

ARE YOU SIGNED UP FOR DRAGONBLADE'S BLOG?

You'll get the latest news and information on exclusive giveaways, exclusive excerpts, coming releases, sales, free books, cover reveals and more.

Check out our complete list of authors, too!

No spam, no junk. That's a promise!

Sign Up Here

www.dragonbladepublishing.com

Dearest Reader;

Thank you for your support of a small press. At Dragonblade Publishing, we strive to bring you the highest quality Historical Romance from some of the best authors in the business. Without your support, there is no 'us', so we sincerely hope you adore these stories and find some new favorite authors along the way.

Happy Reading!

CEO, Dragonblade Publishing

Additional Dragonblade books by Author Elizabeth Heights

Sisters of Ember Hall Series
The Scot's Secret Love (Book 1)

The Earls of the North Series
Gambling with the Earl (Book 1)
Forced to Marry the Earl (Book 2)
Taming the Earl (Book 3)

PROLOGUE

Year of our Lord 1322

THE DAY OF the yuletide hunt dawned clear and bright, but a sharp frost covered the grounds at Wolvesley Castle. Peering out from her tower window, Frida clenched her teeth together in frustration.

Aye, the view was beautiful. It looked almost as if someone had tossed her mother's jewels over the front lawns which shimmered and sparkled in the sunlight. But the icy paths would be treacherous underfoot.

She would not be permitted to ride out.

Frida shook her head, long blonde hair flying our behind her. She was twenty years of age. And mayhap soon to be a married woman! Why did she need the permission of her parents to ride her own horse over lands she had known all her life?

At once, the voice of reason spoke in her head.

Because your horse is young and inexperienced and you have never taken him out in a group.

Because your father has forbidden it.

Frida rolled her eyes. The voice of reason sounded exactly like her father's ward, Mirabel, who was Frida's closest friend. Mirrie was never short of reasons why Frida should be sensible.

Usually, she was willing enough to listen to that voice. But just this once, Frida wanted to throw sensibility to the wind. She might never get a better chance to impress the tall, handsome knight with the flashing dark eyes.

Her brother's friend. *Sir Callum Baine.*

Just thinking of his name sent pinpricks of excitement down her spine. They had danced together last night and she had hoped the music would play on forever. When they withdrew to the fireside to talk, she didn't look over his shoulder for the chance to escape, as was her wont on such occasions. Instead, she gazed into his beautiful eyes and thought that she finally understood what people meant when they talked of their heart skipping a beat.

Frida's heart had been fluttering like a bird in a cage ever since he lowered his lips to the back of her hand. The realisation had been instantaneous.

This is the man I am meant to marry.

She could see it all, laid out before her. His hand, holding hers. Her head resting on his muscular shoulders. They would spend their lives together.

This was no young girl's fancy, for Frida had been blessed with the Sight since birth.

Aye, *blessed*, for that was how she saw it.

She knew that was not a view everyone would share. Some might say her gift was truly a curse. For her mother, it was a constant source of anxiety. But Frida had grown up protected by her family's wealth and status, with no cause to fret over what others might make of her keen insights and vivid visions. She was Lady Frida de Neville, with her father's golden good looks and her mother's adept sensitivities.

The future was hers for the taking, and this was the moment she would stake her claim.

Swearing her young maid to secrecy, she stepped into a snugly fitting woollen kirtle and covered her shoulders with a soft grey cloak. Usually, the de Nevilles wore their family colours to the hunt, but Frida knew she would be spotted instantly in her traditional heavily embroidered emerald green ensemble.

With her hood pulled over her ears, it was easy enough to sneak down the stairs and lose herself in the melange of men, young and old, dressed and ready for a day's hunting. As was customary, the de Nevilles had invited many friends and family members to join them for the yuletide celebrations. Today, their numbers were swelled even further by the addition of local farmers who accepted goblets of punch from waiting servants in the marbled entrance hall. The tempting aroma of freshly baked-bread wafted from the great hall, where so many were breaking their fast. Frida's stomach rumbled, but she knew it would be unwise to linger. Her brother Tristan was circulating amongst their guests, his blonde head easy for her to spot for even at nineteen years of age, he towered above his peers.

But not above Callum.

A small, betraying gasp escaped her lips as she sighted him. His cloak was of deepest blue and the morning sunlight, filtering through the open doorway, haloed his dark hair so he shone even brighter than her golden-hued family. Tristan and Callum chatted amongst a small circle of young knights. As Frida watched, they raised their goblets in a rowdy toast to good fortune at the hunt.

And nearby stood her father, the Earl of Wolvesley, still a tall and charismatic man despite his advancing years. Avoiding his sharp gaze would be a complex undertaking. Frida put her head down and snuck out of the hall, making a beeline for the stable yard.

No one would be charged with saddling Silver, her high-stepping dapple-grey. But that was no bother for Frida, who was as at home in the stables as she was dancing in the great hall.

She spoke to the horse softly as she tacked him up, slipping the bridle over his ears and fastening the girth as tight as it would go.

Her father had oft told the tale of his older brother, Lucan, who had died in his prime from a simple fall in the stable yard. A senseless death caused by nothing more than a poorly fastened girth. Frida gritted her teeth as she tucked in the leather straps. Family history would not be repeated today.

When she was sure that enough hunters had mounted and were circulating the yard that she would draw no notice, she led out Silver. Young and keen, he looked about him with pricked ears.

"We're going to have a good run," she whispered to him, rubbing at the soft fur beneath his mane and quelling a sudden sense of fear. Even the cobbled courtyard was slippery. What would the fields be like? Or the land near the river which often flooded at the time of year? She bit down on her lip, doubting for the first time the wisdom of her decision.

It was not too late to return Silver to his stable and creep back into the house.

But when she raised her head, her eyes met those she had been seeking since he first arrived at Wolvesley.

Callum stood just feet away, holding the reins of a large chestnut horse, but looking only at her. His lips parted in greeting, but Frida silenced him with a subtle shake of her head.

Her lips curved into a smile as she put a finger to them, indicating the need for secrecy.

Callum's answering grin made her stomach churn with excitement. He nodded his understanding and turned to join his friends, but after a few steps he turned again to find her and waved his hand in the smallest of signals.

It was as if they had joined together in a conspiracy against all others.

Frida's worries were no more. She led Silver to the mounting block and sprang into the saddle, not allowing herself to fret when the horse slid over a small patch of ice.

"Steady there boy," she said, her voice calm.

Her father sounded the horn and excitement fairly rippled through the assembled riders. Horses flung their heads up and down, jostling for position in the circular yard. And then they were off, trotting at a fair pace down the lane. Frida held Silver back on a tight rein, knowing she must stay near the back of the pack to avoid being seen. It was her intention to urge him forwards once the hunt was underway and it was too late for her to turn back. Then she could ride beside Callum, as she so fervently desired.

But she saw immediately that her plan was unnecessary, for Callum was also holding back his horse. His eyes burned into hers as he rode up next to her, so close their knees brushed together.

"Good morn, Lady Frida." He nodded his head, his breath pluming in the cold air.

"Good morn, Sir Callum." She was relieved that her voice came out firm and strong.

They were obliged to proceed in single file through an open gate. Callum's horse went side-stepping, clearly desirous to break free of Callum's restraining hold and gallop with his stablemates. But Callum held him easily, his hands light, his voice soothing.

A natural rider, Frida thought. Her mother had long-since instilled in her the importance of treating horses with respect. She thought her admiration for Callum could go no higher. Astride the majestic horse, he was dazzling in the sharp sunlight.

So striking was he that Frida had eyes for nothing else, not even where her own horse was heading. She had not seen the sheer expanse of black ice at the other side of the gate. The ice which had been so skilfully avoided by everyone else. Forsooth, she was still gazing at the muscular expanse of Callum's shoulders when Silver went down. She had only time for the slightest cry of surprise before her head hit the ground and everything turned black.

CHAPTER ONE

Year of our Lord 1324

F RIDA IGNORED THE pain in her newly chapped knuckles as she plunged her hands into a pitcher of cold water. Any expression of discomfort would lead to Agnes shooing her from the kitchen. And Frida didn't want that.

She was determined to prove that an earl's daughter could fend for herself.

Agnes was a woman of few words. If she thought it odd that Lady Frida de Neville insisted on scrubbing her own vegetables, she kept quiet about it.

Gritting her teeth, Frida rinsed the last of the turnips and placed them to dry near the window. At the other end of the room, Agnes leaned over the long, scrubbed table, her long greying plait swinging over one shoulder as she rolled out pastry for a tart. Despite the early-morning chill, Frida enjoyed these times in the kitchen, with sunlight dappling across the plastered walls and glinting off the copper pots and pans. But today had dawned extra chilly, and the big fire beneath the roasting spit had not been lit long enough to generate much warmth.

Frida dried her hands on her apron, trying not to shiver.

"What shall I do next?" She made her voice light.

Agnes looked up from her work and gave her a rare smile. "You can go and warm yourself in the great hall. At least until this fire takes hold."

"I do not feel cold," Frida lied.

"Then milady had best depart now. For soon it will be hotter than hell in here."

Frida schooled her face into an expression of mildness. She was growing accustomed to her cook's plain speaking, even though no servants in Wolvesley Castle had ever spoken to her so boldly. But she was no longer a pampered lady in her parents' grand home. She was many miles north at Ember Hall; mistress of all she surveyed and determined to display no weakness.

"If the temperature rises to such an extent, you must summon my brother. He is forever complaining of the bitter chill in this house."

Agnes let out a bark of laughter. "I'll do that." Her nut-brown eyes lingered on Frida's before returning to her perfectly rolled pastry. "Lord Jonah seems to miss his home comforts."

"I do not know why he has come," Frida found herself confessing. "His injury is little more than a scratch and Wolvesley does not lack healers. I can only think that my father wanted him out of the way to better conduct the business of finding a husband for my sister, Lady Isabella."

Agnes's thin lips pressed together, mayhap to repress her smile. "I've been a widow for longer than I was married, but the ways of men remain constant. Lord Jonah most likely thought you'd greet him with open arms, eager for his council and guidance. You and Miss Mirrie being—" she hesitated.

"Mere women?" Frida supplied.

"Exactly that." Agnes began placing neat rounds of sugared apple onto the pastry.

Frida folded her hands together, preventing her hands forming into fists. How she would love to stride out of the kitchen and demand the truth from her younger brother. Alas, they were no longer children squabbling in the school room. She must at least make the appearance of decorum; especially as she and Mirrie had so recently taken up residence at Ember Hall.

Especially as the servants were already gossiping.

Instead of giving voice to the angry tirade buzzing around her head, she sighed heavily. "You and I both know how much can be achieved by women, Agnes."

"Aye. True enough." Agnes cut a decorative pastry leaf and positioned it with a steady hand. "If we can withstand the pain and blood of childbirth, we can withstand anything."

Frida smiled to hide her shock. As an unmarried woman, she was unused to hearing tales of childbirth. Indeed, as the eldest child of the Earl of Wolvesley, there was much she was unused to hearing. But times had changed and so had Frida's position in English society. Not so long ago, she had been a sought-after prize: a cossetted and fragile flower. Now she was a self-proclaimed spinster; no longer looking to a man to provide for her future, but shaping it herself.

This was the life she had chosen.

Nay, this was the life she had fought for.

She would not allow her sour-faced younger brother to spoil her plans.

Jonah had arrived a sennight earlier, claiming that Frida's healing skills and the peace of Ember Hall would aid his recovery from a slight sword wound gained in training. Frida had been sympathetic at first, but her patience was growing thin. Not least because compassionate Mirrie was running herself in circles tending to his every whim; abandoning her own duties and pleasures in the process.

Frida and Mirrie had come to Ember Hall to live a life free of men, not to serve one.

Mirrie chose that exact moment to stumble in from outside, mist clinging to the ends of her light brown hair. She was wrapped in a faded shawl and over her arm she carried a wicker basket filled with herbs.

"It is like a winter's day out there," she exclaimed.

"Go and stand by the fire," instructed Frida, taking the basket from her.

"Miss Mirabel." Agnes nodded respectfully. "Shall I warm you some ale?"

"Nay please, do not trouble yourself." Mirrie held her narrow fingers out towards the tentative flames.

"What were you doing out at such an early hour?" Frida frowned, noting how her friend shivered despite her heavy shawl and proximity to the fire.

"Picking mint leaves." Mirrie flashed her a small smile. "For Jonah," she added.

Frida shook her head. "Mint is for an open wound and Jonah's scratch had closed e'en before he arrived here." She spoke severely but regretted it when Mirrie's kind eyes clouded over. "'Tis comfrey we need, for the bruising."

"I should have known." Mirrie bit down on her bottom lip. "I will go out again."

"You will do no such thing." Frida placed the basket on the table and took her arm. "You need to get warm and dry before thinking of my brother."

"But I don't mind," Mirrie protested.

Frida couldn't help a lurch of jealousy. Mirrie was her father's ward and had grown up beside the five de Neville siblings. Although Frida and Mirrie shared a very dear friendship, she had always suspected the bond between Jonah and Mirrie was equally strong.

Although the cynic in Frida knew that Mirrie was a compassionate soul. And Jonah had long since learned how to work that to his advantage.

"Let us go to the great hall. The fire there was lit before dawn," she said, evenly. When Mirrie looked to say more, Frida spoke over her. "Do not fret, Mirrie. I shall go out myself and find some comfrey for Jonah." She glanced at Agnes. "I'll take the mint to the store and dry it when I return."

"Very good, milady."

Arm-in-arm, Frida and Mirrie walked slowly along the stone-flagged passageway from the kitchen and emerged into the heat and light of the great hall. Two fires blazed from hearths situated at each end of a wood-panelled wall, while opposite a series of high, narrow windows invited golden light to slant across the polished wooden floor. Although large and ornate, the great hall at Ember was welcoming and somehow cosy. Frida nudged a tapestried chair closer to the nearest fire and waved Mirrie into it, ignoring the burning pain in her ankle.

"Can I fetch you anything?"

"Nay." Mirrie sank back into the chair and stretched out her slender arms to the blaze. "Thank you, Frida." She paused. "Do not feel you have to stay."

Better than anyone, Mirrie knew how Frida hated to be still. Sitting by the fire on a day when there were jobs to be done would be a torment to her. E'en now, Frida itched to be moving. But at the same time, she was reluctant to leave her friend's side.

One question plagued her, this morn more so than usual. Did Mirrie regret coming here?

Mirrie rarely complained, but Frida thought her good-natured friend had struggled to settle here in the northern hills. She openly admitted to missing the colour and gaiety of Wolvesley Castle, and the whirlwind of social engagements therein. But that wasn't the whole of it. Something else tugged at Mirrie's heartstrings; Frida felt it in her bones. Whatever it was—and Frida had a strong suspicion it was intrinsically linked to her eldest brother, Tristan—the arrival of Jonah, complete with greetings and tales from their childhood home, had stirred it all up again.

Frida would never forgive Jonah if he ruined this new arrangement. Her father had been reluctant to permit the two of them to take up residence in Ember Hall. He would never allow Frida to continue living here if Mirrie returned to Wolvesley.

"Frida?" Mirrie spoke quietly, jolting Frida from her reverie. She had been gazing into the hypnotic depths of the fire, lost in thought.

"Sorry." Frida came back to herself with a little shake. "Is there something else you'd like me to fetch for you?"

"There's nothing I need. I shall be quite myself in another moment or two." Her small hand briefly laid over Frida's. "You mustn't fret so."

"Are you happy here?" Frida blurted out.

Mirrie's eyebrows rose in surprise. "Of course."

"Even though it is cold and the work is never done?" Frida ploughed on. "There are no parties and I know how you love to dance." Her gaze flickered down to the polished expanse of wood beneath their booted feet. The hall would be plenty big enough for a dance, if they should choose to hold one.

Mirrie was young and pretty, with bright hazel eyes and heart-shaped lips that were quick to smile. Loyalty to her friend should not force her to miss out on the life that Frida had chosen to leave behind.

Mirrie smiled in return, although there was a sadness in it. "You are kind to speak of parties and dancing, when we both know that a young woman past twenty with an insignificant dowry to her name can hardly expect a choice of dancing partners."

Frida opened her mouth to protest, but Mirrie held up a hand to silence her. This was so out of character that Frida's words dried on her tongue.

"Your whole family has always been kind. Ever since my parents passed away. There has been no barrier between us. Tristan and Jonah are like brothers to me. You, Isabella and Esme are as sisters. But in truth, I am *not* one of you." A log cracked in the fire, as if giving emphasis to her words.

"You are," Frida said, staunchly.

"Nay, I am not," Mirrie persisted. "Truly, the day you asked me to accompany you to live a quiet life in Ember Hall was a blessing to me."

Silence fell between them, broken only by the crackling fire and a faint rattle of wind blowing down the chimney. Frida wanted to believe her, but back then she had been so intent on getting her way that she had never stopped to consider why Mirrie had agreed to her wild proposal so quickly.

"Truly?"

Mirrie nodded, sincerity shining from her eyes. "I had no wish to stand in the shadows, watching the rest of you marry and move on, leaving me as a burden to your parents."

"You would never be a burden," Frida cried out, her denial ringing up to the rafters of the hall. A hound dozing by the fire opened one eye and thumped his tail upon the wooden floor.

Mirrie inclined her head. "They would never say such a thing, I know. But isn't it better this way? You and I can live useful lives. On our own terms."

Frida's heart lifted. "That is exactly what I want."

"And I too." Mirrie squeezed her hand again. "Though I will say this. My options have always been limited. But you are Lady Frida de Neville."

Frida snorted. "You mean that men want me for my father's coin?" She screwed up her face to show her disdain for the notion.

Mirrie leaned closer. "I mean that you carry a great name as well as a great fortune. You are clever and beautiful and gifted." Frida snorted again, but Mirrie would not be dissuaded from her course. "'Tis true, your dancing days may be over, but your future is still bright with possibility. Should you ever decide to return to Wolvesley—"

"I never will."

"You must do what is right for you," Mirrie concluded softly.

"I never will return," Frida repeated. "This is my life now. I will work hard and do whatever I must to ensure the good fortune of the estate. But I shall never marry." She cleared her throat. "I mean it, Mirrie."

Mirrie sat back in the tapestried chair. "Forgive me, Frida. I will not speak of this again."

Frida nodded, not trusting herself to speak until the tight bars of tension in her chest eased. "I will go and gather some comfrey for my dear brother." Her last words were laced with sarcasm, which Mirrie acknowledged with a lifted eyebrow.

"You are not enjoying Jonah's company?"

"I am not enjoying his constant demands for attention."

"He is afflicted," Mirrie began.

"And we have all sympathised." Frida's voice rose higher. "I am sure the days are not easy for anyone born with a wasted leg. But Jonah has many blessings, which he declines to count."

Mirrie looked down at her hands. "He has always lived in Tristan's shadow."

"Then he should go and stand somewhere else," Frida retorted. She folded her arms, rigid with annoyance. "I too know what it is to live with pain."

"You bear it bravely." Her friend's words were softly delivered and Frida felt some of the fight draining out of her.

"I bear it because I have no choice. And because I do not believe that anyone else should be made miserable by it."

Mirrie's mouth twitched. "Jonah does not have your strong will."

"Aye, well." Wind rattled down the chimney and Frida waved away a plume of smoke that billowed towards them. "He will have to strengthen his will if he wishes to remain here long."

"Mayhap that is why God brought him to this beautiful place? So that he can learn to appreciate all that he has, rather than all he has not?"

Muffled, slightly uneven footsteps from the gallery above heralded the imminent arrival of Jonah, the object of their discussion. Whether he was sent to them by God or not, Frida was in no mood to converse with him just now.

She bent down to whisper in Mirrie's ear. "If that is so, let us hope that he learns his lessons quickly."

With a wink to acknowledge Mirrie's hastily repressed smile, Frida swept from the hall as gracefully as her ankle would allow. Her stride shortened as she reached the vaulted kitchen, where Agnes was studding the day's meat with thin slivers of freshly-cut garlic.

"Jonah is up and about," she announced.

Agnes nodded. "He'll be wanting a tray to break his fast."

Frida took a deep breath and tasted smoke from the sputtering fire. "He will have to serve himself, like the rest of us. Don't wait on him, Agnes."

The old woman straightened up, her palms pressing against the small of her back. "Are those your orders, milady?"

"Those are my orders." Frida grinned, suddenly carefree. She snatched up Mirrie's basket from the table. "Is there anything you need from the herb garden?"

"Anything that this cold spell hasn't already killed off you mean?" Agnes thought for a moment. "Rosemary, if any can be found."

"I will dry whatever is left." Frida plucked her cloak from a peg near the doorway. "Is it customary for the temperature to fall so low before Michaelmas?"

"Aye, winter comes upon us early this far north. That is why the farmers couldn't welcome you and Miss Mirabel when you first arrived. They were busy with the harvest."

"There is still the orchard crop to bring in." Frida tied her cloak tightly with the basket hanging off her elbow, regretting once again the impulse that had driven her to declare she would see to the orchard crop herself.

"Mayhap you will need extra help?"

Frida grimaced. It seemed every day they moved further from her dream of a quiet, self-sufficient life. "I shall consider it."

She nodded farewell and stepped out into the mist, squinting to make out the squat shapes of the wattle-and-daub barns across the courtyard. Beyond those, silent figures moved atop the high battlements which her father had insisted on building around the outer edge of Ember Hall. When Frida protested against fortifications in a home that had never been attacked, Angus, her father, had been quick to point out their proximity to the troubled Scottish border. And the vulnerability of two women making a home without a father or husband's protection. His message was clear; if Frida did not agree to guards and a constant look-out at Ember Hall, then she would stay at Wolvesley where he could keep her safe.

Frida had reluctantly agreed, even though the presence of the guards interrupted the peace and healing she had hoped to find in her mother's ancestral home. They were protected by more than mere weaponry up here, amidst rolling hills and woodlands. As a child, Frida had been able to feel the tangible pull of energy around the ancient standing stones nearby. She knew, deep in her bones, that Ember Hall was a place of safety. These soldiers, with their sharpened swords and heavy booted feet, disturbed the tranquillity.

But Frida knew enough about compromise to give up railing against those things she could not change. She had grown used to the guards now. Had even learned their names.

She pulled her cloak about her and walked through the mist to the small store where she kept her herbs and medicines. The pungent scent of dried sage calmed her thoughts as she tied the mint into small bunches and strung them from the ceiling. A quick glance at her orderly shelves confirmed they were well stocked; aside from the comfrey which she would go and gather. Frida breathed deeply; the herb store was evidence she could act with order and purpose, even while everything seemed to be spiralling out of her control.

Nay, not everything, she corrected herself. She should not allow her younger brother to distress her so.

A smile flickered across her face as she remembered the secret nickname she and Tristan had once used for Jonah. *The Scowler.* It was still apt.

Frida carefully closed the door of the store and set off towards the herb garden, before abruptly changing course and walking with new purpose towards the standing stones. Mayhap there she would be able to think more clearly.

Two winters ago, she might have run. Certainly she would have lengthened her stride and revelled in her youth and strength. Now it took all of that same strength to walk at a moderate pace without limping. And when her foot twisted on a sharp stone, she couldn't help a yelp of pain.

Hot tears filled her eyes and she allowed them to fall, knowing that she was unlikely to be observed.

Once a day, and no more, Frida allowed her carefully controlled emotions to surface.

But on this morn, the combination of salty tears and heavy mist was disorienting and she had to stop and look about her to recover her bearings. Thankfully, the way to the standing stones was as familiar as the back of her hand. She had been drawn to them ever since her parents first brought her to Ember Hall at the age of seven. Frida gazed from left to right until she made out the familiar crooked tree which marked the start of the faint rabbit path she must follow. Half-way up the hill was where she usually paused to glance at the sparkling waves breaking onto the small cove below, but today she could not see that far. All about her was quiet and still, suspended in the mist. Frida was the only thing that moved; her breathing the only sound in her ears. Her pulse picked up speed. Mayhap the magic was coming back to her?

Not real magic, the kind that could cast spells and enchantments. But the magic Frida had grown up with: an energy which helped her sense the future and feel connected to the world, both past and present. Losing her Sight had been like losing a limb. It troubled her more than her damaged ankle; more than she would ever tell. No one would understand anyway. This feeling of not being whole wasn't something she could easily explain.

Frida dashed away her tears. She had jibed at Jonah's self-pity and now was indulging in the same.

Seven tall granite stones loomed out of the mist towards her. On a sunny day, these stones exuded a golden hue, but now they were shrouded in white.

White. The colour of my fall.

Gritting her teeth, Frida stepped towards the nearest stone and placed a hand on its rough surface. Years earlier, her whole being could sense the vibrating energy emanating from the ancient site. Standing here she had felt both powerful and humbled; part of something far bigger than herself.

Now, she was just a tired woman touching a cold stone.

Her connection to the spiritual world had been severed.

She hung her head forward, allowing the surge of grief to pass. Her thick white hair fell forward like a cascading waterfall. Impossible to ignore.

Frida had never been vain. Since childhood, she'd known that her sister, Isabella, was the beauty in the family. Consequently, the loss of her honey-blonde curls struck Frida as more of an inconvenience than a tragedy. But there were times when she mourned their loss. Times when the whiteness of her hair stood as a symbol for the colour that had gone from her life, ever since her accident.

My fall.

She always thought of it as her fall. Because accidents were, well, accidental. And with the benefit of hindsight, Frida could see that her own actions had set that terrible sequence of events in motion.

She had been blinded by love. Or by something. For a man she hardly knew.

Sir Callum Baine. A friend of Tristan's. Just the thought of his name was enough to set her heart fluttering. Even now, when she had sworn to live her life free of men.

All men.

But most especially that one.

Wiping away her tears, she straightened her shoulders and tucked her wilful hair back behind her ears. She should tie it in a plait and hide it beneath a bonnet—both for propriety's sake and to save herself the embarrassment of curious stares. But out here, Frida knew she was unlikely to be stared out by anything other than a frightened rabbit. And moreover, she baulked at moulding herself to society's whims. Hadn't she moved to Ember Hall to get away from such rules and restrictions?

Aye. She had moved here for peace. And because Ember Hall was where she had always been most content, comfortable and able to be freely herself. None of that had changed; even though her ankle ached and her senses remained stubbornly ill-attuned to the spiritual.

Frida breathed deeply, dispelling her loss and grief; determined to be positive. Though her ankle pained her, she could still walk. She had the chance of a new, happy life and she was determined to grasp it.

Life. She had so nearly lost it with one fall from her spirited horse. For three days she had lain unconscious, while her devastated parents summoned the best physicians and barber surgeons in the land to Wolvesley Castle. They had shaved off her hair, perforated her skull, applied healing unguents and prayed on their knees. When the sun began to set on the third day, the healers had all but given up, but then her eyes had opened. Eyes that were still bright and cornflower blue, even though her hair, when it grew back, had changed from gold to white.

All she needed now was peace and time.

Time to make peace with what had happened.

Frida smoothed down her skirts and straightened her cloak. She would return to the litany of tasks which now formed the fabric of her days at Ember Hall. Quiet, predictable days which she cherished.

"Frida, come quickly."

The shout came through the mist like an arrow. Frida whirled around to see Mirrie running up the hill towards her; her brown hair flying and her grey shawl gaping over her shoulders.

Mirrie who should be tucked up by the fire, keeping warm.

"Whatever is it?" she cried, walking as quickly as she could to greet her.

"Come quickly," Mirrie repeated, gasping for breath. "A band of warriors have been spotted. And they're coming straight for Ember Hall."

CHAPTER TWO

THE AIR SMELLED different in England.

Mayhap because it was not laced with the scent of blood and despair.

Not yet anyway, Callum reflected, giving his tiring horse a loose rein as they trotted up yet another hill. The landscape here was all rolling hills and woodland. On a different day, the view might have lifted his heart. But he had not yet become so immune to violence that he could approach this particular mission with anything other than gravitas.

Besides which, the fog was so heavy it was difficult to see any further than the brown tips of his horse's ears. But as they approached the summit, the mist thinned, allowing him to take stock of the whereabouts of his small band of men.

Up ahead was Gregor. Thick-necked, strong-headed and silent. They had met just days earlier; Gregor delivering the encoded parchment to Callum at what remained of Kielder Castle, a twitch in his jaw indicating his displeasure at having to wait for Callum to break the seal. It was clear from the off that Gregor wanted sole charge of this mission—to be the man giving the orders and the man swinging the sword.

Beside him, riding so close that occasionally their knees knocked together, was young Arlo; a farmer's lad he had known since birth. Arlo had seen fewer than seventeen summers. He was brave and honest, but not yet as strong as he would one day become.

God willing he would live that long.

Bringing up the rear was Andrew. His friend. A warrior. A lover of women. A teller of tales.

Callum would trust Andrew with his life.

He would not, however, trust him to stay quiet for any length of time. Right now, Andrew was singing a bawdy song about an inn-keeper's wife that made even Callum's reluctant lips twitch into a smile. They had been riding long and hard. Mayhap they needed some cheer.

Callum flicked his eyes down to the youthful face of his companion. Fair-skinned Arlo was turning the colour of beetroot as Andrew's lyrics floated through the wispy mist towards them.

He cleared his throat. "If you've changed your mind..." he began.

Arlo's response was swift. "I haven't."

"'Tis a bloody business, assassinating a man in his own home." Callum saw no sense in softening his words.

"He deserves it. They all deserve it." Arlo's voice broke and sympathy tugged at Callum's heavily barricaded heart. The lad had seen both his parents cut down during the siege of Kielder Castle; Callum's ancestral home on his father's side.

"You're not wrong, lad," he muttered.

Ahead of them, Gregor swivelled in his saddle. "What's this? Are we to take them all out?"

"Nay." Callum's voice came out in a growl. "Then we would be no better than they are."

Gregor shrugged his muscular shoulders. A warrior through and through, he wore his heavy mail shirt as if it weighed nothing. "The English have taken our lands, our women, our children. Everything. And ye ask me to stay my hand?"

"Not I," Callum corrected, resisting the urge to trot up alongside him. "Our orders come directly from the Bruce."

Gregor's response was unintelligible, but Callum knew that for now, at least, he had won.

Evoking the Bruce's name usually had that effect.

The party fell into silence as they rode into the trees; the only sound the steady clop of muffled hoofbeats and occasional lowing from cattle in distant fields.

"Will ye make us ride much further before we slake our thirst? My horse is parched." Andrew pushed his dapple-grey mare into the narrow gap between Callum and Arlo.

"Methinks 'tis you that is parched," Callum replied drily, ducking his head beneath a low-hanging branch. "And it is not much further. If my sources are accurate, the house we seek is on the other side of this hill."

"Ye should know, lad. Being half sassenach yourself."

"My mother was born in England. That does not mean I know every inch of it." Callum shrugged.

That was not the full truth.

In truth, Callum's childhood home lay not far from here. But that was not information he wished to divulge at present.

"And ye learned how to swing your sword in Lindum." Andrew gestured towards the gleaming hilt of Callum's sword, resting at his hip. "Alongside those English knights that now lay siege to Scotland." His horse skittered around a clump of gorse and Andrew gathered up his reins, grinning at Callum to show he spoke in jest.

Andrew and Callum had fought side-by-side in the highlands for more years than Callum cared to count. His friend knew where his loyalties lay. But that wasn't true for all their party.

"Are you going to recount all of my life story? Mayhap for the benefit of Gregor here, who is the only one that doesn't know it?" Callum's voice carried an edge, for he could see by the set of his shoulders that the man ahead was listening.

Callum's parentage was no secret. If anything, the opposite was true. His English birth and education meant he could mix seamlessly with the most important noble families in the realm. He was the perfect spy for Robert the Bruce.

"All that matters is we take our revenge," Arlo spoke up

fervently. His calm cob was plodding steadily along the farm track, but every inch of the youth's body was braced for battle.

An ice-cold warning trickled down Callum's spine.

"What matters is that my heart beats for Scotland," he proclaimed, kicking his warhorse into a canter so he could go ahead of Gregor then swivel round to face all three men. "All our hearts beat for Scotland, am I right?" His horse shied, uncertain of the woodland shadows, but Callum kept his seat easily.

"Aye," shouted Andrew.

"Our orders are to assassinate the English lord who has recently returned to this place. 'Tis a blessing for us we have not had to travel far from the border. And a further blessing that we are not tasked with taking innocent lives."

His men silently nodded, not yet convinced.

"This man is powerful. A danger to Scotland. If we take him out, our people will be able to sleep easier in their beds. Is that not what we all want?"

"Aye," they muttered.

"Who is he?" demanded Gregor.

"The house is Ember Hall." Callum spoke from memory, keeping his voice level. The parchment containing their scant orders had been burned as soon as he digested its contents. Upon seeing the scribbled words some days earlier, his heart had leapt in his chest, for Ember Hall was situated not many miles distant from his childhood home. He recalled an attractive manor house, slowly falling to ruin. It had stood empty for as long as he was a boy, and was likely to remain so given its unfortunate position so close to the turbulent borderlands. Some minor noble must have purchased it for little more than a song.

Or been gifted it by the King in thanks for services rendered in Scotland.

"I mean, what is the man's name?" Gregor's horse pawed at the ground as if sensing his impatience.

Callum shook his head. "We do not have it." Even Andrew looked aggrieved with that answer, but Callum shrugged again.

"There is nothing of note in that. You all know the situation we are in. The less we know, the less we can tell if captured." He paused to allow them to think this over. "We have been riding since before dawn. What say you to resting here awhile? We know not what will be waiting at the other side of the hill."

"Aye." Andrew agreed immediately, swinging one leg over his saddle and landing heavily on the ground. "Ye dinnae need to ask me twice."

Hiding a relieved smile, Callum also dismounted and led his horse over to a small clearing. Rummaging in his saddlebags, he found bread, dried meat and two skins of ale which he passed around. The tension that had been rising between them started to abate as they ate and drank, although Callum could still feel Gregor's eyes boring into him. It was no surprise when the older man edged closer and spoke up.

"Is this your first mission for the Bruce?"

Callum wiped his mouth with the back of his hand. "Nay," he answered shortly, unwilling to speak more on the subject.

And even less willing to tilt his head upwards in recognition of Gregor's height.

Gregor stood half a head taller than he, but Callum fancied that youth would be on his side in a fight, should the man turn nasty. Callum's hair was thick and dark, his tanned face largely unlined. While Gregor's forehead was creased with frown lines and his thinning hair threaded through with grey.

"I have served him since he was little more than a lad." Gregor stated this as a challenge, his sharply articulated words given emphasis by the dense walls of fog all around them.

Callum nodded mildly. "My father's family has long been closely allied to him."

Gregor's face relaxed a little. "Yer father is the Laird of Kielder?"

"He is."

"Rory Baine?"

Callum kept his expression neutral. "The same." Damp air

settled upon him like an unwanted blanket and for a moment, he felt smothered.

"A fine warrior." Gregor took a swig of ale.

"Aye." Callum had no wish to speak of his father either. Why had he urged them to stop and dismount? Why had he allowed this conversation to begin? When would this infernal mist pass and allow him to see clearly?

Gregor slapped him on the shoulder. It was a friendly gesture, but the force of it still made Callum stagger forward. "I'm happy to ride alongside any son of Rory Baine."

Callum's inner beast raged at this. It was not Gregor's place to decide if he was happy with his orders or who he shared them with; it was only for him to follow them without question. But aloud he said, "I am glad to hear it."

Andrew had clearly been following this exchange closely, even as he pretended to check over his horse. He now guffawed loudly and came forward to join them, his booted feet crunching through an early fall of leaves.

"I'll say any man should be happy to ride behind Callum Baine," he declared. "I know of no other warrior so skilled with a sword." He jostled his friend's arm good-naturedly. "They taught him well in Lindum."

Callum decided to go along with the joke. "Aye. I heeded my lessons well."

Gregor folded his muscular arms over his mail shirt. "And what of the men you trained beside? How is it to meet them in battle?"

"It has ne'er happened," Callum answered truthfully. "But I am sure the day will come. Methinks this is a burden we all must carry in these troubled times. Our friend of one day can become our foe the next." Callum curled his fingers around the carved hilt of his sword, both reassuring himself that it was still there, and reminding his almost-adversary of the same.

Gregor grunted. "True enough." But Callum saw that doubt still flickered in his dark eyes.

Andrew pulled off his gauntlet to scratch at his unruly locks of red hair. "Do not doubt the man for the way he speaks. It is an affliction he bears for the good of us all."

Callum's flash of displeasure faded as he saw Gregor's mouth twitch and he spoke up before the moment of levity passed. "'Tis true. I cannot help my English accent. No more than I can help the size of my fist." He clenched and unclenched his large hands reflexively.

"Or the size of anything else." Andrew choked on a mouthful of bread whilst laughing at his own witticism. He spat a shower of crumbs on the soft earth as Arlo hurriedly slapped him on the back.

"I have ne'er had any complaints in that area, friend," Callum grinned. "Are we done here?" It would be best to get going before Gregor could ask any further questions.

The men finished what remained of their food and mounted again; their joviality seeping away as the reality of the task ahead took hold. Callum was pleased to wrap his long legs around his horse's flanks and trot ahead of the men. Their conversation had unnerved him, stirring up memories he would rather forget.

He had spoken the truth. This was not his first mission as a spy for Robert the Bruce. But what he hadn't told Gregor was that he had failed his first—and only other—mission.

It was not a fact he wanted known, for the shame of it still nagged at him. But not for the reason anyone might expect.

Callum had willingly accepted those first orders: to infiltrate the mighty de Neville family, headed by the Earl of Wolvesley, one of the richest and most powerful men in England. Callum could see no harm in living the life of luxury for a while.

Plus, the mission had quietened his father.

Recently returned to his ancestral home in the highlands after the death of his English wife, Rory Baine had been growing increasingly vocal in his demands for his only son to prove himself a true Scot.

Wolvesley Castle had seemed like a good place to start.

Callum had remembered Tristan de Neville from the knights' training academy in Lindum. Although Tristan was two years his junior, tales of his horsemanship, sword skills and accuracy in the joust were impossible to escape. Callum grew to resent Lord Tristan and all he represented about the English aristocracy. The man was entitled and arrogant. Callum would not mind at all being first in line to watch him fall.

At least, that was what he thought at first.

Callum's mouth pressed into a firm line as he ducked under some low-hanging branches, momentarily lost in the swirl of sorrowful memories.

It was one of the Lindum instructors who had secured Callum's invitation to Wolvesley. Even then, the Bruce's connections ran deep. Callum had cared little for the assignment—until the assignment changed from infiltration to assassination. That was the first thing to give him pause. He was not, by nature, a violent man. And Tristan had committed no crime other than to be born a wealthy Englishman.

But worse was still to come. When he arrived at Wolvesley, Callum found a half-starved hound pup shivering in the stable yard. A dog-lover from birth, Callum had determined to hide the hound away and nurse him back to health. But it seemed nothing escaped the eagle eyes of Lord Tristan. And nor was any animal beneath his attention. When next Callum came across the hound, it was being bottle-fed by Tristan himself. The earl's son had even spread a stall with fresh straw so the pup had somewhere warm to curl up.

Callum knew then that he would fail in his duties. He could not kill Tristan de Neville. His only hope was to satisfy the Bruce with some injurious information about Wolvesley.

And then he met Tristan's sister.

Callum closed his eyes at the clutch of pain that still assaulted him whenever he thought of Frida de Neville.

For little more than a sennight he had lived entirely for those moments when he glimpsed her feasting in the great hall, or taking a turn in the gardens, wrapped in a cherry-red cloak. Her golden blonde hair and beautiful smile began to haunt his dreams, until he doubted his ability to take any tales to Scotland that might prove her family's undoing.

Then came the time their eyes met over the banqueting table. And the glorious evening he dared to ask her to dance at the yuletide ball. When their hands first touched, he knew that he could never betray her. And when they withdrew to the fireside for a conversation that flowed more readily than the wine, his heart brimmed with the possibility of something he had rarely known.

Love.

Beneath him, his horse stumbled and Callum came back to himself, shortening the reins and adjusting his seat in the saddle. Gregor would never accept his leadership if he fell from his horse before they even reached their destination.

Andrew rode up alongside him. "Are ye all right?"

"Aye," Callum answered shortly, part of him still grieving for the past.

"Yer not vexed at me for what I said back there?" Andrew jerked his head backwards. "I was only trying to lighten the mood."

"And I thank you for it." Callum flashed his old comrade a genuine smile.

"Ye seem lost in thought."

Callum sighed, too weary to prevaricate. "Two winters past, I left this land vowing to work only for peace between England and Scotland. The lass I loved was dead. Her family in mourning. The last thing I wanted was to move against them. Your man back there, he had a point about facing men in battle that you once trained with." Now it was Callum's turn to jerk his head back towards Gregor.

"I recall you came back to Kielder ready to lay down your sword." Andrew's eyes were solemn. "I could understand it. Though it made your father furious."

"Aye." Callum thought of the scar across his ribs, placed there by his own father's blade.

"But the English cannot be allowed to raze our lands as they please." Andrew's voice became agitated.

"Exactly that. They have all but destroyed my home. Killed many I hold dear." He glanced back towards Arlo, who had watched both his mother and father die in the most recent raid. Callum steadied his breathing. "And so here we are. Ready to wreak our revenge."

As he spoke the words, they emerged out of the woodland into a small clearing. Beyond them, he could discern smoking chimneys and a great wall built of local granite stone. Diminutive figures cloaked in green strode along the top of the wall, making Callum's heart sink.

"Ember Hall is both fortified and guarded," he said in surprise, remembering too late that he had claimed to be unfamiliar with these lands.

"It changes naught," declared Gregor. "I am ready to take down any number of English guards."

"And I have no intention of turning this into a massacre," retorted Callum. His mind's eye conjured the pile of bloodied and broken bodies piled beside the curtain wall of Kielder Castle. Pushing the memory away, he ploughed on before the challenge in Gregor's eyes could be articulated. "As Andrew said earlier, my English accent is an asset to us in times like this." He paused for emphasis. "Leave the talking to me."

"So we continue with our plan to assassinate the English lord?" Arlo chewed nervously on his bottom lip.

"To the last. But stay behind me and follow my lead."

In a single line, they trotted down a winding track which skirted the perimeter of Ember Hall. Glancing up, Callum saw an elegant stone-built manor, four-square and strong. Mullioned windows looked out onto sweeping fields. Aside from the guards, it looked to be a place of peace and welcome. His heart lurched at the devastation they were about to bring upon it; but he could not allow recent events to go unpunished. The English would pay for what they had done to his home and his people.

Hardening his heart, Callum held out a hand to slow his men to a walk as they rounded the corner and approached the main gate. A liveried guard stood waiting for them beneath the archway, one hand on the hilt of his sword. Callum's eyes lingered on the golden standard emblazoned on the man's tunic. Something snagged at his memory, but there was no time for him to consider it.

"Halt," the guard commanded. "Who goes there?"

Callum dismounted and tossed his horse's reins to Andrew, who caught them neatly.

"Stay there," he muttered, not waiting to see if his men agreed.

Straightening his own cloak, he walked the few paces to the gate and bowed his head. "I wish to see the lord of the house."

"State your business to me first." The guard stood firm, hooded eyes boring straight into Callum's.

Callum remained calm. "My business is with the lord of the house."

A sudden flurry to the right drew his eyes to a tall, slim young woman hurrying towards them. She was clothed in a serviceable woollen shawl, her light brown hair escaping from beneath its folds.

She stopped some distance away and dropped into a short curtsy. "May I ask your name, sir?"

She spoke too well to be a servant, yet was not dressed as fine as a lady.

"I am Sir Callum Baine."

He was confident that his father's name would not be known in these parts, but the lady's hazel eyes opened wider.

"Sir Callum Baine," she repeated, more loudly than he thought necessary.

Was this a trap?

"Aye." He widened his stance. He could reach his sword in

less than a second. "I am of Egremont House," he added, evoking his mother's ancestral home. The place where he grew up. The house his father had wrenched him from within days of his mother's death.

The lady nodded, as nervous as a rabbit. "I am Miss Mirabel Duval."

God's bones. Why did he know that name?

There was too much here not adding up. Callum swung his gaze around to his men, reassuring himself of their presence. The mist had closed in around them, giving him a strong sense of being all alone.

She straightened her spine. "There is no lord here for you to speak to. But I will carry a message to my lady."

Her words made no sense to him. Callum repeated them stupidly. "No lord?"

"No lord." Mirabel was emphatic. She folded her arms about herself, holding the shawl closed.

Callum cleared his throat, grappling with the blow of all his carefully laid plans unravelling. "May I speak directly with your lady?"

"She is not at home."

It was a lie. He could tell by the strain in her voice and the anxious darting of her eyes.

"That is most unfortunate." Callum glanced towards the guard, stood just feet away and closely watching their exchange. If Callum made any attempt to enter the gate, he could tell that he would have a sword pointed at his chest within moments. He looked back towards Mirabel. "When do you expect her to return?"

"I do not," Mirabel protested, her voice scarcely carrying through the mist.

Callum took a small step towards her. One more question and she would cave, he was sure of it.

But before he could frame that question, all capacity for rational thought deserted him. His mouth gaped open as an ethereal figure appeared behind Mirabel, walking steadily towards him as gracefully as a swan gliding across a lake.

Her figure was tall and slim. Her face angelic, framed with cascading hair that was whiter than winter.

Her hair had changed colour, but he would know those piercing blue eyes anywhere. They had once looked up into his, bright with laughter. He had held her hand and not wanted to let it go.

Is she real? Or am I haunted by an apparition?

His mouth went dry. Blood roared in his ears.

This was Frida de Neville.

His deceased love.

CHAPTER THREE

*I*T IS HIM.

The man she wanted to see least in all the world.

And he had recognised her, she was sure of it.

Frida stood tall, ignoring the chill wind whipping through her uncovered hair. She should have pulled up her hood. Nay, she should have run back to the kitchen and bolted the door behind her.

"I am the lady of the house," she declared. "You can state your business to me."

Callum was just as she remembered him, although she had never before seen him clad in chain mail. He stood taller than most men; taller than Tristan, she would wager. And his shoulders were broad and strong. At first glance, he was a man you might depend on, lean on.

But appearances could be deceptive.

Right now, Callum appeared quite unsteady on his booted feet. His dark eyes had grown wide with fear. Frida didn't understand why, but she allowed herself to enjoy the jolt of power it gave her.

"How may we assist you, sir?" she said, after several seconds of silence had passed.

He looked her up and down, surprise and wonder darting across his rugged face.

"You are Frida de Neville," he declared, his voice little more than a croak.

She lifted her chin higher. "That is correct."

He staggered backwards and she saw his men, still mounted on horseback behind him, exchange worried glances. A biting gust of wind wrapped Callum's midnight blue cloak around him, covering his armour. For a moment, he stood before her as a man, not a knight.

"Are you unwell, sir?" she asked, her voice carrying through the mist.

He took a deep breath before offering her a courtly bow. "Forgive me, my lady. We have ridden long and hard to reach you."

She allowed a beat to fall. "And why have you done that?"

He straightened and she found her gaze rising with him. Their eyes clashed and a frisson passed through her.

A frisson that she would pay no heed to.

"Perchance you do not remember me, my lady? I am a friend of your brother, Lord Tristan."

Aye, she remembered him. Stolen glances across a hall strung with mighty boughs of pine. A dance that she'd hoped would never end. An ill-advised hunt that had changed her life forever.

She would give all the coin she had if it meant she could forget him.

Beside her, Mirrie was all but trembling with anxiety. Frida wanted to send her away, lest she said something that spoiled her charade of nonchalance. But to do so would only alert suspicion. And part of her drew comfort from Mirrie's presence.

"My brother Tristan has many friends," she answered steadily, folding her arms across her cloak. If only she had dressed in expectation of visitors. In expectation of *him*.

Frida pushed the thought away, angry at herself. Why should she spare a thought to her appearance? And what did it matter what she wore when her very soul had changed beyond recognition? The Frida who had danced with Callum beneath festive greenery, breathless with anticipation and the heady scent of pine, was a different person to the woman she was now.

White-haired, weary, limping.

"I once visited your family at Wolvesley Castle for the yuletide celebrations," he said, surprising her. Sudden vulnerability showed in his rugged face, as if he wanted her to remember him.

Aye, she remembered him.

But she was not ready to abandon all her carefully-crafted defences and admit it.

Although that flash of humanity in his eyes had stirred something she'd long since buried deep inside her heart.

"I lose track of the knights who have visited Wolvesley, sir. My parents enjoy company."

He swallowed, his muscular chest rising and falling beneath the folds of his blue cloak. Had her sharp words wounded him?

"I'm afraid Tristan is not here. Nor is he expected to be. There is only my youngest brother, Jonah; mayhap you are acquainted with him?"

Why had she said that? It was nerves that made her chatter on so. Nerves that grew tighter with every second that passed.

Indecision raced across his face, but then his expression closed and became unreadable.

"I met Lord Jonah at Wolvesley, of course." His mouth tightened. "He is a poet, is he not?"

Frida allowed herself a short laugh. "A poet one day, a painter the next. A struggling artist of all kinds. Most unlike Tristan, who lives only for the thrill of battle."

Callum nodded his head. "It was Tristan who sent me."

Beside her, Mirrie let out a small sound of either excitement or distress. Frida shot her a warning look.

"Tristan? How so?"

Callum glanced back towards his men, seeming to steel himself. "To offer protection, my lady, against growing unrest on the border." When she raised her eyebrows quizzically, he continued. "Our spies tell us that Robert the Bruce plans to strengthen his position against the English."

Mirrie put a hand to her heart and turned anxiously towards her. "This is grave news."

But Frida shook her head impatiently. "'Tis unnecessary caution. You see we are already well-defended, sir." She gestured to the high fortifications and the uniformed guards.

Callum, however, did not back down. "Tristan did not believe it unnecessary. In fact, he urged me to ride with all possible haste."

Frida's stomach twisted as she sensed the situation slipping beyond her control. She could not, in good conscience, turn away a man who had been ordered here by her brother. But neither could she countenance *this* man staying.

Her lips tightened at the thought of Tristan sending soldiers to her home without so much as a hastily-penned message to notify her of his intentions. 'Twas a high-handed move, even for her brother.

Indecision swirled in her gut. And Frida was not usually indecisive.

For better or worse, Mirrie took charge of the situation. "You must come in and take some refreshments. You and your men."

Callum bowed. "That is most kind."

Frida's breath caught in her throat at the prospect of Callum Baine stepping into her sanctuary.

Defiantly, she remained in his path. "Do not feel you have to stay, sir, out of courtesy." To Mirrie, she said, "Mayhap Sir Callum would prefer to be on his way. 'Tis a long ride back to Egremont House."

Immediately she berated herself for revealing this proof that she had been listening so attentively.

"I would much appreciate the chance to eat and drink away from this wind," he contradicted her, standing so close she could catch his scent.

Horses, leather and something indescribably male.

Her heart jumped in her chest. "It would not be wise of me to invite four armed men into our home," she said tautly.

She expected a denial, but Callum paused as if considering her words. "Nay, indeed." He inclined his head. "My men will be pleased to take shelter anywhere."

Mirrie clucked her tongue. "The barn roof is damaged. But if they will be happy to eat in the dining chamber used by the guards, I will take them there."

Frida took her elbow and led her a few paces away. "Have you taken leave of your senses?" she whispered furiously.

Mirrie's hazel eyes widened with surprise. "How so?"

"We do not know these men."

"But Tristan sent them," said Mirrie, as if that fact alone was the most important. "And you do know Callum, as do I. We both recognised him straight away."

A flush threatened to creep up Frida's neck. "I do not wish to be alone with him."

"But Jonah is inside." To Mirrie, it was very simple. "And I will be along presently."

Frida couldn't ignore a deep sense of foreboding. "Take Matthew with you," she ordered, nodding to the guard who had first intercepted Callum.

"Very well."

With a regal wave of her hand, Mirrie beckoned the three men in through the gates. She and Mathew then led them towards the stables, where two young stableboys waited to take the horses.

Leaving Frida alone with Callum.

He cleared his throat, momentarily looking as discomfited as she felt. But then the shutters came down on his face again.

Enough. They could not stand here staring at one another.

Frida turned on her heel and began walking towards the hall. Callum hurried to catch up with her.

"Your hospitality is greatly appreciated, Lady Frida."

"Call me Frida," she said impatiently. "You will find we do not stand on ceremony here, Sir Callum. Nor do we offer such a grand welcome as you are perchance accustomed to."

"If I am to call you Frida, then you must call me Callum."

As if driven by the same impulse, they both slowed and glanced at the other. Again, Frida felt a traitorous blush creeping over her cheeks.

"I am a man of simple pleasures," he muttered. "I expect no grand welcome."

Frida's throat tightened. "I am glad to hear it." She quickened her pace, ignoring the biting pain of her ankle and abandoning any attempts to disguise her limp. She must get inside, away from Callum, as soon as possible. They were approaching the side of the house and chickens scurried from their path. Soon they would be in sight of the big windows of the great hall. Frida thought that she might never again be so pleased to catch a glimpse of Jonah.

But Callum had other ideas, catching at her arm whilst they were still in the shadows.

"Forgive me," he said, pulling her around to face him. "I mean you no harm."

Frida tried to pull herself free. "Unhand me then, sir, this instant."

He did so, his breathing jagged and his stubbled cheeks mottled with red. "'Tis only that I may not get this opportunity again."

Blood rushed to Frida's ears. She should walk away, but her feet were rooted to the soft earth beneath her. Mist covered them like a blanket, but Frida was far from cold. She was flushed and anxious and more alive than she had been in years.

Two years, to be exact.

"You are Frida de Neville," he said, wonderingly. "You are alive."

This was so close to what Frida had been thinking that a smile chased at her lips.

"I am alive," she confirmed.

"I thought you were dead."

His words landed heavily between them. Frida gave a short intake of breath, digesting this.

"I saw you fall from your horse," he continued, his voice little more than a whisper. "Saw you carried into the castle." His face creased with pain and Frida fought the compulsion to put a hand to his cheek.

"I did not die," she said, steadily.

He shook his head as if to dislodge a long-held belief. "I have grieved you." His dark brown eyes bore into hers.

Frida did her best to keep her memories of that time far away, but now she remembered waking on the third day to find her family in tears of joy. No one, bar her mother, had believed she would survive.

She narrowed her eyes. "Yet you left Wolvesley without waiting to see if I lived or died?"

She should not have said that. It was as good as an admission that she remembered the time they had spent together—and she was not willing to make herself so vulnerable. But Callum did not appear to have noticed.

"I did not wish to intrude upon your family at such a time."

It might be a reasonable sentiment, but all the same, it was not one that her heart was prepared to accept. If the feelings between them had been truly sincere, he would have stayed.

Frida pulled herself together. She was in danger of falling under his spell all over again.

"Of course, you were right to do so. I believe most of our yuletide guests did the same."

Her words put a barrier between them. She knew he felt it as strongly as she.

"Let us go inside," she continued, turning from him without waiting for his response.

It took all of Frida's self-control not to break into a run. She needed to be alone. She needed space and air to calm her thoughts. But instead she led the way to the arched front door and pushed it open. The scent of home was a comfort; lavender from the rushes on the floor and woodsmoke from the fire. The entrance hall was small and narrow, set with wooden panelling.

Frida could sense Callum gazing about him, taking it all in, but she didn't pause. Together, they walked quickly beneath a blazing wall torch and emerged into the great hall.

There, praise be, was Jonah.

Her brother was sitting in the tapestried chair earlier used by Mirrie. He had pulled it even closer to the fire and an abandoned tray of soft cheese, cold meat and freshly-baked bread rested on the wooden floor beside him.

"Sister," he greeted her, without rising. "And a friend."

Frida swallowed her stab of impatience. "Jonah, you will remember Sir Callum Baine?"

Callum gave a small bow while Jonah's cool gaze raked him up and down. Her youngest brother had inherited the de Neville colouring of fair hair and blue eyes. He may not have the height and strength of their father, but he was as skilled with a sword as their brother Tristan.

A skill that not many people expected of him.

Jonah had been born with a club foot and a penchant for poetry. From an early age, he had learned to embrace the differences between himself and his siblings. Less was expected from him, meaning he was largely free to do as he pleased.

Only Frida and Tristan saw their brother clearly. Others cosseted and indulged him, including their usually clear-headed mother.

A rare smile transformed Jonah's pinched face. "I do indeed remember Sir Callum Baine." He rose to his feet and extended his hand, which Callum took politely. "You are most welcome, sir."

Frida bristled. It was not Jonah's place to welcome anyone to her home.

"He will take refreshments with us." Frida pulled on the rope by the fire, even though she would usually serve herself from the kitchen.

Jonah sank back down into his chair. "Pray, take a seat," he drawled towards Callum, making Frida bristle again.

But Callum took matters into his own hands, pulling over a

tapestried chair for Frida and then a wooden stool for himself. After a moment's prevarication, Frida sat down. Immediately she wished she was further from the fire.

"What brings you to Ember Hall?" asked Jonah, his long fingers beating a pattern on the arm of the chair. He wore an elegant green tunic shot through with golden thread, making him appear every inch the attendant lord.

Callum cleared his throat, but his voice was strong. "I am sent by your brother, Tristan."

Jonah's eyebrows shot up. "How come?"

"That's exactly what I asked," Frida interjected.

Both men ignored her.

"Tristan has received word of increased trouble on the Scottish border." Callum rested his elbows on his long legs, looking both out of place and entirely comfortable on the small stool.

"That is most worrying." Tristan echoed Mirrie's words from earlier.

"I have explained to Sir Callum that we will not require his services." Frida attempted to nudge her chair away from the vigorous orange flames, but it was too heavy and would not budge. She should at least have removed her cloak before she sat down. Callum's arrival had thrown her all out of sorts.

Jonah looked at her as if she were a small but interesting creature who had just crawled from beneath a log.

"Why will we not?"

"Because we are already well-defended, with guards enough for the King himself." Frida took a breath. Exaggerations would not help her cause.

"If Tristan has deemed it necessary…" Jonah left the rest of the sentence unsaid.

Frida clutched at the fabric of her chair in annoyance. "Jonah, you are the last person to believe Tristan's word should be followed as law."

Amusement crossed his finely-drawn face. "Occasionally, even I must concede to our dear brother's wisdom."

"This is not one of those times." Frida cursed herself for mishandling this so badly. She should have known that Jonah would say exactly the opposite of what she wished.

"I would think it is exactly one of those times." Jonah's gaze rested on her for a moment, before turning to Callum. "And you, sir, must believe so?"

If Callum was at all entertained by this display of sibling rivalry, he did not let it show. "The situation could turn grievous with no or little warning," he said gravely.

Frida refused to look in his direction. "That is nonsense. The guards spotted your arrival. Why should they miss an approaching army?"

Callum leaned closer. "Because me and my men made no attempt to hide."

She would never win this argument, especially with his earnest eyes gazing into hers. Frida sighed in exasperation, abandoning any attempts at decorum and tugging her heavy cloak from her shoulders. Beneath it she wore only a plain woollen day dress; ideal for scrubbing turnips, less so for entertaining a visiting knight who made her pulse pound.

She folded her hands in her lap and lowered her gaze to them, realising that she must accept the inevitable. Callum and his men would remain at Ember Hall. But she would not go down without a fight.

"Ah, here is Jennifer with the tray."

Was Jonah deliberately provoking her with this show of lordly behaviour?

Glancing across at her brother behind her lashes, Frida concluded that her brother was doing just that. As if aware of her scrutiny, he placed a tentative hand on his right shoulder, over his recently-acquired wound, and opened his mouth in a slight moue of pain.

The wound was little more than a scratch. Frida had packed it with honey and covered it with bandages last night. There was no sign of infection, and she still believed it a ruse of some sort.

Though for what purpose, she could not imagine.

Resolving to ignore him, she rose to help the young kitchen maid balance her laden tray on the small wooden table, but Callum had beaten her to it.

"Allow me," he said, in his voice as deep and smooth as molasses. Standing, he towered over them all. Jennifer nodded her thanks and scuttled away. Frida tried not to notice the way Callum's eyes followed her back to the kitchen.

"Are you going to pour, Frida?" Jonah enquired lazily.

She flashed him a glance. "I suppose I must."

Again, Callum held out a restraining arm, his mail shirt glinting in the firelight. "A man can pour his own ale," he said. "And one for a lady, of course."

Frida did not wish to drink ale, but she supposed holding the cup would give her something to do with her hands. Jonah also accepted a measure, despite having broken his fast so recently.

Frida rested her cup against her chin, thinking hard. "If the situation is so dire, how is it that Tristan has not come here himself?" she demanded.

Callum had declined to sit back down on the stool and was now standing near the fire. She fancied he must also regret positioning himself so near the source of heat, especially clad in heavy chain mail. For a moment, his dark eyes were opaque.

"I cannot tell you. Perchance he is busy with other affairs."

"He has only just returned from Scotland," Jonah piped up. "Allow the man some leisure time."

Frida thought a shadow passed over Callum's face, but it may have been a trick of the light.

"I still do not understand why he should send you," Frida said abruptly. "We have not seen you for two winters."

And apparently, you believed me dead, she added silently.

"Do not be so disagreeable," Jonah muttered. "We are no longer in Wolvesley, but that does not mean we should abandon our manners entirely."

Callum opened his arms. "Egremont House is well situated in

proximity to Ember Hall. We are but half a day's ride away. Mayhap Tristan's other friends are more distant?"

His calm words dispelled the fury that had begun to rise in Frida's belly. She had been within moments of throwing her ale in Jonah's face.

What a spectacle I am making of myself.

Her father had made her mistress of Ember Hall. It was time to assert her authority.

"I have made my position clear," she began, drawing surprised gazes from both of the men. "I do not wish to have more soldiers at Ember Hall."

Jonah chuckled and made to speak, but Callum silenced him with a sharp look.

A look that almost silenced Frida as well.

"This is my home and I shall decide who stays and who goes." She paused. "But I cannot ignore my brother's wishes." She glared at Jonah. "It seems I am cursed with two brothers who are equally impossible to ignore, however much I might wish it."

Callum smiled, relief radiating from him. "You will allow us to stay?"

His smile was almost her undoing.

Frida sat straighter in the chair, frantically marshalling her thoughts. "Mayhap I spoke too rashly before. We can always find a use for strong men. As Mirrie said, the barn roof is in need of repair. And the orchard crop must be gathered before the first frost." She forced herself to meet his eye. Forced herself to remain composed, even as her heartrate steadily increased. "You may stay, Sir Callum. Not as men-at-arms, but as labourers."

It was an impertinent speech. Even Jonah floundered for words. Callum should have been affronted, but instead he seemed to be considering her proposition carefully.

"You would like us to surrender our weapons?" he suggested.

Frida nodded. "At once." She continued before her courage failed her. "I'm afraid we have no grand chamber to offer you. We were not anticipating visitors. You and your men will have to share quarters with the guards, above the stables."

This would also mean that she did not have to sleep under the same roof as him.

Frida doubted she would sleep a wink knowing that Callum slumbered so near.

"One question, Lady Frida." He hesitated. "Will our weapons be close at hand, should we need them?"

She nodded. "They will be locked in the armoury, alongside our supplies."

For a long moment, he held her gaze. "Then I am pleased to accept your offer."

Frida released the breath she did not know she had been holding. "Welcome to Ember Hall."

CHAPTER FOUR

CALLUM STOOD IN the cobbled courtyard, his gaze fixed on the patchwork vista of rolling hills visible beyond the outer wall. The afternoon sun had finally burned away the last of the mist, bringing the beauty of his surroundings into sharp relief. Birdsong floated up from the trees nearby, but there was no other sound save the slight whisper of wind.

What on earth should I do now?

Callum's instincts usually served him well, but right now he had no clear sense which path he should take through the maze that had sprung up before him. Holy hell, he was not even certain which direction to face. Just hours earlier, he had thought himself the commander of a tangible mission. Now he saw that the mission was as unclear as his ability to execute it.

"I'm damned whatever I do," he muttered to himself.

Marching footsteps broke him out of his reverie, and he straightened up in time to nod to two guards changing shift on the wall. They barely acknowledged him as they passed, green cloaks swaying around their booted legs. But he knew how they watched him. Him and his men.

Ember Hall was better defended than they had anticipated. But the presence of so many trained guards was by far the least of his problems. His head reeled with what he had learned.

Firstly, that Ember Hall was owned by the de Nevilles, the family he had baulked at betraying two years earlier.

Secondly, and most importantly, that Frida de Neville lived.

When he first beheld her, he had believed her to be an apparition, come mayhap to reprimand him for his planned assault. Come to haunt him for his past misdeeds. Either way, he wanted only to gaze at her familiar, beautiful face.

And then came the tumult of realisation. Frida was not only alive, she was also well. And she was standing right in front of him.

This had been enough to blow all other thoughts from his mind. For long minutes, he had forgotten the reason he was here.

He'd wanted to kneel at her feet. Nay, he'd wanted to take her in his arms and follow on from where they had left off, over two years ago in Wolvesley Castle, when he had felt the possibility of happiness come so tantalisingly close.

And yet, the lady herself seemed not to recognise him.

If anything could dull the joy of the moment, it was the polite disinterest in her expression.

Callum allowed himself a short, guttural shout of frustration which reverberated around the empty courtyard. It mattered not if Frida recognised him. Forsooth, it was better if she did not. What mattered was this; Frida was mistress of Ember Hall.

And she ruled alone, with no lord by her side.

He put a hand to his forehead, rubbing at the ache within his temples and doing his best to recall the exact wording of the Bruce's orders. They had been scant, but the instruction was clear. Callum was to assassinate the lord recently returned to Ember Hall: a man considered a danger to Scotland.

One name now reverberated through his head.

Tristan de Neville.

The man he had once thought of as a friend.

Callum closed his mind to this. Again, it mattered not. Tristan, the revered knight, was not in residence.

Surely his orders were not to strike down Jonah? He was little more than a youngster; more at home with a quill than in combat. Jonah was no threat to peace and stability in Scotland.

There must be some mistake.

Callum wrapped his fingers around the hilt of his sword and drew it partially from its scabbard. The polished metal shone brightly in the sunlight. His sword was a prized possession. He would not use it against a young man who was ne'er likely to ride into battle.

What then? He could leave. Ride away and pretend all this had never been. But that would mean walking away from Frida.

Callum's gut twisted. He simply could not do that; not when he had so recently found her again.

Time is what I need.

One fact shone clearly through the mists of his confusion; he could not bring violence to Ember Hall—to Frida's home. Though his men may see things differently. The English were their enemies. And the de Nevilles were a powerful English family.

Callum closed his eyes against the vivid reel of violent images playing through his mind. The siege of Kielder Castle had left its mark, with memories rising unbidden to torment him. He saw again the pale and lifeless bodies piled against the curtain wall; the steep grassy embankment soaked red with blood. The stench of death and the sorrow of so much needless destruction.

Aye, the English must be punished for what they had done. But still, he baulked at bringing retribution to Frida's door, or that of any of her kin.

Even if Tristan was involved in the siege of Kielder Castle?

Had Jonah not admitted that Tristan had recently been in Scotland?

The prospect made beads of perspiration spring out on Callum's forehead. He struggled to reconcile the friend he once knew with the monster who had ordered the deaths of women and children. But who knew how the passage of time might change a man?

Callum returned to the same conclusion. Time was what he needed. Time to talk to Frida. Time to discover Tristan's likely whereabouts. Forsooth, he might be on his way here even now. They were a close family. 'Twas not beyond the bounds of possibility that he might visit his sister's home.

Mayhap we just arrived too early. He had been right to agree to Frida's conditions, however belittling they might be.

Now all he had to do was explain it to his men.

Stifling a sigh, Callum turned towards the back door of the house. Mirabel had shown him where his men waited, ensconced in a small chamber above the kitchen. But he had begged a breath of air before facing them.

Before facing Gregor, at least. That man could start an argument with a priest.

He climbed the narrow stairs like a man approaching the gallows, but by the time he had reached the waiting guard, Callum's face was set with determination. He nodded to dismiss the guard, as arranged with Mirabel, and shouldered open the wooden door.

Andrew was the first to greet him, jumping to his feet and striding forwards. His bright eyes and fiery red hair seemed subdued in the shadows.

"What news?" he demanded.

Callum held up a hand, bidding his friend to pause while he scanned his surroundings. The room was small and square, lit with two flickering candles as well as the dim light filtering through the tall window. He took in a wide window seat, upon which Andrew had been reclining, and an array of wooden furniture. Arlo and Gregor faced one another across a round table, upon which a pitcher of ale sat beside an empty trencher. Refreshments had been brought up, as promised. There was no hardship here, save the stuffiness of the small chamber.

"We are to stay," he told them, shortly.

His announcement was greeted with silence. Arlo's pale blue eyes flickered between Gregor and Andrew, as if gauging their reaction.

"As guests?" Gregor's voice was incredulous.

"Speak softer, man," Callum warned him. "We do not know who might be listening." Moving with deliberate slowness, he pulled out a chair and sat down at the table, stretching out his long legs with a sigh. "Nay, not as guests," he finally answered. "We are to help work the land."

Not a muscle moved in Gregor's face, but his eyes remained fixed on Callum's.

It was vital to bring him on side.

Callum leaned forwards, placing his elbows on the table and realising too late that he had chosen to sit by a puddle of ale.

"This house is owned by the de Nevilles," he said, in little more than a whisper. Andrew crossed the room to stand closer, his shoulders hunched against the low ceiling. "They are a powerful family."

"I know right well who they are." Gregor's voice carried a warning.

"We must tread carefully," Callum continued.

"We must strike now, when they least expect it." Gregor banged his fist on the table for emphasis, caring little for keeping their plans quiet.

"We cannot kill the lord when he is not here." Callum tried hard to keep his tone reasonable.

"We can kill those that are." Gregor's eyes flashed with fire as he glared across the table. "'Tis no more than the English did to our own women."

Callum snatched a deep breath, knowing he must disguise the cold fear flooding his veins. His mind conjured an image of Gregor stalking toward Frida, his sword outstretched and ready to strike. "That would be going against our orders."

"Is the lord expected back?" Andrew asked. A lone voice of sanity.

Amidst his growing panic, Callum glimpsed a way forward. "Aye. He visits regularly. They expect him any day."

He looked from one to the other in the dim candlelight, his heart racing. He had not intended to tell an outright lie, but the words were out now. There was no going back.

He cleared his throat. "Given these circumstances, 'tis clear enough to me there has been some mistake with our orders. If we stay a while, we may yet rectify the situation. I have the trust of the family. If all else fails, we can question them to discover the whereabouts of Tristan de Neville and intercept him on the road." He lowered his voice further. "But we cannot take this fight to his father's seat at Wolvesley Castle. 'Tis too well-defended. Our best bet is to bide our time here and await his arrival." Arlo's question was hesitant. "Is it safe for us to stay?" He glanced towards the window, through which the regular trampling of booted feet could be heard. The guards of Ember Hall remained ever vigilant.

"Nay. I cannae think it is." Andrew looked towards Callum, confusion clouding his brow.

Callum poured himself a cup of ale, hoping that the tremors in his hand would not betray him. He took a mouthful and smacked his lips. "Aye, it is safe," he declared.

As soon as his proclamation landed, he knew it had failed. Even Arlo sucked in his breath as the narrow room seemed to palpate with tension.

"How so?" Gregor was the first to voice his challenge. "You may speak like the King himself, but we dinnae. It will take just one suspicious servant to work out where we're truly from." He sneered. "And 'tis not Egremont House, where'er that is."

Callum held his gaze. "You will have to stay quiet, all of you." He avoided looking towards Andrew.

"As if we are mute?" Arlo's eyebrows disappeared beneath his untidy thatch of hair.

"Or dumb," Gregor sneered. The big highlander rocked on his chair until the spindly legs creaked with protest.

Callum leaned forwards, meeting his challenge. "Naught so extreme. Just keep your words few and far between. Is it not the basic task of a spy to avoid suspicion?"

"I am nae spy, man. I am a warrior."

"Then just keep yer big mouth shut."

Callum was gratified to hear Andrew speak up in his stead, but one glance upwards told him that his old comrade was far from convinced. Andrew's green eyes were wide with worry.

"This is nae the job we came here to do," he appealed to Callum.

"You are right." Callum reached up to clap him on his shoulder, knowing that he was asking too much.

For the sake of a woman he barely knew.

But she was the woman he had ne'er been able to forget.

"I ask only for a couple of days. No more, I promise. When Tristan de Neville arrives here, I will do what needs to be done." He quelled his inner turbulence and gazed steadily at Gregor until the man caved and met his eyes. "I will fulfil the Bruce's orders, to the very letter." He smiled, bringing Arlo and Andrew back into the fold. "And we can all go home."

Fresh tension reverberated through the chill air as they considered his words.

"And until then, what?" Andrew raised his hands, palm up. "We till English fields for wealthy English nobles?"

Gregor deliberately spat on the wooden floor. Callum did not react.

"We do what we need to," he answered mildly. "As every man must." He scratched at the growth of stubble on his cheeks. "As the Bruce expects."

This was his winning line.

Arlo nodded, his face serious. "We blend in, so as not to attract attention."

Callum could have hugged him. "Exactly that." But a muscle twitched in Callum's jaw. He had not yet told them the worst of it. "We must surrender our weapons." He saw immediately how this would go. Gregor's expression became thunderous. Even Arlo looked discomfited. "At least, we must appear to," Callum amended, thinking quickly.

"What madness is this?" Gregor looked ready to rise and walk from the room.

"Think on it, man, there is no good reason for us to be so heavily armed." He indicated the gleaming swords each man carried at his hip. Knives, he knew, were secreted elsewhere on their persons. Along with heaven knew what else.

"I will nae walk about as defenceless as a bairn," Gregor stated.

"And nor do I ask it of you." Callum leaned over the sticky table, ignoring the sickly-sweet scent of spilled ale. "Let us surrender just half our weapons. The rest we shall hide, until we have need of them."

"I am not leaving this place without my sword." This from Andrew, who had lowered his brow.

A warrior's bond with his sword was near sacred.

"Again, I'll not ask it of you." Callum opened his arms to indicate his sincerity. "Every last blade shall be recovered before we depart Ember Hall."

"Right ye are," Andrew sighed. "I can spend two days of what's left of my life here." He rubbed at his beard. "I suppose on a good day, if we squint, we can see Scotland."

"Thank you, all of you." Callum nodded at each of them. "I am sorry for this unexpected turn. But our mission will come good. I will make sure of it."

Arlo and Andrew both smiled. Gregor did not, but the friction in the room had eased slightly.

Callum resisted the urge to put his head in his hands. He had won this first battle, but he had no idea how he might make good on his promise.

How could any good come out of this?

CALLUM SPENT A restless night and was relieved to hear the cock crow as the first pink rays of dawn spilled over the horizon. He and his men had slept in a low, boarded chamber above the stables, just a thin row of slatted wood separating them from the guards. There was no opportunity for even hushed conversation, for which Callum was grateful.

His threadbare reasoning had withstood enough scrutiny.

At the other side of the wooden partition, he heard heavy footsteps and murmured exchanges as the guards returned from the night shift. Callum lay still and silent, his ears straining to catch any reference to the small band of men who had ridden through the gates yesterday. He could make nothing out, which meant either that their arrival had caused no suspicion, or that the guards were as aware as he was about the flimsiness of the wall.

Most probably the latter.

But if it wasn't for the turmoil of his thoughts, he might have spent a restful night, for they had been provided with warm rugs and straw pellets thick enough to hide those weapons too large to conceal within their saddlebags. The building was weatherproof and, oddly enough, a feeling of calm had settled upon him as soon as he laid down. Mayhap it was the distance he had travelled from Kielder Castle that allowed some of the horrors to recede from his mind?

A brusque knock on the door broke his reverie.

Callum rose from his pallet, careful not to bang his head against the low-hanging beams, and picked his way across the narrow chamber. Andrew and Arlo slept on, but Gregor's eyes followed him in the half light.

He unbolted the door and pulled it open. "What is it?"

A tall guard stood at the top of the outer steps, smothering a yawn. "Miss Mirabel is here to see you."

Callum blanched with surprise. "Here?"

The guard jerked his head backwards. Behind him, thick, uneven stone steps had been built into the wall of the barn. "In the yard."

"Thank you."

The guard swivelled on his heel and trampled back down.

Callum rubbed his eyes.

This was unexpected.

Last night, he had removed his chain mail and slept in his hose and tunic. He glanced downwards, taking in his crumpled appearance. It could not be helped, for they had not come to Ember Hall equipped to stay for any length of time.

But the morning air carried a chill. He would need his cloak.

Callum walked back to his pallet at the end of the room and rummaged through the items he had piled on the floor. Dust motes rose around him, making him blink. In times past this room had clearly been used to store hay, for the sweet smell still lingered.

"What is happening?" Gregor's voice was rough, either with sleep or displeasure.

Callum tied the strings of his cloak. "As soon as I find out, I will tell you."

Before further questions could be asked, Callum strode away, closing the door behind him.

It was something of a relief to hurry down the stone steps and breathe the fresh, clean air of the morn. Yesterday's mist had cleared away and the faint early sunshine held the promise of warmth. In the centre of the yard he spied a lone female figure, clad in a long grey cloak with the hood pulled over her hair.

Mirabel Duval was ward of the Earl of Wolvesley. Callum could remember her clearly. When last he saw her, she had worn a dress of shimmering green which matched the holly and pine decorations for the Twelfth Tide Ball. *What brought her to this remote outpost*, he wondered.

He bowed smartly and walked to her side.

"Miss Mirabel."

She gave an answering curtsy. "Sir Callum. I trust you passed a comfortable night?" Her hazel eyes looked up at him, something shining in their depths that he could not read.

"Most comfortable, thank you." He gave her a quick smile. "I am afraid that two of my men slumber still."

"It is no matter. I came only to speak to you." Her eyes darted about the courtyard as if to confirm they were alone.

He was half intrigued, half wary. "How can I help you, Miss Mirabel?"

"Oh please, call me Mirrie. Everyone does." She folded her hands demurely in front of her. "I came to ask a favour."

Callum's attention was caught by a small parade of guards making their way from their sleeping quarters to their day-time stations. He counted six of them, before turning back to Mirrie.

"I will be pleased to hear it."

"How gallant you are." She turned, indicating he should walk with her across the courtyard. A soft wind blew, rustling the folds of their cloaks. "Are you always willing to help a lady in distress?"

Callum's mouth twitched. Miss Mirabel was teasing him. Under the circumstances, it was not what he had expected. Banter and light-hearted conversation had been in short supply recently.

"I should hope so," he answered lightly. Their exchange put him in mind of the last time he had exchanged pleasantries with well-dressed English ladies: at the Twelfth tide ball in Wolvesley.

She flicked him a glance from beneath her hood. "The favour concerns my good friend, Lady Frida." She paused. "Frida, I should say. We are not formal here. There is no cause to be."

At the mention of her name, Callum's pulse sped up. It did not slow in any way when he realised that Mirabel was watching his reaction closely.

"You must tell me more," he declared. "Before anticipation proves my undoing."

Her laugh was like a peal of bells. "I remember your wit from Wolvesley."

He bowed his head. "And I remember you, most especially your grace on the dance floor."

She looked away. "You are too kind, sir. But you are right. I did so love to dance."

This was his moment. Callum took the plunge. "I am pleased to know that you recall our earlier meeting. I fear that Lady

Frida—Frida," he corrected himself, "does not."

Mirrie came to a halt. They had reached the corner of the courtyard formed by the outer walls of the hall itself. She leaned one hand against the stone. "May I speak candidly?"

"I always favour candour."

But Mirrie's expression had grown serious. She tucked a wilful strand of hair behind her ears and met his eyes boldly. "You know that Frida had a terrible fall?"

He nodded. "I saw it myself." A chill went through him at the memory.

Mirrie inclined her head. "Frida was unconscious for three days. When she awoke, much had changed."

Callum spoke without thinking. "Her hair." He had wondered at its shimmering whiteness yesterday.

"Her hair," Mirrie agreed. "Although mayhap that is not the most important thing." She broke his gaze, an expression of doubt dancing across her heart-shaped face.

"Tell me, pray. I will help if I can," Callum said quickly. A chicken pecked about his booted feet but he hardly noticed it.

Mirrie pursed her lips. "There are some things that Frida has," she paused, "forgotten."

He looked at her, not understanding. "Forgotten?"

"Aye." She nodded. "I should like your help in getting her to remember them."

Callum dragged a hand through his own hair, which was tousled and tangled, having not seen a comb this morn. "What things might those be?"

Mirrie fixed her gaze at some point over his shoulder. "I have always admired Frida's self-discipline, but in times past, this was softened by a sense of hope and joy." She sighed. "I sound whimsical, I am sure, but 'tis this softer side that she has put aside. Forgotten, I would say."

He had to draw on all his training as both a warrior and a spy to disguise the jolt of emotion he felt at her words. "I am not sure I am the right person to help Frida recover her sense of hope and joy."

Perchance I am the last man who should try.

She gave him a smile like sunshine after rain. "On the contrary, Sir Callum Baine, you are mayhap the only person who can do so." She stepped closer and took his arm, the sincerity of her gaze impossible to escape. "If you are willing to try?"

His heart threatened to jump through his ribs. He could not prevaricate beneath her all-seeing eyes. "Then I will do all I can."

"That is exactly as I'd hoped." Mirrie's manner became playful again as she turned them towards the arched front door, but Callum still held back.

"What would you have me do?"

Mirrie shrugged, her eyes dancing. "Speak with her. Spend time with her." She nudged him with her elbow. "I cannot prescribe every detail. But I have dragged you from your bed and not offered you any refreshment. Forgive me. You and your men are welcome to break your fast in the great hall."

"I am not hungry." His mind raced too fervently to allow hunger. "But my men will be." He glanced back towards the outbuildings. "I will fetch them."

"Nay, do not trouble yourself. I will show them to the hall when I give them their tasks for the day."

A day when Gregor, Andrew and Arlo would act as labourers for those they saw as their enemies. Despite his excitement over the chance to spend more time with Frida, a new clutch of anxiety made him pause.

He cleared his throat. "What will those tasks be?"

"Frida is keen that the barn roof be repaired before the onset of winter." Mirrie drew the folds of her cloak together. "Which is near enough upon us." She met his eye again. "Frida is already at work in the orchard, gathering in the fruit crop. We are late in doing so."

Callum realised what she was trying to say. Immediately, all thoughts of his men were forgotten. "You would like me to go and help her?"

Mirrie nodded, a smile playing about her lips. "There are

apples at the top of the trees that she will not be able to reach without assistance." She leaned closer, her eyes dancing. "If she tries to send you away, do not let her succeed."

CHAPTER FIVE

F RIDA LOVED EARLY mornings at Ember Hall. There was a sort of magic in the slanting sunlight and melodic birdsong, a feeling of peace and wonder that was further enhanced by their solitude in the northern hills. Having grown up amidst the constant hubbub of Wolvesley Castle, tranquillity was something that Frida cherished.

But the events of yesterday had threatened all the solitude and tranquillity that she held dear.

Frida tugged at the branch of a fruit tree, ignoring the dew soaking through the hem of her dark blue dress.

Why did I allow it to happen?

Six rosy red apples winked up at her, as if they knew the answer well enough. The apples were a thing of beauty, glistening in the dawn light. On rare occasions like this, Frida envied her brother Jonah his drawing talent. How lovely it would be to capture this fleeting moment forever.

But Frida had always been of a more practical mindset. With one hand holding the branch steady, she plucked off the apples one by one and placed them carefully in her basket.

She should have brought gloves, but they would have grown damp with dew within minutes. Besides, what did propriety matter when she was alone? No one knew she was here, aside from Mirrie.

Frida had escaped from the house at first light, desperate to be distracted from the endless circling of her thoughts. Winter was coming, and the surprise arrival of Callum Baine would do nothing to mitigate that fact. The orchard harvest must be brought in with all possible speed. She had declared her intentions of starting the job today, as she and Mirrie broke their fast in the cosy solar behind the great hall.

"On your own?" Mirrie's brow creased with concern.

"I work best alone." Frida chewed her bread as quickly as good manners allowed. She wanted to leave the house before Callum—or any of his men—set foot inside it.

Mirrie pursed her lips. "I would join you, but I promised Agnes that I would help her with brewing the ale for winter."

"It is no matter." Frida shook her head emphatically.

"But you will scarcely be finished before dark."

Frida stood, brushing crumbs from her heavy skirts. "A good day's work never hurt anyone." She patted Mirrie's shoulder to take the sting from her words. "I shall see you at supper."

Frida had hastily pinned up her hair and pulled on an old straw hat. The day was dry and the sun had strength to it, so she was quite warm enough in her usual grey-green cloak. *This may be the last nice day of the year*, she reflected. It was quite sensible to spend it usefully in the orchard.

And if the high surrounding walls offered her privacy and concealment, so much the better.

Still, the scale of the task was a little overwhelming. Ember Hall was blessed with more than a dozen apple trees as well as several mixed plum and pear trees. All of which were groaning with fruit.

It would take days to gather it all; days they did not necessarily have. But 'twould be a shame, mayhap even a sin, to see any of it go to waste.

Frida sighed, rising onto her tiptoes to grasp the next branch. Their long-anticipated move to Ember Hall had been delayed by her father insisting on building a high fortified wall all around the property. When she and Mirrie had finally arrived, they discovered that the building works had interrupted harvest by some weeks. All local labourers were immediately deployed to the fields, and happily the main crops had been brought in safely. But the orchard harvest had been left until now.

Unfamiliar with the scale of the task, Frida had blithely dismissed the locals, thinking she could gather the crop herself over time. But time was in short supply for their hard-working household.

We will be better organised next year, she promised herself, straining to reach the apples furthest along the branch.

Alas, her booted feet slipped on the damp grass and the branch sprang upwards, showering her with raindrops. She winced as several apples thudded to the ground. They would be spoiled now, good only for the animals.

"May I offer assistance?"

The familiar deep voice sent shivers scooting up her spine, but Frida remained where she was; facing the tree whilst awareness of his close proximity caused her flesh to tingle. At least she had managed to remain standing.

"I can manage, thank you," she said, primly.

"I have brought you a ladder." Callum's voice came closer this time; he must be standing just feet away from her.

Frida closed her eyes, reaching for her composure. "That was thoughtful," she conceded.

"And a crooked stick I found in the store. It will be useful for reaching the higher branches."

There was nothing for it but to turn around. As she expected, Callum stood almost within touching distance. He had propped a wooden ladder by a wide plum tree and was proffering a long stick with a curved top, shaped almost like a sceptre, towards her.

Like an offering.

Her heart thudded as she took him in. In two years he had grown older; the boyish glint she remembered in his brown eyes was all but gone. Now his expression was serious, solemn even. Stubble coated his strong jaw and tousled hair hung almost to his shoulders, but nothing could mask the raw, male beauty of him. His crumpled tunic only emphasised the hard lines of muscle across his chest.

"Thank you." She managed a small smile as she reached out for the stick.

He folded his arms, his nut-brown eyes following her every move. "Better yet, I have brought you an extra pair of hands. Mine."

Nay, she could not handle that.

"You are kind, Callum." With difficulty, she avoided adding the *Sir*. "But this is not difficult work. I am well able to pick apples unaided."

"There are a lot of apples to pick." His tone was dry.

"And I am a fast worker." She held his gaze for as long as she was able before the traitorous flush again began creeping up her neck towards her cheeks.

"As am I." He gave a low bow. "Frida, you accepted my presence here in return for work on the land. You e'en made explicit mention of bringing in the orchard crop. Was that job not meant for me?" His dark eyebrows raised in question, making her body tingle with awareness once again.

Frida shook her head, aware of her hair coming loose beneath her bonnet. "I should not have mentioned the orchard crop." He had her at a disadvantage now. "The barn roof is in most grievous need of attention. This, I can manage alone." She waved her arms to encompass the laden fruit trees. Every fibre of her body was willing him to turn and leave. His presence brought back thoughts, memories, *feelings* that she had worked so hard to lock away.

"The barn roof will be mended before nightfall. I understand Mirabel is setting my men onto the task as we speak."

"I am sure they would benefit from your assistance," she interrupted.

"I assure you, my men will not tarry."

An edge came to his voice and she looked at him more closely. "Have they served you long?" She had but dim memories of the soldiers who had waited behind the gates while she conversed with Callum yesterday. All of her attention had been fixed on the man in front of her.

His expression became guarded. "They do not serve me, not exactly. 'Tis more that we all serve the same lord." He cleared his throat. "And he has put me in charge of this mission."

She gave her head a little shake, puzzled by his words. "But I thought you were here at Tristan's bequest?"

"Aye, that is correct. My lord was happy to release us upon the request of Tristan de Neville."

"I see." Frida shaded her eyes from the morning sunlight and forced a smile. "I am sure your lord would not like to think of you, a skilled knight, picking apples."

He met her smile with one of his own. A smile which cut straight through all her defences. "He knows I like to be busy. And helpful." He swept up an empty basket and hooked it over his elbow where it dangled incongruously against his muscular body. "Especially when there is a lady in need."

"But I am not in need." How she wished she could drive away the genuine smile which was now tugging at the corners of her mouth. 'Twas as if part of her body worked against her, wanting, even longing for his company—even as the sensible, rational part of her knew that it would be safest to step away. She had not spent two long years rebuilding her life, only for Sir Callum Baine to bring it crashing down once again.

"Are you not, Frida?" he asked in little more than a whisper. The air between them became charged as his brown eyes met hers. "Are you not in need of anything at all?"

This would not do. In another moment she would be blushing like her sister Esme at her first ball.

"Indeed, I have all I need," she replied airily, looking down to brush an imaginary speck from her cloak. "At least I did, before my peace was disturbed." She raised her eyebrows in what she intended to be a reprimand, but she couldn't help the laugh that escaped her when she encountered his face creased in mock penitence.

"All the more reason for me to help you, to atone for my most grievous fault."

Before she could think of a response, Callum had walked towards an apple tree and started efficiently divesting it of fruit. He worked quickly, his long arms easily reaching the heights of the tree. Frida had to force her eyes away.

There was nothing to it but to join him. Frida went back to the first tree, discovering that the long, crooked stick did indeed come in handy for pulling down the tallest branches. She soon got into a rhythm and her awkwardness dissolved. It was difficult to be annoyed whilst surrounded by nature's bounty, her ears filled with birdsong and her skin warmed by the morning sun.

But when Callum removed his cloak and hooked it from a branch, she couldn't help her gaze being drawn to his shoulders. Beneath the fabric of his light-coloured tunic, his muscles rippled as he reached and dipped. It was like a graceful dance. And she, an audience of one.

"'Tis hot work," he commented.

Frida hurriedly switched her gaze to his brimming basket. Had he seen her watching? She would have to hope otherwise, else wilt with embarrassment. "You have done well," she allowed.

He grinned at her. "This is not my first time."

"Oh." Frida's cheeks grew hot and she cursed herself for it. Their exchange seemed intimate, bold even.

But also very compelling.

"May I ask you a question?"

Surprised, she answered faintly. "You may."

Callum rested one hand against the trunk of the tree. His face was flushed with hard work and sunshine. It was hard to keep her gaze from the suntanned triangle of flesh visible at the top of his tunic. "Do you really not remember me?"

She should have been ready for this. Should have an answer

prepared, one that would save both her blushes and her heart.

Instead Frida turned away and reached for another branch, her fingers shaking. Could she tell an outright lie?

"From Wolvesley, you say?"

"Aye." His eyes burned into her back. "I remember you well."

Her grip slipped and the branch sprang upwards. She ducked her head as the loosened apples showered downwards, falling on the soft grass with small thuds.

"Damnation," she swore, not quietly enough. She was hot, uncomfortable and embarrassed.

But Callum was by her side in an instant, swooping down to pick up the apples and place them carefully on a flattened tree stump. "The horses will thank you for these," he said.

"Thank you." She swallowed as he straightened and turned to face her. They were so close she could make out each one of his long, dark eyelashes.

"We danced together," he said abruptly.

"Did we?" Her heart hammered beneath the bodice of her dress.

"And we talked." A frown flickered about his brow. "I dare to claim our conversation was worth remembering."

Aye. It was that and more. She had ne'er been able to chase it from her mind.

Frida put a hand to her brow. "I apologise." Her voice quavered. "There were many balls at Wolvesley. Many dances."

"Many conversations?" he finished for her.

She nodded, unable to look again at his honest brown eyes.

"As you know, I suffered a fall."

"I know it well." He reached out as if to clasp her hand and then thought better of it. Awkwardness hung in the air between them. "I am pleased and relieved to see you so recovered."

"I am not the same person I was." The words burst from her before she could stop them. "I am much changed." She glanced upwards and was immediately a prisoner of his dark, intense gaze.

"Nay." He shook his head. "You are Frida de Neville. I see you still."

His proclamation unlocked something inside her. Something reckless and ill-advised.

Frida reached up and untied the ribbons of her bonnet. Her hair had already fallen free of its pins. She tossed the bonnet on the grass and shook out her long tresses. "My hair was all shaved off by the barber-surgeon who saved my life. When it grew back, it had lost all colour." She heaved a breath. "My ankle was all but shattered. The physician told me I would never walk again." She straightened her shoulders, swallowing down a lump of sorrow. "I shall certainly never again dance at Wolvesley."

She had expected, e'en hoped, that her bold words would shock him. But if anything, Callum leaned closer. "Your hair is beautiful," he whispered. "You are beautiful. And I will carry the memory of our dance always in my heart."

Her heart fluttered and jumped as if she had fallen from a log. *This is not supposed to be happening.*

"And yet, you do not remember me?" he continued. It was a question, not a statement. She could see the doubt flickering like a flame in his eyes. "I should not take this as a personal slight given the injuries you suffered. But I confess that my heart grieves this loss."

Frida's mouth went dry. How could she continue to deny it?

How could she continue to deny *him?* The one man who had made her feel whole and happy. But she was not ready to open herself up to further pain, nor make herself vulnerable when she had worked so hard to recover her strength.

"There are things I have forgotten." She indicated her head, even though the lump received from her fall was no longer present. It was true, kind of, for Mirrie always declared that Frida had forgotten how to laugh and hope and be carefree.

But she had not forgotten Callum, nor any of the events or people in her life. Though she knew this was how he would interpret her words.

"Of course." Regret washed over his chiselled features.

What right did he have to feel regretful, more than two years after the event?

What right did he have to come here and disturb the peace Frida had worked so hard to achieve?

A question pricked at her mind. "You say you are close with Tristan?"

His eyes widened, mayhap surprised by her change of subject. "We trained together at Lindum."

"And you became friends? That is why you came to Wolvesley that time?"

Was it her imagination, or did his expression harden?

"Of course."

It was Frida's turn to frown. "I would have thought my brother would have informed his friends that his sister still lived."

A beat passed. "The fault was mine. I expected the worst and was most grieved by it." He tightened his lips. "I went straight from Wolvesley to fight in France. My path has not crossed with Tristan's since."

His answer was delivered smoothly, but Frida was still not satisfied.

"And when Tristan asked you to come to Ember Hall, for whose protection was that?"

Callum's gaze did not falter. Above them, a blackbird broke into a piping song. "He asked only that I ride to the aid of his family."

There was something he was not telling her. Knowledge slid inside her, like a knife into butter. It was the sort of insight Frida had been used to receiving when she had the Sight. But this was no sixth sense. This knowledge stemmed from the fact that deep down, she knew this man. And he knew her.

And they both knew that neither one of them was being entirely truthful.

Without shifting her gaze, Frida took in his dishevelled hair and the lines of tiredness running around his eyes. Why would he deceive her?

Why would any man ride out to the far north of the country, sleep in an old hayloft and spend the morning picking apples?

Frida's stomach flipped. Could it be that Sir Callum Baine was interested in her? Just as she had once dared to believe?

Her breath caught in her throat. For a long, dizzying moment, she pondered this possibility, before pushing it resolutely away. As she did, she broke Callum's gaze, looking instead at the trampled grass and the wicker baskets filled with glistening fruit.

She had come dangerously close to forgetting the most important thing.

She had come to Ember Hall to live a life free of men. Her hard-won strength and independence rested on this one fact.

"I see."

Brimming over with annoyance, mostly with herself, Frida stepped around Callum and stalked over to the plum tree. Without pausing to think, she climbed the ladder, relieved to disappear into the laden branches and hide her flaming cheeks.

God's bones. She didn't have a basket.

So be it. She would gather the plums into a fold of her cloak.

Frida worked steadily, stripping the nearest branches and placing the plump purple fruit carefully into her cloak. Noises below indicated that Callum had also returned to the task in hand.

Good.

They would work, not talk.

She would just have to be careful never to talk to him alone again.

All too quickly, the plums threatened to spill out of her hastily-fashioned receptacle. Frida began to lower herself down the ladder, moving slowly so as not to drop any. She had taken less than two steps when the ladder moved beneath her, tipping her further into the tree. She cried out, half in alarm and half in frustration, as the plums scattered.

"What is it?"

This was the last thing she needed; to look a further fool in front of him.

"'Tis nothing. I will right myself in a moment."

But as her injured foot searched for the next rung, the ladder lurched again and this time Frida could not prevent her fall. She scarcely had chance to scream as sharp branches whipped past her face and a rush of air lifted her skirts. She braced herself for impact, but instead found strong arms closing around her.

Then Callum cried out as his feet slipped beneath him and they both landed on the soft grass; Frida's face falling against the soft linen of his tunic.

His heart beat directly in her ear. Her breath mingled with his. She inhaled his scent of horses and leather. Long moments passed.

"Are you hurt?" His voice was gravelly.

"Nay." She raised her head so that it hovered over his. "Are you?"

"Nay." His eyes looked directly into hers.

As her panic subsided, Frida became aware of the hard muscles of his chest. His face was an open book. His lips inches away.

She could kiss him. If she wanted to.

She didn't want to. It was a preposterous idea.

She tried to push herself up, but found her skirts tangled in his long legs.

"Wait," he cautioned, twisting beneath her in an effort to free them both. Every inch of her lower body seemed welded with his and time stretched painfully before he finally rose to his feet and extended a hand to help her up.

Frida contemplated ignoring the hand, but she was shaken and could not deny a pain in her left arm.

"You *are* hurt," Callum exclaimed as she came to stand beside him.

"It is but a scratch," she replied automatically, although red blood dripped from her elbow.

Callum closed long fingers about her wrist, sending tremors

through her as he examined the wound. "'Tis a deep cut. It must be tended to."

"I can do it." She wrestled with the desire the leave her wrist where it was. The better part of her knew she should pull away.

"You are a healer?"

"I have some training." She must do something to alleviate this tension—this *connection*—between them. Her breath was coming so quickly it was as if she had run across the fields. "It is for that very reason that we are blessed with my brother Jonah's presence," she blundered.

Callum's eyebrows raised a notch higher. "He is also hurt?"

"So he says." Frida exerted great self-control in lifting her arm free of his fingers, but the sudden flow of warm, sticky blood brought a wave of dizziness upon her. She put her right hand to her forehead, staggering slightly.

"Steady." Callum placed his hands on her shoulders, righting her once again. His concerned face swam before her. "You are losing a lot of blood."

"'Tis nothing," she persisted.

"'Tis only nothing if it is treated properly—and quickly." He tore off a strip of his tunic and wrapped it tightly around her arm. It stung, but Frida was more distracted by the smooth expanse of bronzed flesh she could now see at his waist.

She averted her eyes. "Thank you."

"Let us get you inside."

"I can walk well enough," she protested, feeling his arm come about her shoulders.

"You are swaying," he pointed out.

She paused, recognising the truth of his words and wanting to right herself. "I am in shock, that is all."

"Aye, and is shock not reason enough to merit some assistance? 'Tis a long walk to the main house."

"I can manage," she said, through gritted teeth. But when she started forwards, the grass beneath her rose up into a steep slope and her vision blurred.

Moments later, she was lifted snugly against Callum's broad chest, her head resting on his broad shoulder. "We will make faster progress like this," he declared, pre-empting her objection.

She tensed her body. "You are carrying me as if I am a child."

"I am carrying you as if I am a knight," he corrected her.

"But I do not want to be carried." She did not speak the truth. Warmth from his body enveloped her.

"And I do not want to explain to your brother why I let you bleed out in the orchard." He set off, long legs striding forwards. "I have carried men from the battlefield with lesser wounds."

"That is a lie." With her good hand, she beat him lightly on the chest. "Do not patronise me, Callum Baine."

His voice trembled with laughter. "At least you remember my full name."

It was on the tip of her tongue to admit that she remembered it all. Not only the dance they had shared, but the stolen glances across a crowded banqueting hall. The times she had lingered in the garden, hoping to catch a glimpse of him.

That icy morning, when she had known it was risky to take her young horse out on the hunt.

Frida's head spun and she closed her eyes against another spell of dizziness.

Callum was at once kind, loyal and attentive. And the man who had upended her life.

She couldn't allow him into her heart a second time, even if his arms felt like home.

CHAPTER SIX

HOLY HELL, IT felt good to hold her.

For the smallest moment, Callum allowed himself to concentrate fully on the press of Frida's body against his and the lavender scent of her hair. When she had tumbled from the plum tree, something more than the honed reactions of a warrior had propelled him into position to catch her.

Aye. He had sprinted to her aid with the instincts of a lover. E'en before she cried out, he had known she was in trouble. So it had been for him back in Wolvesley; as if he and Frida were not two people who had recently met, but a couple long attuned to the subtle workings of one another's hearts.

They had reached the inner courtyard, within eyesight of the guards and servants of Ember Hall. Plus his own band of men, working on the roof of the barn. He must release her. Gregor's temper was turbulent enough without witnessing his enemy in his leader's arms.

Besides, Frida would hate to be seen by the others as weak and vulnerable. 'Twas one thing to hold her close when they were alone, quite another to make a public display.

Regretfully, Callum paused and placed her gently back on the ground.

"Are you well enough to walk from here?" he asked, quietly enough not to be overheard.

"Perfectly." Her arch reply was softened by a smile.

She is pleased I was sensitive enough to put her down, thought Callum.

The tourniquet he had wrapped around her arm had staunched the flow of blood, but Frida's usually healthy colour was still a shade too pale for his liking.

"We must go inside," he urged. "Is there a healer I can summon?"

"I am the healer in this house," she reminded him, taking his arm and leaning against him. "Once we are inside, I shall tell you what to fetch and where to find it."

They made halting progress up the stone steps and through the arched doorway. Callum grew conscious of her limp, which he had not noticed the day before.

"My ankle was all but shattered," she had said.

He winced for her pain, and for the incident that had struck her down in her prime.

Although Frida de Neville was still very much in her prime, as far as Callum was concerned.

Inside, all was calm and peaceful. Woodsmoke drifted into the panelled hall, together with the smell of roasting meat from the kitchens. It was a relief to be away from the bright glare of the sun.

He paused awkwardly. "Where should we go?"

Yesterday he had only been so far as the great hall, but he sensed instinctively that Frida would not want to go there. Not until her wound was treated and she had regained some of her customary strength.

Frida inclined her head to the side. "Let us walk through the great hall to the solar beyond," she said. "It should be empty at this time of day."

The great hall was also empty, aside from a brown-coloured hound stretched out by the fire. The dog bounded to its feet at first sight of Callum and approached with its teeth barred.

"Sit down, Samson," Frida commanded. "Callum is a friend, not a foe."

The hound sat obediently, though he pricked his ears as if considering his next move. Callum had always been fond of dogs and horses. He threw him a smile.

"Good boy," he tried.

The dog's tail thumped on the floor as Callum and Frida passed him.

The day before, Callum had been struck by the warmth and welcome of Ember Hall. As he nudged open the door to the solar and helped Frida into a high-backed cushioned chair, he thought he had never seen a room so inviting. It was the light, he realised, which blazed through a high arched window to cast pretty patterns onto the plastered walls. And the scent of late roses from the garden beyond. Through the open shutters, he glimpsed a green vista of rolling hills, topped with trees and dappled with autumn sunlight.

It was a room one could settle into and forget all about the perils of the world.

"Thank you," Frida said.

He realised he was standing, hands on hips, gazing about. "Tell me how to help." He nodded towards her arm.

Frida's blue eyes met his own. "Are you brave enough, Sir Callum, to enter a lady's chamber?"

He blanched. "Aye, if the lady grants me permission." He paused. "And if her brother does not run me through with his sword."

Frida's laugh was a balm. "I doubt Jonah will even notice. I have healing herbs in the store outside, but what I would like is a special salve and that, I'm afraid, is up in my chamber."

They both paused as heavy footsteps sounded in the great hall. For a moment, Callum felt as if he might be caught in an act of wrongdoing. He would never have dared spend time alone behind a closed door with Lady Frida at Wolvesley Castle. But here at Ember Hall, the usual rules seemed not to apply.

The footsteps turned towards the kitchen, and he shook away his fears with a mock salute. "I believe I am equal to the task."

She smiled, leaning her head back against the cushions. "Very well. You must climb the stairs and cross the gallery. My chamber is at the very end. You will find the salve within a wooden box which I believe rests upon the window seat." She sighed. "I left it there after treating Jonah last night."

"Am I likely to encounter your maid, mayhap wielding some sharp implement to chase me away?" he asked lightly.

But Frida's face was serious. "Nay. Mirrie and I did not make the move here to continue our lives as pampered misses. We have only a few servants and there are no ladies' maids at Ember Hall." She indicated her unadorned hair. "We fend for ourselves. 'Tis small payment for living amidst such beauty and peace."

Her quiet words touched him. "That is the kind of life you seek? A peaceful one?"

"Aye. Anyone who doesn't is a fool."

Frida's tone had turned sharp and Callum's eyes widened with surprise. But a red bloom of blood on the fabric wrapped around her arm reminded him of the task ahead.

"I will fetch your salve." He bowed his head in farewell and slipped from the chamber, his heart beating more normally as he put distance between himself and Frida.

God's bones. She affected him just as much now as she had two years previous. More, mayhap, for her girlish gaiety had been replaced by a calm resolve which reached out to his troubled soul.

Aye, his soul was troubled because of the war wreaked upon his home and family by English nobles exactly like the de Nevilles. Whenever Callum closed his eyes, he saw again the bloody devastation of Kielder Castle. Heard the crying of children blend with the impotent raging of his father.

"Curse the English," the old man had raged, forgetting in his delirium that he had wedded an English bride; that his only son was half English, born and raised south of the border. "Curse them all."

And gazing upon the horrors around him, Callum had agreed.

Which was why he had come to Ember Hall. To take his revenge on a powerful English knight. Not to fetch and carry for an English lady, however enticing her cornflower blue eyes.

However much she had become lodged in his mind.

Callum paused on the gallery, his elbows resting on the smooth oak banister overlooking the great hall below. The fire flickered in the grate, the dog snoring gently beside it. He thought again how this was a place of peace. 'Twas impossible to reconcile the mission he had embarked upon with the reality of life in Ember Hall.

His thoughts circled back to their usual place—the fact that there was no powerful knight currently in residence. Though he had pledged to his men that they would await the return of Tristan de Neville, Callum had no idea if his former friend had any plans to visit. He must ascertain the facts. Gregor would not be fooled for long.

And what if Tristan *was* on his way? What then?

Callum breathed deeply. He had been in this position once before, and subsequently failed in his duties to the Bruce. But those times had been different. Back then, Kielder Castle had stood strong and proud. Children played happily in the lanes. Villagers worked the fields and fed their families, little realising the fate awaiting them.

He had not been so angry then. Nor had so much to avenge.

His hands clenched into fists when he recalled what Jonah had said as he sat by the fire below. At the time, Callum's attention had been mostly on Frida. He could scarce continue with the act of normality for want of celebrating her presence; her very *life*. But e'en so, Jonah's words had pierced his haze.

Tristan had just returned from Scotland.

Did that mean that Tristan de Neville, the man he had once spared, had played a part in the storming of Kielder Castle?

Wouldn't he have recognised him, if that were the case?

Callum had fought long and hard on the battlements during that terrible siege, his blade slicing into his enemies as he gave his all to protect his home and his father's people. But once it was clear they were over-powered, he had given the order to retreat. Instead of greeting the invaders with his sword, Callum's attentions had turned to protecting those who still lived. Boys like Arlo. Men and women, some older than his father, who had lost everything. Nay, Tristan de Neville could have ridden through the main gates and hung his standard from the battlements without drawing Callum's eye to him. Callum had been occupied with leading his people to sanctuary in a cave by the river by then. He would not have known.

His throat constricted at the idea; his pulse pounding harder than it had in the orchard when Frida fell upon him, her long skirts entwined in his legs. But even as the familiar swell of rage ascended, Callum worked to dispel it.

Scotland was a big country.

And lives had been lost on both sides of the border when wiser men than he jumped to false conclusions.

Right now, Callum's best course of action was to remain at Ember Hall; to gather information and plot a course forwards.

Whether Tristan had plundered Kielder Castle or not, Callum could not abandon Frida.

Releasing his fists, Callum tuned back into the present moment. He had dallied overly long. The last thing he wanted, despite Frida's assurances, was to be apprehended by a disapproving housemaid.

The gallery was lit with soft light from a circular window. He found the door to Frida's chamber and turned the handle easily. The fragrance of lavender spilled out as he opened the panel, soothing his troubled thoughts. This was Frida's private sanctuary. He felt as if he were somewhere almost sacred. His family chapel at Kielder evoked less reverence in his heart than her neatly-made bed, heaped high with cushions and topped with a practical nightrail of pale green.

Closing his eyes against a vision of Frida wearing that very garment, Callum walked softly into the chamber, noting the rugs on the floor and the highly-polished, if modest, wooden furniture. A round table flanked by two chairs waited by an unlit fire and a long trunk rested by the foot of the bed. The window seat was also piled high with cushions. It was impossible for him to approach without first admiring the view, and second picturing Frida curled up here, gazing out into a darkening sky—perhaps with him joining her.

Callum had long since closed his heart to notions of love and marriage. But the domestic scene unfolding in his mind's eye was so compelling, he felt a short stab of grief that it could never be.

The medicine box was, as Frida had said, laying upon one of the square cushions on the window seat. Before his imagination could betray him further, Callum snatched it up and left.

THE MORN HAD not gone according to plan.

Forsooth, it had gone terribly wrong. But Frida could not help from smiling as she recalled Callum's chivalry. Against all odds, he had broken her fall from the fruit tree and carried her home like some gallant knight clutching a fainting maiden. And then, most importantly of all, he had allowed her to stand tall and walk inside on her own, just as the lady of the house should.

Her heart, long hardened, was beginning to open up. Something about Callum's arrival here, at Tristan's bequest, still nagged at her. But she had to admit that the knight had been naught but helpful.

Helpful and apparently sincere, especially when he recalled the detail of their last meeting.

Mayhap his tale has the ring of truth, she pondered, gazing out of the long window towards the sun-dappled gardens. In such serene surroundings, breathing in the heady scent of roses, anything seemed possible.

Frida pinched her hand, frowning at her fancies. She must not allow herself to become carried away. Once before she had believed Sir Callum Baine to be her future. That had ended in disaster. Though 'twas not his fault her horse had slipped on the ice.

"I have grieved you," he'd said, as they stood outside in the clinging mist.

She had not allowed herself to be moved, thinking only of how he had abandoned her. *But if he believed her to have perished…*

She was jolted from her thoughts by the man himself returning. In his hands he carried the slender wooden box in which she kept her balms, salves and bandages. A gust of wind caused the door to slam behind him and they both startled.

Callum recovered first. "Would you like me to reopen it?" He nodded towards the door.

Propriety dictated they should.

Frida shook her head. "It is no matter. No one is likely to come upon us."

"And you trust me, Lady Frida?" He came closer, placing the box gently upon a side table by her chair.

She tilted her head to look up at him, noting the intensity of his brown eyes and the rasp of stubble on his suntanned cheek.

"I do."

Perchance she should have demurred, or made some fancy speech about the honour and integrity of Lindum-trained knights. But Frida merely spoke what was in her heart. When last she met Callum, she had still enjoyed the gifts of her Sight. And she'd known instinctively that he was trustworthy.

More than that. She'd known instinctively that he was the man for her.

But then he had abandoned her.

Callum held her gaze as if he was reading these secrets of her soul. It was too much. Too intense and too bewildering. Frida snatched her eyes away, focusing instead on the crackling fire.

Callum cleared his throat, the sound echoing through the square-shaped room. "Shall I remove the tourniquet?"

Her wound. She had almost forgotten about it. Mayhap that was why her thoughts wandered so. She had lost too much blood to be of rational mind.

Frida sat up straighter in the chair and forced herself to concentrate. "Please do. I think the bleeding has stopped."

But his proximity, when he crouched beside her and began unwinding his makeshift bandage, was almost too much to bear. His hands were large but his touch was gentle.

"Aye, it has stopped." He looked up at her, his eyes reflecting the orange sparks of the fire. "Though it should be cleaned before we apply any salve."

Frida smiled, although her heart thudded with embarrassment for of course he was correct. How could she call herself a healer and forget something so basic?

It was because of Callum. His presence made her near enough forget her own name.

"You can fetch a basin from the kitchen." She paused. "Tell Agnes I sent you."

He nodded wordlessly, rose up and strode from the chamber, leaving her to press a hand over her heart and reach for her faltering composure. By the time Callum returned, Frida was more herself.

He squatted again by her side, placing a basin of water on the table beside the box. "'Tis warm water; Agnes had some heated on the stove," he said. "Miss Mirabel was there as well. She asked if we needed assistance."

Frida held her breath. Was this surreal interlude already over? "And what did you say?"

He flashed her a smile and her insides turned over. "I said I had treated many a battle wound and could manage well enough. But of course, if you would prefer to have her tend you?"

Frida shook her head. She wanted Callum's touch. Callum's company.

"She is busy," she said, by way of an excuse. "There is work enough for this household without Mirrie or the other servants tending to me as well."

He nodded, soaking a cloth in the warm water and dabbing gently at her arm. She flinched at the first stab of pain, then gritted her teeth together, determined to show no further weakness. After a while, there was something soothing in the warmth of the water coupled with the dexterity of his fingers. The only sound in the solar was the crackling of the logs in the fire.

"Which is the salve?" he asked.

"In the box, the largest of the round jars."

He found it quickly and returned to her, twisting open the jar and scooping out the thick salve. Frida closed her eyes and turned away, readying herself.

"What is it?" His voice was alarmed.

She kept her head turned towards the plastered wall. "It stings at first."

"Should I continue?"

"Aye." She nodded quickly, sucking in her breath when sharp pain clamped around her arm. Callum worked competently, wrapping a bandage snugly over the wound and then repositioning the sleeve of her dress.

"'Tis done," he said.

She opened her eyes to find his face hovering inches from hers. He had not moved from the floor, though it must be uncomfortable to sit so long on his heels.

"Thank you," she whispered.

His hand crept over her good one. "I would do all of that and more for you, Frida."

Sincerity shone from his nut-brown eyes. She found her fingers linking with his. It was impossible to look away.

"Do you really not remember me?"

She could not hold up the pretence any longer. She no longer remembered why she had started it in the first place.

"Frida, are you hurt?"

It took several seconds for her to realise that Jonah had entered the solar and it was he who asked the question. Callum did not shift his position, but instead of gazing into her eyes, he busied himself with rolling up bandages and screwing the lid back onto her jar of salve.

"'Tis nothing but a scratch," she replied, as evenly as she could.

Jonah stood by the open doorway, his blue eyes swinging from his sister to the kneeling knight.

"You tended her?" he asked.

Callum swivelled his head around. "It was my honour to do so."

Jonah took a few steps forwards. "Allow me to see?"

"There is nothing to see." She lifted her bandaged arm closer to him.

But Jonah nodded as if satisfied. "I give you my thanks," he said, a note of joviality creeping into his voice. "I admit, when I saw the fastened door, I suspected the worst."

"'Twas the wind that closed it," Frida interjected.

Jonah clasped his hands together. "I should have known my sister would be safe with any friend of Tristan's."

Something changed in the atmosphere. Something Frida didn't understand.

Callum stood up slowly. "Entirely safe, I assure you."

"Good." Jonah gazed at Callum for all the world as if he were about to challenge him to a duel. Frida gave her head a slight shake, wanting to signal to her younger brother that he had no reason to act so.

What a time for Jonah to become concerned with her wellbeing.

"There is no cause for vigilance on your part, brother." She made her voice deliberately light, smiling brightly at them both.

Callum seemed to relax. He placed her jar and roll of bandages neatly in the box and fastened the lid. "There is always a cause for vigilance," he replied, his tone equally cordial. "Jonah is right to be concerned."

"Thank you, Callum." Jonah clapped him on the shoulder, having to reach up a little to do so. "As we are all friends here, let us sit awhile."

"Very well, but I must return to my men before long," Callum replied, following Jonah's lead and sinking down onto the settle.

Frida couldn't help bristling, at the interruption as much as the inference that as a mere woman she could not look after herself. "I maintain that Jonah had no need to be alarmed," she stated. "You do not need to guard me, brother."

Jonah's laugh sounded genuine enough. "Forsooth, Frida, I have no wish to face Tristan's wrath should anything happen to his favourite sister."

Frida only just resisted the urge to throw a cushion at him. "Naught is going to happen to me. Besides, who says I am his favourite sister?"

"'Tis a well-known family secret." Jonah turned to Callum. "What say you, as Tristan's friend? Is Frida here his favourite sister?"

Callum appeared uneasy, and Frida could well guess why. To what end was Jonah asking such awkward questions? She opened her mouth to excuse the need for a response, but Callum was already speaking.

"I am sure that Frida would be anyone's favourite sister. Just as, if I were his brother, I would no doubt wish to avoid Tristan's wrath." He smiled genially at them both, so genially that she thought she must have misinterpreted his earlier discomfort. "At Lindum, we all feared being drawn against him in the joust."

Jonah nodded, his eyes still fixed on Callum. "Ah yes. You trained together at Lindum." He paused. "And did you fight alongside Tristan more recently?"

Callum's response came instantaneously. "I have been in France this last year." He angled his body so that Frida could no longer see his face, addressing his next question entirely to Jonah. "And where did you say Tristan had been?"

"Scotland."

This time there was a pause. "Aye, that was what I thought you had said." His voice was strained.

Perchance with the effort of making so much light conversation.

Frida got to her feet. "I have been idle here long enough." She looked expectantly at the two men, hoping that Jonah would melt away and that Callum would mayhap offer to return to the orchard.

But even as the traitorous thought formed in her mind, she knew that propriety had stretched thin enough between herself and the handsome knight.

He would take his leave. As he must.

As would undoubtedly be for the best. When she next saw him, she must ensure her thoughts ran more evenly.

As expected, Callum rose to his feet and bowed. "I shall bid you good day and find my men." His voice was short and it seemed he was deliberately avoiding her eye.

Frida swallowed down her disappointment and curtsied as gracefully as her ankle would allow.

"Thank you again, for everything."

She hoped for a smile, even a small one, but Callum's face was dark as he turned to leave.

She waited until his heavy footsteps had passed through the great hall before turning on her brother.

"Jonah, must you always spoil everything?"

He scowled in response. "Take care, sister," he said quietly, his long fingers drumming a pattern on his knees. "That man is not all that he seems."

CHAPTER SEVEN

CALLUM KEPT HIS temper in check until he had made it out of the house and across the courtyard. Listening hard, he could discern Andrew's ribald singing coming between bursts of hammering, and he used this as a cue to find the damaged barn where his men were working.

Here, just inside the shady entrance, he allowed his rage to surface in a guttural bellow. At the same time, he swung his fist so that an ancient, blackened beam by the door caught the full force of the blow.

Holy hell, that hurt.

He shook out his fingers, wincing from the pain. It was a foolish thing to do, given that a broken hand would not aid him in any way. But his temper was brewing inside him so fiercely that he needed a release.

Both the hammering and the singing ceased, the sound replaced by lowered voices. Within moments, his men would appear and questions would be asked of him.

Callum was in no mood to answer questions.

He should not have come here. Not yet.

Quickly he slunk away, running lightly away from the open barn towards a low building where a slatted door stood ajar. All he wanted was to be alone so he might think.

Callum paused at the door, nudging it gently so that it swung open and revealed an empty chamber.

It was not until he had walked through the door that he real-ised he was inside a modest chapel. Modest in its size—it would not hold a congregation of more than twenty—but far from modest in its execution. Painted glass softened the light and cast rainbow-hued patterns onto plastered walls which were adorned with frescoes so intricate he could not help but gaze at them, his breathing becoming more even as he made out a glorious pattern of intertwined stems and leaves twisting about the mullioned windows. Callum sank onto the nearest pew and rested his elbows on his knees. Silence pressed upon him heavily.

So Tristan had been in Scotland. There was no doubting that fact now.

Callum's anger was so intense he thought he might weep. Albeit, there was still no proof that Frida's brother had played a part in the storming of Kielder Castle. But the probability was rising.

Why else would Callum have been dispatched to this very place if it were not to assassinate a man who had brought death and destruction to his homeland?

He clutched his hands together, wondering if he might send up prayers asking the almighty for a sign as to how he should proceed.

It was then that the irony of the situation fell upon him like a rug thrown from on high. He was momentarily smothered, gasping for breath in the quiet chapel.

Callum had done exactly this in Wolvesley Castle. He had asked for help from on high when his feelings for Frida grew stronger than his will to serve his master.

His subsequent decision to leave England and abandon his quest meant that Tristan de Neville was left alive and free. Free to attack Scottish lands.

Free, perchance, to attack Kielder Castle.

A groan ripped from him as he realised the weight of these implications. The razing of Kielder Castle, the killing of the innocent, the destruction of his father's lands; the blame for all of this and more could easily belong to him. For he had spared the man who had likely led the attack.

The strength drained from his body into the wooden pew. He felt as weak as a child.

He should have listened to his father. Obeyed his orders. Abandoned any fanciful notions of kinship with an English noble sworn to an English King.

Fanciful notions of connection. *Nay,* of romance, with the daughter of an English earl.

Callum rubbed the heel of his hands into his eyes. He had lived long enough on this earth to know that regret was baked into the very fabric of existence. One could never second-guess the future and there was little to be gained by reimagining the past.

What mattered was the present.

A present in which he vowed to take his revenge upon Tristan de Neville. God's bones, if he must bide here a year or scour the earth to track the man down, so be it. He would do whatever it took to look the man in the eye and demand if he had led the raid on Kielder Castle.

If he saw, by the merest flicker of an eyelid, that the answer was yes, then friendship be damned. Tristan de Neville would know punishment for his myriad crimes upon the innocent.

In fact, enough time had been wasted. He would talk to Jonah on the morrow and establish Tristan's present whereabouts. What he'd said to his men was true: Wolvesley Castle was far too well-defended to attempt an attack. But Tristan must travel on the roads at some time.

Breathing deeply, Callum straightened his back and fixed his gaze on the soft swirls of light emanating from the painted glass.

His mother would not approve of him thinking such dark thoughts of vengeance in a place of worship. But he had not known the benefits of her calm counsel since his sixteenth summer. And his father's guidance ran to a different tune entirely.

An eye for an eye.

Violence answering violence.

Rory Baine had long demanded that his son wreak revenge upon their enemies. And if Callum had answered that demand two years ago, his father may not now be scrambling for coin with which to order the rebuilding of their ancestral home.

Coin that Callum was to provide, in part at least, with this mission.

Callum stilled on the pew as the hairs on the back of his neck prickled. Someone was watching him. Without turning his head, Callum looked as far as he could towards the open door on his left.

A shadowy figure stood within the chapel.

Immediately Callum leapt to his feet. One hand instinctively sought the hilt of his sword before he remembered that he had turned his weapon in as Frida requested. No matter. He had his fists and a knife secreted in his boots.

"Who is there?"

"'Tis only I." Callum relaxed as he recognised Arlo's strained voice. The boy walked further into the pink-hued light and bowed his head in apology. "I did not mean to startle you. Nor did I wish to interrupt your prayers."

Callum snorted. "I was not praying."

"I came here to find you."

"Why?"

"'Tis Gregor." Arlo pressed the palms of his hands together as if in supplication. "He is most unsettled."

"He and I both." Callum shook his head in exasperation. Could he not enjoy two minutes of solitude?

Arlo swallowed. "Aye, but Gregor intends mischief. I'm sure of it."

Now he had Callum's full attention. "Where is he?"

"He left the barn headed for the loft where we slept."

Where our stash of weapons is hidden, Callum silently added. He didn't waste time asking more questions, knowing Arlo to be a sensible youth who not raise any alarm without reason.

"Come," he said, already striding out of the chapel. Before they emerged into the sunlight he glanced back over his shoulder. "If trouble is brewing, I want you to stay out of it."

The courtyard was empty, save a clutch of hens scratching in the soft earth. For the first time since arriving at Ember Hall, the uniformed guards were nowhere to be seen. Callum picked up his pace, hoping to intercept Gregor before he left the loft.

Before any showdown between them became a public spectacle.

But as he rounded the corner, he saw the tall highlander crouched low, running towards the stone steps leading to the hall's entrance. Light glinted off the blade clutched in his hand.

A jolt of alarm brought the scene into sharp relief; pink roses nodding in the breeze, ancient stone basking in sunlight.

A lone figure intent on spilling blood.

"Halt." Callum infused the command with all the authority of his rank. He was the son of Rory Baine. He was the spy trusted by Robert the Bruce.

He would not stand for insurrection.

His boots trod heavily over the stones as he closed the distance between them. Gregor had paused, as requested, but his dark eyes shone with defiance. He made an unpleasant sight; unwashed and crumpled with a straggling growth of beard and lank hair hanging about his pointed face.

"I have naught to say to you." The man spat at his feet.

Callum did not flinch, though he wished he had his sword to hand. Gregor's blade was lowered, for now.

"What is the meaning of this?" He kept his voice low, his words clipped.

Gregor pushed back his shoulders and looked at him scornfully. "I will nae follow a coward."

"Callum is nae coward," Arlo spoke from beside him.

Callum fought an urge to tell the lad to go away. Somewhere he would not be harmed by flying fists or blades. Instead, he put his hands on his hips and fixed his gaze on Gregor. "Your orders were to work on the barn. Why are you headed for the house?"

"To do what ye are too afeared to do."

Cold pinpricks of apprehension washed down his spine. "I am the one in charge of this mission. I will decide what we do and when."

"Ye are nae in charge of naught." Gregor spat again. "All day ye have been picking apples and fawning over lady Frida de Neville. Ye are a warrior man, the lady's enemy. At least, that is who I thought ye were."

The courtyard still appeared empty, but armed guards could be listening to their exchange even now. This was no place for a discussion. Much less for threats and accusations. If they weren't careful, all three of them would wind up with swords pointed at their chests.

His heart beat hollowly, but he drew himself up to his full height and ensured his voice carried an edge of menace. "This is not honourable, Gregor. No true Scotsman would launch an attack on defenceless women."

"Ye dare speak to me of honour?" Gregor snorted. "When ye have lied from the very day we arrived?"

Callum bade his voice be steady. "What is this you accuse me of?"

"Ye lied outright when ye told us that Tristan de Neville was expected here within two days."

Callum froze. He had not anticipated being caught out so quickly.

"Dinnae try to deny it. I asked the lassie who thinks herself the boss o' me now. Miss Mirabel. She said *Lord Tristan is not expected*. Those were her exact words. *Not expected*." Gregor spun his knife in his hand, triumph glinting in his dark eyes.

Arlo was following the exchange closely, his eyebrows disappearing under his thatch of hair.

"But why else would we ha' stayed?" the lad interjected.

Gregor let out a bark of laughter. "Why else? That is what I have been asking meself." He lifted his chin, eyeing Callum as if he were a flea-ridden hound. "Shall I tell ye what I have concluded?"

Arlo looked to be struck dumb. Callum forcefully re-entered the conversation. "Aye, why don't you do that, Gregor. Continue with your entertaining tale."

Anything to turn the conversation away from his lies over Tristan's whereabouts.

"Yer a friend to the de Nevilles and a traitor to yer own kin."

"I am no traitor." He ground out his reply with force, Gregor's accusation having struck a recently-exposed nerve. A shutter banged somewhere nearby, but Callum did not shift his gaze from the highlander.

"I am thinking ye intend to betray us three to yer friends here. That is why ye demanded we surrender our weapons."

Callum heard Arlo's sharp intake of breath, and this wounded him just as much as Gregor's insults. Coming so soon after his own barrage of self-abuse, it was too much. Red mist descended before his eyes.

He took a step closer to the older man, squaring up as if for a fight. "I dare you to say those words again."

Gregor leaned closer, his sour breath filling Callum's nostrils. "And I dare ye to do what we came here to do. Kill the de Nevilles."

"I will not harm Frida de Neville. Nor any of her kin within these walls." His voice was too loud and carried too far around the courtyard. He must not lose control. "Jonah is scarce old enough to bear arms. Is this the man you truly are, Gregor? One who would strike down a youth?"

His adversary's eyes glittered with triumph. "Yer Lord Jonah has seen more winters than young Arlo, I'd wager. Here's more proof that ye value English blood higher than Scots. That boy in there is capable of swinging a sword, and if ye won't face him, I will." Gregor spun around and resumed his journey towards the front steps.

Callum was not entirely sure of the sequence of the ensuing

events. His rage erupted in a fierce roar. He grabbed Gregor by the shoulders, dimly aware of Arlo shouting a warning. Then Gregor was on the ground, his knife still clutched in his fist, and Callum's own fist was stinging from the blow he had landed.

For a moment the man lay still. Slowly the ringing in Callum's ears lessened. He shook his head to clear his senses.

"Get up," he ordered.

The man did not move. Arlo crouched down beside him. "I think ye have killed him," the lad said, breathlessly.

"I have not felled a man with one punch to the head." Callum flexed his fingers, mayhap wishing he had.

Gregor groaned, his long limbs flailing on the grass.

"Get up," Callum repeated, conscious of the scene they were causing. The tramp of booted feet came from around the corner. If the guards were to hear anything amiss, they would be upon them in seconds.

It seemed to take an age, but eventually Gregor stood, waving away Arlo's hesitant offer of assistance. "At least ye fight like a warrior," he declared.

Callum was taken aback, but he didn't let it show. "As one warrior to another, I ask you to leave now, Gregor. I cannot risk your doubts and suspicions sabotaging my ability to carry out the Bruce's orders." He ensured his words were forceful even as his voice was as low as a whisper.

Gregor put a hand to his head. "Ye will let me fetch my things?"

"Aye." Callum turned around the inspect the courtyard. Even the chickens had moved on elsewhere. 'Twas hard to believe, but their terse exchange appeared to have gone unnoticed.

Though the banging shutter snagged in his memory. Callum stepped closer to the hall, wondering which window the noise had come from. Had Frida been sitting and watching all along? The thought made his heart ache.

He might wish to put Tristan's sister from his mind and his heart, but she had carved a space for herself in both places. She would not be leaving any time soon.

Arlo shouted a warning, breaking into his spiralling thoughts. He felt warm hands on his back, pushing him to one side. There was a sickening thud and a gasp, almost of surprise.

Callum waited for the pain to hit him. When none came, he turned around.

Then came the pain.

Young Arlo lay face down on the grass. The curved handle of Gregor's knife sticking from his shoulder blade.

Gregor stood a few feet away, his expression unreadable.

Callum's moan of anguish was almost inaudible as he sank to his knees by the lad's prone form.

"Arlo," he said urgently, putting a hand to the lad's warm cheek. Blood soaked through the boy's shirt, pooling on the trampled grass. A sickly-sweet smell wafted up towards him. Breathing heavily, Callum lifted his eyes to Gregor. "What have ye done?"

"I didnae mean to strike the lad," the highlander protested. His black eyes flickered past Callum and what he saw galvanised him into action. He scuttered backwards, then turned and broke into a run. Before Callum realised what was happening, Gregor was pounding along the path to the main gates.

"Stop him," bellowed Callum. Far away, the guard at the gates stepped into position, blocking Gregor's path with his sword at the ready.

Callum shifted his attention back to Arlo. "Stay with me, lad," he begged.

He started to see Jonah dropping to his knees on the other side of Arlo. The English lord placed his fingers on Arlo's neck, searching for a pulse and smiling in confirmation when he found one. "He lives still." Jonah met Callum's eye. "Do not remove the knife until Frida is here."

"Can we send for her?"

"She is already on her way." Jonah smiled briefly. "I was watching you from the solar."

Distantly, Callum registered that this represented a new danger. What exactly had Jonah seen? More importantly, what had he heard?

"I heard you speak up in defence of Frida," Jonah answered his unspoken question. "And in defence of me."

"I would do naught else," Callum replied, his attention still fixed on Arlo.

"Aye, I see that now." Jonah stood with surprising grace considering his club foot. "You have proven my suspicions invalid, Callum. I am sorry for doubting you."

"I did not know of these doubts," Callum declared. "But all I can think of now is the preservation of this young life."

He spoke with sincerity, straight from his heart. Even when beautiful Frida hurried down the steps, he was little moved by the fierce determination in her eyes and voice as she directed willing servants to assist her.

The turmoil of his thoughts had abated. His focus had narrowed to one thing. Arlo's life.

Callum could not bear to be responsible for another senseless death.

CHAPTER EIGHT

FRIDA TOOK IN the scene as she rushed down the stone steps. Callum knelt by the fallen boy, his tanned face ashen with shock. Jonah paced back and forth, his gait customarily uneven. The boy lay between them, the narrowness of his shoulders giving away his youth. She reckoned he could be no older than her youngest sister, Esme.

Too young to have a knife stuck in his back.

Breathing deeply, she steeled herself for the horror of what she must face.

"What has happened?" she asked briskly, falling to her knees opposite Callum. Her ankle protested, but she ignored the pain. While the knight framed his reply, she felt for a pulse, relieved when it thrummed steady and strong beneath her fingers. The boy, however, was unconscious.

"My man Gregor threw his knife. It was meant for me."

The bald statement surprised her, but this was not the time to question it.

"Did he hit his head?"

"I did not see him fall." Callum dragged a hand through his hair, leaving a smear of blood on his craggy forehead. "Can you save him?"

She did not yet know.

"What is his name?"

"Arlo." Callum leaned forward, distress writ large over his

handsome features. His hands shook as he waved them near the knife handle. "I do not know what to do."

Frida leaned closer to the boy, breathing in the smell of damp earth and fresh blood. "Arlo?" She tried, speaking close to his ear, but he did not react. "We must get him inside." She pushed herself awkwardly to her feet, beckoning to two guardsmen who tarried behind her with a long wooden board. Her eyes found Agnes amongst the rapidly growing throng. "We need boiling water and linens."

"Very good, milady." The cook scurried back to the kitchens.

'Twould be the second time this day Agnes was called upon to boil water to treat an injury. Though Frida's own incident paled in comparison to the life-threatening wound before her.

"Carry him to the solar," she ordered the guards, who were carefully lifting Arlo onto the board.

"The solar?" Callum's gaze locked with hers. "Thank you, Frida."

"It will give him the best chance of recovery."

Jonah was at her side, uncommonly agitated. "What can I do?"

Her eyebrows lifted, but it would be churlish of her to express surprise. "The man who threw the knife. Gregor?" She glanced at Callum for confirmation. "Enquire with the gatekeeper if he was apprehended. He should be punished."

"Most certainly he should." With no further prevarication, Jonah began walking haltingly towards the outer gates.

Frida watched him for the briefest of moments. What had transpired to make Jonah so keen to be helpful?

But her brother was not her main concern. Ahead of her lay the greatest test of her abilities she had ever faced.

Frida was naturally skilled with herbs, a gift which her mother always said came from her great grandmother. Back at Wolvesley, for several summers she had worked side by side with the healer, but only treating minor afflictions found within the day-to-day workings of a prosperous castle. A baby with croup.

An old woman with an aching back. A farm-worker accidentally cut with an axe.

She had never been near a battlefield in her life. Never treated an injury inflicted with malice. Never before been the one to mark the difference between life and death.

But the boy, Arlo, must be saved. He was too young to die.

And she was the only one who could help him.

This suddenly struck her as ridiculous. At Wolvesley Castle, they had both a healer and an apothecary within the bailey walls. What had she been thinking to set up home so far removed from such support? With meagre staff to top it all.

She clutched her hands together to stop them from trembling. Callum had already rushed ahead of the stretcher-bearers to clear their path. She could not dally out here any longer.

Walking as steadily as she could, Frida followed the throng back inside the hall. The cosy welcome of the great hall was jarring, almost unsettling when so much violence had crossed their path. A small group of servants hovered near the fire, watching her with wide eyes. The girl called Jennifer stepped forward.

"I would be of assistance, milady. My pa trained as a barber-surgeon. I am well-used to the sight of blood."

Frida released a breath she had not known she'd been holding. "Thank you, Jennifer. Come with me to the solar. The rest of you should help Agnes in the kitchen. We need a regular supply of hot water. And all the clean linens you can find."

Glad to have a purpose, the girls scurried away. Frida led Jennifer to the solar, careful to keep her nerves under wraps. The guards had pushed back the heavy furniture and made room for the boy on the floor. Frida frowned when she saw this, she had intended he be laid on the couch. But perchance they were right not to move him too much. At least the room was warm.

But she did not want an audience.

"I thank you all for your help," she declared. "Can everyone please leave us now, except Jennifer. And Callum," she added, noting his entreating gaze.

In truth she would prefer Callum to go. His very presence unsettled her, which was the last thing she needed when every moment and every decision carried so much import. But she could see in his eyes how much the boy's welfare meant to him.

His concern did him credit, she decided. It touched her heart, which had started opening to him e'en before this.

The guards shuffled out and moments later, two young housemaids rushed in with their arms full of linens. Agnes followed them, panting slightly, with a large basin of hot water.

"There is more coming," she said, answering Frida's unvoiced question.

Frida knelt on the rug by Arlo's side. His breathing had become shallow. There was no time to waste. She glanced up to Jennifer.

"Can you hold him still?"

"Aye." The girl placed her hands on Arlo's shoulders, well clear of the knife. Her calm certainty helped steady Frida's nerves.

Frida did not want to do this, but she had no choice.

Breathing deeply, she grasped the handle of the knife and pulled. The blade came free easily, followed by a sickening spurt of blood, which Frida hastily suppressed with a wad of folded linens, passed to her by Jennifer. Her first attempt to staunch the blood failed, as did the second. She could not apply enough pressure, partially because of her injured left arm. Steadying her rising panic, Frida swathed her right hand with a clean cloth and jammed the heel of it into the boy's wound, pressing down with all her strength. Opposite her, Callum muttered something that may have been a prayer.

She met his anxious gaze over Arlo's prone body and smiled with what she hoped was reassurance.

"I do not believe the blade came into contact with the boy's shoulder blade."

"That is good?"

"Aye, that is good." Long moments passed and the bleeding

at last began to lessen. She turned her head to Jennifer. "We shall need honey, strong thread and a sharp needle."

"I'll go at once, milady."

"Can you save him?" Callum asked again.

"I shall try," she promised. They were momentarily alone in the quiet chamber. A log cracked in the fire and the boy stirred, moaning slightly. Frida put the back of her hand to his smooth cheek, registering his coolness. "Can you cover him with a rug?" She nodded to the soft, hand-stitched rug laid over the chair behind Callum.

He reached for it. "It will be ruined." He paused. "Shall I fetch a rough one from the loft where we slept?"

"Nay. Do not be foolish." She shook her head, her hair swinging below her shoulders. "A rug has no value next to a life. Besides, I imagine Arlo is comforted by your presence here."

Callum snorted, even as he folded the rug over the boy's legs and torso with the greatest of care. "I do not deserve his esteem."

"How so?"

"'Tis my fault he is like this. I should have kept him safe."

Her eyebrows raised with surprise. "But you were not the one to throw the knife."

A look of anguish passed over his face, making Frida all the more confused. But all he said was, "I should have known what Gregor was capable of."

Frida's legs were growing cramped on the floor. Her back burned through proximity to the fire and her efforts to staunch Arlo's bleeding had brought perspiration out on her brow. "We can never know what lies ahead," she said, steadily. She knew that more than most.

But Callum was right, she thought. He *should* have known the nature of the man who rode beside him.

He looked down, before she could properly confirm if his dark eyes were glassy with tears. "If he dies, I shall ne'er forgive myself."

"Because of Gregor?" A slight nod of his head confirmed it.

"Was there a quarrel between you?"

"I only met him a sennight since."

Not a proper answer.

Frida frowned. "That is not what I asked."

When he met her eyes, his gaze was steady. "I did not trust him, nor did I trust his temper. But the man I serve holds Gregor in high esteem." He shrugged his shoulders. "Arlo, I have known for many summers. I promised him my protection."

She dared release some of the pressure on the boy's shoulders, easing the tension in her own body in the process. The bleeding had all but stopped. "Should we send word to his parents?"

"He has none." Callum's voice was gruff. "They were killed in a raid at midsummer."

She stifled a gasp of dismay. "A Scottish raid?"

He lowered his eyes. "The Scots were involved, aye."

"These are troubled times. I fear for my brother Tristan every day he is gone from Wolvesley."

Callum's lips parted as if he were about to speak, but no words came out. His anguished eyes conveyed the tumult of his thoughts. Frida resisted the urge to reach out to him and looked back down at the boy whose wellbeing hung in her hands. The frayed edges of his linen tunic were now mattered with so much blood it was hard to distinguish cloth from skin.

"Ember Hall has always been a place of peace." She spoke the truth of her heart without pause. "I never imagined bloodshed on our doorstep."

"'Twas I who brought it to you. I am sorry for it." His words came out in a fierce rush, the violence of his expression belying the sentiment he expressed.

Again, his show of emotion confused her. Callum Baine was a knight, surely well-used to seeing comrades fall. *He must take his responsibilities to the boy seriously,* she thought, *especially if Arlo is now all alone in the world. And he had promised him protection.*

Tentatively, she rinsed a cloth with warm water and began

the painstaking process of cleaning the wound. It was deep, and she must not risk starting the bleeding up again. The actions soothed her. 'Twas a relief to fix her attention on something other than the handsome man kneeling opposite, so close she could feel the warmth of his breath on her fingers.

Jennifer returned, her footsteps quick and light across the stone flags. As she laid out a needle, thread and a jar of honey on the low table, her hazel eyes sought Frida's.

"Lord Jonah is in the great hall. He said to tell you that the man, Gregor, got away."

Frida knew a swell of frustration, but Callum's reaction was more extreme. He rose to his feet and turned away from them both, his hands clenching into fists at his sides.

"Lord Jonah asked if we should send the guards after him?"

Frida bit down on her lip. She was minded to refuse, but Callum appeared in sore need of justice. Her mind raced with indecision, for she had been resolved to preside over Ember Hall without ever deferring to a man's judgement.

But her father had always taught her that a wise leader must adapt to changing circumstance.

"What do you say, Callum?" she asked, softly.

Still facing away from her, he released his fists and lifted his chin. "I say your guards are better placed defending Ember Hall than in chasing a worthless man far and wide."

She nodded her agreement, still carefully prying Arlo's tattered tunic away from the knife wound. Her left arm stung beneath the bandage and she sent up prayers that it would not impede her more.

"Very well. I dare say he will not return. If he does, the guards should take him prisoner." She lifted her gaze back to Jennifer. "Can you see that the message is delivered?"

Jennifer nodded, but her expression remained anxious.

"What is it?" Frida asked.

"Lord Jonah said something else as well." The maid swallowed. "He said the guard told him that Gregor spoke with a

Scottish brogue."

Frida paused, one hand in the basin of cooling water. "Did the guard think him a Scot?" Her eyes flew to Callum, who stood curiously still. "Is it possible that you rode here with a Scotsman? On a quest to protect us from increased Scottish raids?"

Her mind immediately conjured visions of musclebound highland warriors, robed in tartan, shrieking vengeance as they stormed across the hills. Mayhap her father had not been wrong to order fortifications be built at Ember Hall.

But when Callum turned to her, he looked unperturbed. "We live close to the border, this far north." He shrugged his shoulders. "Bloodlines are mixed. 'Tis true e'en of the French and the English. And in the most noble households."

Again, he did not answer my question.

But she could not deny the truth of his words.

A faint moan from Arlo chased away all such thoughts. It was good news if the boy was regaining consciousness. But 'twould be better still if she could stitch his wound before he fully recovered his senses.

"Pass me the needle," she said quickly to Jennifer.

"I have already threaded it," the girl replied.

Frida worked quickly, closing her mind to the horrors of the gaping wound and the layers of muscle she could glimpse through the ragged flesh. She did not allow doubts over her competence, nor the neatness of her stitching to take over. And when she had finished, she scooped up honey and wadded it into the wound before swathing it with bandages. The boy perchance had a long journey of recovery before him, but she had done all she could.

All she knew how.

Her head dropped with both fatigue and a wave of distress which came in place of the adrenaline that had fuelled her actions thus far. Callum clearly held himself responsible for this young man. And Frida felt the same.

But was she equipped to restore balance when so much harm

had been wreaked?

In times past she might have looked to the spirits for an answer. Now she stood alone. And she had never felt the isolation more.

She closed her eyes to ward off tears that were already brimming.

Shock, the rational part of her mind declared.

Callum's voice broke through her growing sorrow. "Jennifer, might you fetch us some wine?"

As the girl's footsteps passed through the chamber, Callum's warm hand fastened about her wrist. She sensed him drawing closer and it took all her remaining strength not to rest her aching head against his muscular chest. To seek comfort in one so willing to offer it.

"You did well," he said, softly.

Frida opened her eyes, relieved that no tears spilled down her cheeks. She sniffed and inclined her head towards the boy. "We must ensure no fever sets in."

Callum nodded. He had come to rest on the rug beside her, not so very much closer than they had been while she tended to Arlo. But now his body was angled towards Frida.

His hand remained about her wrist, anchoring her to hope and banishing the fears that flickered at the edge of her consciousness. She breathed in woodsmoke from the fire, mingled with Callum's particular masculine scent.

"You have given him a chance." His voice was thick.

She nodded, swallowing down a lump of emotion. "Let us hope, a strong chance."

"Aye." His brown eyes looked down into hers, as if calling her home. Without shifting his gaze, his hand left her right wrist and skimmed up over the length of her arm, sending flickers of awareness through her stiff body. When his palm cupped her cheek, she could do naught but lean into it, batting her eyelids shut as his thumb carefully nudged away a stubborn tear. "Frida," he said.

With one word he lit a fire inside her.

Her eyes flew open to find his face inches from hers. Acting purely on instinct, she reached up to place her own hand over his. Her breath caught in her throat as their fingers entwined.

"You are remarkable," he whispered. "I knew it from the first."

A smile hovered around her lips, despite knowing all the reasons she should dispute his praise. For one, the proof of her skill with Arlo remained to be seen. For two, she had solemnly vowed to live a life clear of men.

But this man had found a place in her heart, however much she might try to deny it.

"I simply do my best." She paused, anticipation tingling down her spine. "As we all must."

Her heart raced beneath the bodice of her dress at the notion—the crazy notion—that he might press his lips upon hers. But in another moment, his face had clouded over and he was drawing away from her.

"Aye," he said. "We all must."

Frida felt a blush heat her cheeks, but 'twas not from the fire. What had she said that was wrong? She swallowed and attempted to straighten her aching limbs; she had been kneeling so long that a cramp was setting in. She put a hand to her skirts before realising that both were covered in blood.

Callum rose up with enviable ease and folded his hands behind his back as he looked down at Arlo.

"I will watch over him." His voice was gruff.

Frida blanched. Was she being dismissed?

From the solar of her own house?

She was at a disadvantage on the floor while he loomed over her so. Using the table as a support, she hefted herself onto her feet, stumbling a little on her weak ankle. Immediately Callum came to her aid.

"Steady," he said.

But he did not meet her eye and his touch was perfunctory;

there was no tenderness to it.

She mustered her dignity, ignoring the stains on her dress. "I can manage, thank you."

A movement at the door caught her eye. It was Jennifer, carrying a tray with two goblets and a pitcher of wine.

Wine that she did not want.

Frida lifted her chin. "Thank you, Jennifer." She fixed her gaze on the servant, not allowing herself to even glance at the knight stood by the fire. "And thank you for your help. Alas, I am needed elsewhere, but I am sure Sir Callum will be glad to partake of refreshment."

With that, she hobbled from the chamber.

Mayhap Sir Callum would enjoy the company of the pretty serving wench while he drank his wine.

Frida did not allow herself to care.

CHAPTER NINE

THE SABBATH DAWNED damp and cold, so cold that Callum's breath hung mistily in the air ahead of him as he trudged up the hill to the wood store.

Two days had passed since that fateful afternoon. Days in which Callum did everything in his power to keep distance between himself and Frida. Not because he wanted to avoid her, but because he no longer trusted himself in her presence.

No one else was about at this early hour. Even the cooing of the woodpigeons sounded muted. Above his head, grey clouds scuttled across a grey sky. Callum shivered a little, despite the warmth of his blue cloak. But cold was good. Cold kept his senses sharp and alert.

Exactly as he needed them to be.

He had almost kissed her, that afternoon in the solar. He'd been just moments away from tilting his head and claiming her sweet lips with his own, giving in to the craving that had haunted him ever since his arrival at Ember Hall.

But then she had spoken words about doing one's best, invoking the strict moral code by which Callum's mother had raised him. And Callum had floundered.

How could he be doing his best when he was lying to the woman he wanted to kiss?

How could he be doing his best when a boy who believed in him lay injured, fighting for his life?

How could he be doing his best when Frida, if she knew the truth, would doubtless order his arrest?

Were it not for this new knowledge about Tristan's time in Scotland, Callum wondered if he might, in a moment of weakness, have confessed all to Frida. For living like this was purgatory. And the longer he spent at Ember Hall, the more entrenched in his heart she became. Even as he took steps to avoid her, he lived for those moments when he glimpsed her hurrying across the yard, her silvery hair tumbling down her slender back, her head held high and proud.

But how could he pledge his love to a woman whose own brother may well have ordered the destruction of Kielder Castle, initiating the siege which saw so many innocent lives lost?

He could not.

His hand wrapped around the smooth wood of the axe handle and he swung it upwards, relishing in the moment of greatest power, when the heavy metal axe head hovered at its highest point. He brought it forcefully down and a log splintered in two, falling in the damp grass at his booted feet.

Damn Tristan de Neville to hell.

Callum grunted with satisfaction. At least he could depend on physical labour to vent his surging frustration. There was no shortage of work to be done. And with Gregor gone, Arlo laid up and Andrew tending to him, Callum was determined to pull enough weight for the four of them—making amends for his deception in the only way he could.

At least Arlo was recovering, he reflected, positioning a new log on the stump and readying his stance. The boy had regained consciousness some hours after Frida had tied off her last careful stitch. Callum was simultaneously overjoyed and over-anxious lest he say something—in pain or delirium—that gave them away.

As soon as he was decently able, Callum had Arlo moved from the solar to a comfortable pallet in their loft above the stables. It was safer for him, for all of them, to be away from the main house. Frida came twice a day to check on his progress and change his dressing. At such times, Callum had given Andrew and Arlo strict orders to hold their tongues and say as little as possible. Andrew was thus far embracing his role as a tongue-tied simple peasant, and Arlo was still too weak for much conversation.

Callum swung his axe again, then piled the newly-cut logs inside a barrow. Physical exertion had begun to warm his limbs and he untied his cloak, relishing the cool breeze that whispered across his skin.

So far, his men remained safe. So far, no one suspected them. But he was playing with fire. At any moment they could be discovered.

If only they had left earlier, before Arlo was so grievously injured. It would be several days more before the lad could feasibly mount a horse. And Callum would not risk his recovery by stealing him away earlier. Nor could he abandon him.

He swallowed a curse, releasing all his energy into the fall of the axe and taking grim satisfaction in the cleanness of the cut.

"You shall have us ready for winter before the bell tolls for chapel," spoke a voice he knew well.

Callum spun around, newly aware of his crumpled tunic and dishevelled appearance. He had washed his face and hair last night, but with no looking glass in the loft, he had not been able to shave, nor properly tame his unruly dark curls.

Frida stood just feet away beside a low stone wall. She was dressed in a rich gown of dark green covered with a fur-lined cloak in a lighter shade. Her long hair hung in a neat plait over one shoulder; her hood raised against the chill of the day.

He bowed. "Good morn, Frida." The words came with difficulty, his tongue seemed glued to the roof of his mouth.

She nodded in response. "Callum." Her blue eyes sought his, but as soon as he met her gaze, she looked past him towards the log store. "I thank you for your efforts here."

He shrugged awkwardly. "I must earn my keep. Especially with my men unable to do so."

"All men are entitled to rest on the sabbath." She smiled, but with more politeness than warmth.

He could not rest. If he sat still, his spiralling thoughts would soon drive him demented.

"'Tis my belief that the good lord knows when there is work to be done. And forgives a man for doing it." Unable to gaze any longer at her beautiful face, he half-turned and gestured to the grey expanse of sky. "'Tis also my belief that we will have snow before the sennight is out."

He felt rather than heard her gasp of surprise. "Snow? Before All Saints Day?"

"Have you ne'er wintered this far north?" His tone was glib, but he regretted it when he looked upon her face and saw fear stamped upon it.

"I have not." She clutched her cloak around her.

"We shall be well prepared." He nodded towards the log store.

"Aye, thanks to you." She gave a ghost of a smile, which could not banish the anxiety from her blue gaze.

It occurred to him that he may no longer be at Ember Hall once the foulest of the winter weather arrived. Frida might have to face the frost and snow without him.

"I shall be sure to fix the barn roof before then." He nodded emphatically, keen to provide all the reassurance he could amidst his sudden sense of loss.

Frida straightened up, wincing a little as she balanced her weight on her injured ankle. Again, Callum had a strong urge to offer her comfort.

An urge he pushed down with all the others.

"As I said, we are grateful for your efforts." She nodded towards the low wall and he realised she had placed objects upon it. "I have brought you a skin of wine together with bread and cheese."

He pursed his lips, not liking to think of Frida waiting upon him. Nor of her giving him special treatment.

"That was not necessary."

He thought he saw her flinch, but her gaze remained steady and cool. He must have imagined it.

"You did not break your fast with the others in the great hall. Whene'er workers are in such demand that they must miss meals, 'tis my custom to bring refreshments out to them."

No special treatment then. He was just another man working the grounds of Ember Hall. 'Twas what he wanted, so why was he disappointed to hear it?

"You are kind," he muttered.

She tightened her lips. "I only follow the lessons my mother taught me."

Her mother, the Countess of Wolvesley. He recalled a petite woman with a radiant smile. Another whose hospitality he had trampled upon.

"Thank you, Frida," he said, summoning warmth into his words, for his torment made him as cold as ice.

She nodded once. "You must take care with that axe. It is sharp."

She was about to leave. Suddenly he didn't want her to go. This realisation cut through the clamour of his confusion like his axe splitting the log. He stepped forward. "Are you headed for chapel?"

"Aye, Mirrie and I will walk down into the village."

"Not the chapel here?" He thought of the peaceful chamber with the vivid murals.

"'Tis important that we meet the local families." She looked down at the damp grass for a moment. "Would you care to join us?"

He held her gaze. "Is that invitation extended to all who work at Ember Hall?"

This time she did not flinch. "Of course."

His urge to say yes was in direct conflict with his rational mind. He must put distance between them to deny to himself the alluring connection which sparked in the air whenever she was near.

But he didn't want to deny it any longer. He was tired of pretending to be something he was not. For this one moment in time, he wanted to own the desires of his heart.

He wanted to be special to her—not just another worker, nor just another knight.

He took a second step closer, noting her physical reaction to his increased proximity. A pulse fluttered at the side of her neck. How he wanted to kiss it.

"I would go with you chapel if I might sit beside you," he said recklessly. He was suddenly uncaring of propriety, and e'en more uncaring of keeping up this pretence of indifference. He was already in trouble.

And he may as well be hung for a sheep as a lamb.

"As a friend of the family, that would be entirely acceptable."

He was stood directly in front of her now. Close enough to hear the raggedness of her breathing. He caught one of her gloved hands in his. "What if I was not a friend of your family? What if I was just Callum Baine, desirous of your company?"

"My company?" she echoed. Her pupils had grown wide and liquid, her sweet lips parted just enough for him to kiss them.

"More than your company," he declared. Greatly daring, he brought her gloved fingers to his mouth. If she pulled away, he would release her.

But she didn't.

He pressed his lips to her knuckles, gazing all the while into her darkened eyes. When she made no move to resist, his lips travelled upwards, skimming her wrist until he had pushed away the fabric of her sleeves. When his mouth brushed against the bare skin of her forearm, Frida gasped.

A gasp of pleasure.

She tasted of lavender.

He kissed her there again, wrapping his other arm around her waist and drawing her closer until less than an inch separated them.

"Frida," he said.

Now that she was so close, so yielding, he was paralysed by his own desires. 'Twas not proper to embrace an unchaperoned young lady out in the open where anyone might come across them. But for the life of him, he could not step away. Moments passed. He closed his eyes, gathering both his strength and his commonsense.

And then both deserted him in a sudden wave as Frida raised herself onto her tiptoes and began kissing him. Her mouth was soft and hesitant, her body warm against his. With a groan of willing submission, he crushed his arms about her and kissed her back. He was gentle at first, but as she wound her arms about his shoulders, desire defeated his reason and he parted her lips with his tongue, running his hands down her spine and pulling her against him.

The gift he had longed for was here, in his arms.

Frida de Neville. The girl he had loved from afar. The woman he had not been able to forget.

She pulled away, lifting her chin so that he was scorched by her blue gaze.

"I'm sorry." The words fell from his lips.

A beat passed before she frowned. "Why so?"

"I should not have kissed you so." His hands were still upon her body. He should release her, but he could not bring himself to do so.

"'Twas I that kissed you," she whispered. "I only wanted a moment to check this was real." Her nostrils flared. "And that it was what you wanted."

In answer, he claimed her mouth again, slanting his lips over hers and kissing her thoroughly. "It is what I want, Frida," he said. "It is what I have wanted for the longest time." His hands skimmed over the gentle curve of her hips. He wanted to explore beneath the heavy folds of her cloak but knew that territory was forbidden.

And that his self-control hung on a knife edge.

She rested her palms against his chest, her touch burning through his tunic. "I vowed to live a life free of men."

He regarded her steadily, drinking her in. Her eyes, glowing with passion. Her oval face, framed with loosened strands of silver hair.

"I would recommend you live a life free of *other* men," he said, solemnly. "But I plead for leniency for this particular man."

Her laughter brought a bolt of joy to his heart. "I believe I have already granted it."

He kissed her again. His senses, which minutes earlier had registered the chill of the morn and the mournful cry of the birds, were now awash with Frida. Her lavender fragrance, the rich wool of her cloak, the way her body slotted against his so perfectly.

"Frida?" The call pierced the misty haze, causing them to spring apart.

"'Tis Mirrie," Frida said. Her lips were swollen from his kisses, her eyes wide and dark. She rocked to one side and he shot out his arms to steady her.

He wanted to suggest that they hide in the wood store until Mirabel had gone, but deep down he knew that this precious interlude was already over. Frida was smoothing down her cloak and re-positioning her hood. Her breathing steadied as she looked over her shoulder.

"I'm here," she called in return.

Callum made his own breathing slow down. For want of something to occupy himself with, he picked up his cloak and slung it back over his shoulders. A tall shape loomed out of the mist.

"There you are," Mirabel said. She dropped into a small curtsy and Callum bowed in return. Like Frida, Mirabel was dressed in a warm cloak with the hood pulled over her head. He had not spent much time in Mirabel's company, but he thought there was something odd about her eyes. As if she was trying overly hard to repress a smile. "Are you ready for chapel?" she asked Frida.

Composed as ever, Frida nodded. "Let us depart."

Callum bowed again. "Fare thee well, ladies."

Mirabel nodded and took Frida's arm. The two of them walked away from him, down the slight incline to the courtyard, leaving Callum alone with his thoughts. Before they disappeared around the corner, Frida threw him one last look, but she was too far away for him to properly see the expression on her face.

It looked as if she was smiling.

Smiling in farewell? Or smiling in anticipation of seeing him once more?

Callum turned back to the pile of waiting logs with a barely smothered growl of frustration. This turn of events did not make his path forward any clearer.

In fact, with every day that passed, his vision of the future became increasingly muddled.

CHAPTER TEN

RIDA'S ANKLE TWINGED as she walked with Mirrie through the main gates and down the path towards the village. It was some distance from Ember Hall to the local place of worship, so much so that Frida had contemplated inviting the priest to lead a weekly service at their own chapel when they first took up residence.

But she also knew it was important that she and Mirrie be known and accepted by the locals. If they were to not only survive, but thrive, in this remote locale, then they would need the support of those who lived nearby. This summer's delayed harvest had already proven that.

Which was why, every sabbath, Frida and Mirrie donned their most respectable attire and made the halting journey down the hill to the small wattle-and-daub chapel which nestled above the river in a copse of trees. It was a pretty, peaceful place. Despite the effort involved, Frida usually found the services deeply soothing.

But not today.

Today, she hardly noticed the rolling fields and ancient woodlands revealed by the gentle turns of the narrow lane. When Mirrie pointed out the glorious golden canopy of autumn leaves in the distance, Frida nodded without e'en a glance in that direction.

Mirrie swung around to face her, taking hold of both her

hands. Frida found herself drawn into her friend's inquisitive gaze.

"Aren't we going to talk about it?"

"About what?" Frida hedged.

Mirrie looked behind them, checking they were all alone. But the only other creature nearby was a shy woodpigeon who fluttered away into a tall tree. "I saw you," she declared.

Frida's heart began to pound all over again. From the way Mirrie's eyes danced, she knew there was no point trying to deny anything.

Frida exhaled in a rush, her breath hanging in the cold air between them. "You saw?"

Mirrie nodded. "I did not intend to spy upon you, but nonetheless, I saw."

Part of Frida wondered if she had imagined the whole thing. It had been like a scene from a dream. The handsome knight, the warmth of his arms, the searing heat of his kiss. She had pressed her palms against the hard ridge of muscles on his chest and his stubble had rasped against her cheek.

She tightened her grip on her friend's gloved fingers. "Then you can tell me it was real?"

"Aye." Mirrie smiled. "What I saw was real enough."

Frida's strength threatened to desert her. "Oh Mirrie," she whispered.

Acting with insight born from familiarity, Mirrie fastened her arm supportively around Frida's waist, allowing her to lean her weight against her. The slope of the lane combined with the coolness of the morn and Frida's near feverish excitement did not create a steady situation for her ankle.

"There is no cause for distress, Frida. None that I bore witness to." She giggled, like a peal of church bells. "Unless you are swooning with happiness?"

"I hardly know what to think," Frida whispered. They were approaching the top end of the village and she did not want to be overheard. "Save that I have acted in a way my parents would disapprove of."

She recalled her father's uncommonly stern gaze as he helped her into the carriage that would bear her from Wolvesley Castle to an as-yet-unknown life at Ember Hall.

"Take heed, child," he'd said, *"I only permit this due to your proven sensibility. Retain that wisdom, whatever the days ahead may bring. Do not be lured into decadence simply for want of my supervision."*

She had clicked her tongue and reminded him of her deep desire to put distance between herself and decadence.

But was her behaviour this morn not decadent?

She had been lured into… *something!* By the passion stirring in Callum's wondrous brown eyes.

She swallowed awkwardly, feeling heat rising to her cheeks. It would not be proper to enter chapel whilst remembering how it had felt to stand in his arms with his hands running over her body. But those memories—sharper and more vivid than the chill wind at her back—would not be easily quashed.

Mirrie steered them both safely around a muddy puddle which had opened in the rutted path.

"The Earl and Countess of Wolvesley always seemed very approving of happiness to me." Mirrie paused, glancing sideways at her friend. "Is that not what you are feeling right now, Frida? Happiness?"

A smile tugged her lips as she pondered the question. She was undoubtably light of heart. A frothy, giddy sort of feeling bubbled up inside her, as if all problems were surmountable and all good things were possible.

She had not felt like this since her fall from the horse.

"I think you're right," she whispered. They were passing beneath the wooden arch which marked entry to the church yard. "I am happy."

Mirrie's answering smile was even larger than Frida's own. They squeezed each other's hands and then, of one accord, moved apart so they could properly greet the small group of waiting villagers.

Frida nodded and smiled and passed comments about the inclement weather, all the while thinking of one thing.

Callum.

Mirrie was right, he made her happy.

More than that, he made her feel whole.

Whole, after being broken for over two long years. Broken because of her ankle. Broken because of her altered appearance and altered spirit. But mostly, broken because she had lost her Sight; that connection with the natural world that had always helped her feel strong and complete.

But now Callum filled up the emptiness inside of her.

Frida sat beside Mirrie on the narrow wooden pew at the front of the chapel, bowing her head respectfully as the ageing priest delivered his sermon, but she hardly heard a word. Part of her was reliving every moment of that extraordinary kiss. The first time she had e'er been embraced with such passion.

And the other part was asking herself an important question.

Can I break down my barriers and confess the love in my heart?

Callum had made his feelings clear. He remembered her from Wolvesley. He had grieved her. Although she couldn't allow herself to feel guilty about that. 'Twas not her doing that the man left Wolvesley before she recovered consciousness. And 'twas not her fault that Tristan had never thought to send word to him in France.

Men are funny creatures, she mused. So preoccupied with battles and warfare that they rarely attended to what was really important. Tristan, for example, was apparently blind to the fact that beautiful Mirrie, sitting on this uncomfortable pew beside her, had held a torch for him since they were in the school room together.

What if her instincts had been correct during the Twelfth tide revels at Wolvesley? What if Callum was the man meant for her?

Frida took a deep, rattling breath, drawing curious stares from the genteel family seated on the opposite pew across the stone-flagged aisle. Mirrie nudged her sharply and Frida dragged her attention back to the service. People were kneeling to pray.

Frida shuffled forwards and carefully lowered herself onto a hand-stitched cushion positioned beneath the pew. She pressed her palms together and closed her eyes, allowing the priests' lilting entreaties to wash over her.

Frida prayed for a sign.

Should she stay true to her vow and live a life free of men?

Or should she open her heart to the possibility of love?

THE REST OF the service passed in a haze. She followed Mirrie back down the aisle and out of the chapel, shaking hands with the priest and wrapping her heavy cloak around her as protection from the brisk wind which caused the shutters to bang and children to shriek.

The long walk home was made longer by the unprepossessing grey cloud and a creeping chill which even the noontime sun could not banish. Mirrie talked of pressing apples and preserving berries, but Frida could not properly concentrate. When they were in sight of the stone gateposts of Ember Hall, Mirrie tugged on her elbow until she paused.

"What is it?" Frida shifted her weight onto her right leg, rotating her left ankle as far as she could inside her restrictive boots in an attempt to ease the aching.

"I know you didn't want to talk about it at chapel." Mirrie jerked her head back towards the village. "And most likely you don't want to talk about it now. But I must say this." She took a breath. "I think it's good, what's happening between you and Callum."

Frida pressed her lips together. "Truly, I do not know what is happening."

Mirrie continued as if she hadn't spoken. "He's brought a light back to your eyes that I feared was gone forever."

"But what of my promise to you, to live in Ember Hall for the rest of our lives, just the two of us?" The words burst from Frida's lips before she could hold them back.

"I don't hear wedding bells ringing just yet," Mirrie answered wryly.

Frida looked away, mortified. "Of course not."

"But if that's where things are headed, if that is what is meant to be, then I will be truly happy for you," Mirrie said, sincerity shining from her face. "And I would certainly not stand in your way."

"I am not saying that is what the future holds." Frida folded her arms to hide her discomfort. Tiny droplets of rain began to fall around them.

"We none of us know what the future holds."

"True enough." The rain cast a sheen on Mirrie's hood. Frida took hold of her arm and beckoned her forward. "Let us both get inside before we freeze."

"But you should fight for your happiness," Mirrie persisted, seemingly determined to drive this point home.

By now they were within earshot of the guards. Frida nodded to the man on the gate and waited until they were closer to the walls of the house before saying more.

"When did you become such an expert on matters of the heart, Mirabel Duval?"

She had meant the question lightly, but Mirrie flinched as if she had wounded her.

"Forsooth, I am no expert. Truly." Her voice wobbled, betraying her emotions.

Frida cursed her lack of insight. At one time she would have been able to divine what troubled her friend, without making matters worse by asking her, forcing her to express that which caused her such pain.

"'Tis not the company of my foolhardy brother, Tristan, that you are missing, is it?" Frida guessed. Seeing Mirrie's hastily concealed look of alarm she added, "I know you long ago had feelings for him."

Mirrie dropped her eyes. "I was not aware you knew."

"Aye. I have eyes in my head." Frida smiled, but Mirrie pursed her lips in response.

"Twas long ago, as you say." She sniffed. "We were but children."

"That is what I thought." Frida nodded emphatically. "You are far too sensible and wise to fall for Tristan's charms."

"Such as they are." Mirrie wrinkled her pretty nose.

"Aye, such as they are." Frida smiled again and this time, it was returned.

"Sorry, Frida, your question came out of the blue. I should not have reacted so." Mirrie shook down her hood as they passed through the back door into the kitchen.

"Do not think on it again," Frida assured her. "Mayhap it is the biting cold that affects us both?"

"That must be it." Mirrie hung up her cloak with a shiver. "Will I fetch us some warmed wine? We can sit by the fire in the great hall?"

Tempting as the offer was, Frida shook her head. "Thank you, but nay. I must tend to Arlo. I did not have chance to change his dressing this morn."

Because I went in search of Callum instead.

"You are not going out again so soon?"

"The sooner I go, the sooner I shall return," Frida promised. Her head was already in the low-ceilinged loft over the stables where Arlo lay recovering just feet away from Callum's tidy pallet.

With a farewell smile at her friend, Frida picked up her box of remedies and ducked back outside, her hood pulled up against the rain, which was now falling relentlessly. She walked as quickly as she could across the cobbled courtyard, keeping her weight on the toes of her left foot. She knew this gave her a hobbling sort of gait, but it was also the easiest way to get about without straining her ankle. The old stone steps running up the side of the outbuilding were slippery with rain and she ascended them carefully, rapping against the wooden door at the top before she pushed it open.

Immediately her heart sank, for the loft was empty except for Arlo. She had hoped for a glimpse of Callum, e'en though his habit was to keep himself busy on the land.

Arlo was laying on his side, propped up with rugs and cush-ions to prevent him rolling onto his wound which was healing nicely. His blue eyes lit up when he saw her, and he smiled in welcome.

"Good day," she greeted him. "How do you fare, Arlo?"

The boy had intelligence in his gaze and Frida was careful to always address him with that in mind, but in the short time she had known him, he had said less than ten words to her. At first, she had put this down to him being awkward and in pain, but now part of her wondered if he might be simple-minded.

Callum's other man, Andrew, who oft sat with Arlo, was equally inarticulate.

She wondered at his choice of travelling companions. Two simpletons and a Scottish rebel. But then she recalled that Callum was in service to the Lord of Egremont House. Mayhap Callum had no choice in who he rode out with.

She crossed the wooden floor and lowered herself carefully beside Arlo's pallet. Well-accustomed to their daily procedure, Arlo had already shifted onto his stomach so she might better view his wound. Frida unwound the bandages, pleased to note no whiff of infection. The deep cut had closed nicely, with thick scabs already forming.

Frida touched his shoulder, gently. "You will be up and about in a day or so, I'll wager."

Arlo made a noise which she couldn't properly decipher. His face was pressed into a cushion, so it was hardly surprising she couldn't decipher his speech. But his next words were clear enough.

"Thank ye."

"You are most welcome."

She once again packed his shoulder with honey, covered the wound with a linen pad and wound fresh bandages across his body. The position of the cut meant she must wrap her bandages all around his ribs, going over and under alternate shoulders to keep the dressing in place. Arlo sat up so that she might accomplish this. Usually Andrew was here to help him into a sitting position, but today he managed well enough on his own.

"Very good," she smiled, encouragingly. "Perchance on the morrow you might try to stand?"

His eyes met hers. "Aye, milady," he whispered.

She wished he might converse more easily, so she could get to know this young man who had been so grievously injured on her property. A youth who Callum clearly held in great affection.

Sighing, Frida helped him back down, positioning him again so that he was on his side, facing the door.

"Will your friend be back soon?" she asked. "Andrew, isn't it?"

Arlo opened his mouth as if to reply, but then closed it again. He nodded vigorously, an elaborate pantomime that saw his pallet shift and Frida's jar of honey, which had been precariously balanced on the corner fall to the floor. She tutted as it rolled across the wooden floor and disappeared beneath Callum's pallet.

"'Tis no matter," she said reassuringly, for Arlo's eyebrows shot up his face at her concerned expression. "I can reach it."

But that was easier said than done. Frida had to lower herself into the narrow gap between the two pallets, relieved that Arlo was facing away from her and would not bear witness to her undignified wriggling. Once in position, she blinked until her eyes grew accustomed to the gloom and squinted to make out the glint of the glass jar.

The gleaming blade of a dagger glinted back at her.

Frida quickly stifled her sharp intake of breath, realising that not one, but several blades lay concealed on the dusty floor beneath the pallet. This was no less than a stash of weapons.

A stash that Callum must know about. *Nay,* must be responsible for.

Her fingers trembled as she reached out for the jar of honey, which had settled near the carved wooden handle of a lethal looking dagger.

Did Arlo know about this, she wondered. Either way, she must move quickly else she would risk rousing his suspicion.

"I have it," she declared, somewhat breathlessly.

Arlo grunted in response.

Frida pushed herself to her feet, dishevelled and dusty from the floor. She placed the honey back in the box and snapped the lid shut.

"That will be all for today," she trilled.

Arlo nodded again and smiled. Footsteps outside had her starting with something like fear.

Misplaced fear?

Frida no longer knew. But she held herself steady and composed, half hoping and half dreading that Callum would appear through the wooden door.

But 'twas not Callum, 'twas Andrew. And Frida had never been so aware of his height and strength.

He smiled slightly and nodded his auburn head in greeting. Over the past two days, Frida had grown accustomed to the silence of these men, but now it struck her as menacing.

What if they were not simple, as she had previously thought? What if they were in league against her?

Did that mean that Callum was also in league against her? Frida's heart pounded at the possibility. Surely that could not be?

In the moment, all that mattered was that she got out of the loft and into the fresh air, where she might breathe freely and unravel her tangled thoughts.

Swallowing hard, Frida walked past Arlo and made her way towards the door. By necessity, she must pass close to Andrew, who shrank back against the stone wall to let her pass.

"Milady," he grunted.

"Andrew." She adopted what she hoped was a bright smile and nodded her head.

She half expected him to shoot out a muscular arm and stop her progress, but Andrew merely held the door politely for her. She clutched her box and descended the narrow steps more speedily than caution should have dictated, only allowing her muscles to unclench when she was more than half way across the courtyard, well within sight of the hall. Then her shoulders shook and she let out a sob that she didn't realise she had been holding in. Her silvery plait swung in front of her eyes and her stomach rolled with nausea.

Had she been betrayed by the man she most wanted to trust?

Frida longed for some support. It seemed her ankle would never hold steady for the remaining walk across the courtyard. She had overdone it, walking to and from the village in the cold. But the main reason for her unsteadiness was shock.

Those concealed weapons! All the while she had treated Arlo in the loft, they had lain just feet away from her.

Gleaming, sharp, lethal.

Blades that had inflicted injuries, mayhap even killed men.

And she had bade Callum to give up his weapons. More so, she had been the one to take receipt of four heavy broad swords. Even now, they were locked in the armoury.

Frida could feel her face crumpling in a most unbecoming fashion. Hot tears threatened at the corners of her eyes. This was a man she had kissed, just hours earlier.

A man who made her heart sing.

A man who has deceived me.

She could not let this pass unpunished, she realised. The only question was, what should she do?

CHAPTER ELEVEN

"**F**RIDA, WHAT AILS you?"

Never before in her life had she been so pleased to recognise Jonah's voice. She glanced up to see him hobbling down the front steps.

"Jonah," she gasped, sniffing away her tears. "My ankle is weak. Can you help me?"

He gave a small chuckle as he splashed towards her. "'Twill be the lame leading the lame, but I will do what I can."

Her ankle burned as if a knife was twisting inside it. Relief flooded through her as she took Jonah's arm, even though he had to shuffle his feet and brace his knees to support her weight.

"We must make a comical pair," she grimaced.

He dropped his mouth to just above her ear. "I do not believe anyone is watching."

She looked up into his laughing blue eyes, so similar to her own. Rain had already darkened his golden hair and was running in rivulets over his richly decorated tunic.

"You do not have a cloak."

"Nay indeed." He began walking them both slowly towards the front door. "I was looking out from the solar and saw you staggering. Does a gentleman hunt for a cloak before helping a lady in distress?"

His jovial tone helped to lessen the weight of grief in her heart. But she could not repress her sisterly retort. "Chivalry has not always been your strong suit."

They both made heavy work of side-stepping a puddle. Water had found a path beneath the neckline of her cloak and the cold trickle made her long to be beside a roaring fire in the great hall.

Jonah waited until they had re-established their balance before replying. "Mayhap your steady influence is bringing out the nobler side of my character."

"Pah."

"You do not think so?"

He was making an effort to be charming, she realised. A trait she would usually associate more with her brother Tristan than the boy they had christened *the Scowler*.

"'Tis more likely to be the absence of strong liquor and inappropriate companions," she retorted.

"Perchance," he agreed with surprising equanimity.

They had reached the arched porchway leading to the heavy oak front door. It was a strong relief to be out of the rain and Frida paused, leaning against the plastered stone to catch her breath.

"Thank you," she said.

Jonah gave a mock bow, his club foot ahead of him so that his weight rested on his good leg. He was an attractive man, Frida thought, when he was not scowling.

"The pleasure is mine," he said solemnly. "Though my quest shall not be complete till you are settled before a fire with a rug over your knees. Let us proceed."

He offered her a rather soggy elbow, which Frida accepted. Heat enveloped them as soon as they were through the front door. She inhaled the scents of lavender and woodsmoke, more than grateful to be home.

Although her gratitude brought her a step closer to weepiness and she sniffed once again, remembering what she had found in Callum's loft.

"I vowed to ask you no questions until we were both ensconced in the warmth. Forsooth, sister, do not make me break my word."

She summoned a smile. "I shall not."

Walking side by side, they traversed the stone-flagged entrance hall and turned left into the great hall, which had never looked more welcoming. Flames flickered in both grates and the tapestried chairs seemed to be waiting just for them. Jennifer appeared, as if by magic, and Jonah politely requested she fetch them some warmed wine.

Frida felt a traitorous stab of relief that Mirrie had not come out to greet them. Her friend would have divined the distress in her eyes within moments. And Frida could not quite bring herself to divulge her recent findings so soon after confessing her indiscretion with Callum.

At least Jonah does not know about that.

Jonah helped her into the nearest chair and solicitously pulled a rug over her knees before taking his own seat with a sigh of relief. His head rolled against the cushioned back of the chair for a moment, before he shuffled forwards and held his hands out towards the blaze.

"So, Frida, will you tell me what ails you?"

"Naught but the damp and cold," she said staunchly, reaching down to stroke her favourite hound who was slumbering by the fire.

"Do you think me a doddypoll?" He raised an eyebrow quizzically, prompting a low chuckle from her. "I spy my unflappable older sister weeping in the rain and I am to believe this is simply because she grew chilled?"

"Nay." She shook her hands at him, silently asking for a reprieve while Jennifer set down her tray and handed each of them a goblet of wine. "I will tell you," she sighed, once the servant had departed.

She didn't want to, but she had to confide in someone.

But where to start?

She sipped her wine, wrapping her cold hands about the goblet and enjoying the rush of warmth through her body. The wine was rich, sweet and fragrant with spices. It occurred to her that she could gulp it down and drown her sorrows, the way Jonah had so often behaved back at Wolvesley.

But overindulgence in liquor would not achieve anything beyond a sore head. She had witnessed this often enough with Jonah and his ill-chosen friends at the numerous Wolvesley balls.

"I am waiting," Jonah chided.

"I will speak." Frida set down her goblet and linked her fingers together. "It concerns the men we have staying with us." She pursed her lips as she recalled Jonah's suspicious line of questioning in the solar days earlier. Had he realised their duplicity before she did?

If so, 'twould be a relief to unburden herself to one who would show no surprise.

I will deal with my heartbreak later.

"Callum?" His blue gaze was hypnotic. Frida felt she was caught in a trap, much as she felt when confessing some childhood misdemeanour to her father.

"Aye."

Jonah inclined his head to one side. "What have you discovered?"

She took a deep breath. "I do not believe he is trustworthy." The words came out in a rush that made her pulse pound. But at least the deed was done. There would be no hiding from it now.

Jonah took a long swig of wine. "I admit that when he first arrived, I too had my doubts."

"I thought you were wrong at the time," she interjected.

Jonah silenced her by leaning forward and taking her hand in his. "I believe I was."

Nonplussed she could only sit back in her chair, gaping at him. A log cracked in the fire and the dog's tail thumped lazily against the floor.

Jonah flashed her a smile. "On the day the young boy was stabbed, I was resting in the solar. I heard a disturbance and decided to listen by the open window." Jonah released her hand, opening his palms before him. "What I heard was reassuring."

Frida felt her head beginning to spin. This was not the conversation she had been anticipating.

"What did you hear?"

"I heard the other man, Gregor, threaten you. I heard Callum answer that threat with the same valour and determination that I would have voiced myself." Jonah's smile became pinched. "Aye, sister, e'en our esteemed brother Tristan could not have defended you more vigorously."

Frida's heart was beating heavily now. *Can this be true?*

But she directed a level glare at Jonah, pretending that her very soul was not clamouring for Callum's innocence. "Can we leave your eternal feud with Tristan out of this?"

"I find that Tristan enters everything, in the end." Jonah paused. "I wrote him into this tale myself."

Frida took a moment to digest this. In the background, she heard swift footsteps walking along the passageway to the kitchen.

Mirrie.

She would dearly love to hear all Jonah had to say before Mirrie came upon them.

Not because Mirrie was not a cherished friend and confidante. But because Mirrie knew how Frida felt about Callum. And right now, Frida could not manage Mirrie's disappointment alongside her own. Although perchance there was no need for disappointment. Her brother had offered her a lifeline, but she had not yet reached out to grasp it.

"You are speaking in riddles, Jonah," she declared.

Jonah pushed a hand through his thick blonde hair. "It comes down to this. When Callum and his men first arrived, I was suspicious of their story. When I entered the solar and found you and Callum there alone, I grew ever more suspicious of his motives."

Frida took a breath, keen to dispute this implication, but Jonah caught her eye with a questioning smile.

"Do you want me to finish or not?"

"I want you to finish," she allowed.

"I dispatched a message to Tristan, checking Callum's claim that he had been sent here to provide additional defence against Scottish unrest."

Jonah reached for his wine, allowing Frida's thoughts to race unchecked.

"I had only fleeting doubts over that tale," she breathed. She had been more concerned about her old history with Callum.

About protecting my heart.

Jonah inclined his head. "You have not been trained to doubt."

She suppressed a desire to kick him. "Just because I did not train as a knight in Lindum does not mean that I am not capable of rational thought."

"Nay indeed." The glimmer in his blue eyes told her he was teasing.

"What did Tristan say?"

Jonah shrugged. "I have not yet received a response. But 'tis no matter. For after hearing Callum's words in the courtyard to the man Gregor, my doubts are eased."

Frida parted her lips. If only she could find such conviction for herself. "What did he say to change your mind so utterly?"

"'Twas not so much what he said, as the passion with which he said it." Jonah thought for a moment. "He declared that he would not harm you, nor any of your kin within these walls. Methinks Gregor had challenged him to do that very thing. Whatever it was, it enraged Callum. I would say you may consider yourself safe in his company, sister."

A lump was forming in Frida's throat. She wanted to be reassured by Jonah's tale, but still could not reconcile these events with Callum's stash of hidden weapons.

"I am not sure of it," she whispered.

Hearing the emotion in her voice, the slumbering hound opened his big brown eyes and gave a little whine in her direction.

Jonah said nothing, wisely waiting for her to continue.

Frida took a breath. "When Callum arrived at Ember Hall, I asked him to surrender his weapons."

Her brother nodded. "I have seen the swords myself, locked in the armoury. Great heavy things they are."

"Today I discovered that Callum did not fully comply with my request. He has concealed a number of knives, daggers and the like beneath his pallet in the hayloft." She paused as a new thought occurred to her. "There may even be more, hidden elsewhere."

Jonah pursed his lips. "This is what you had found, before I met you in the courtyard?"

"Aye."

"Gadzooks, sister, I had imagined much worse." Jonah took another mouthful of wine, a smile playing across his lips. "You cannot expect trained warriors to come to a strange place and relinquish all that makes them feel safe. Weaponry is part of a man's identity. Especially a trained knight, like Callum."

At first his words made little sense to her. Frida's mind refused to give up the notion that something was awry.

It all came down to this: Callum betrayed me.

But Jonah's nonchalance was more than a little affecting.

She gazed into the orange flames of the fire, puzzling it all out. "You do not think it suspicious?" she tried.

"Let us imagine our brother, Tristan, e'en our father, arriving some place and being asked to give up his weapons." Jonah looked at her over the rim of his goblet. "Do you think either one of them would truly surrender every one of their weapons, leaving them with no protection?"

She shook her head. "They would not."

"For the sake of etiquette, they may relinquish one or two items. But most certainly, they would retain more." He tossed her a grin—de Neville charm at its finest. "Mayhap even conceal them beneath a mattress?"

Frida smiled; relief was tapping her on the shoulder.

"Then you do not think I have reason to fear? *We* have reason to fear?" she amended quickly.

Jonah grew solemn. "I did not say that, sister. We live in turbulent times. Robert the Bruce aims to be king of an independent Scotland, while our king has every intention of ruling over Scotland himself. Overseas, our best men are fighting in France. 'Tis not the time to lower our guard." He met her troubled gaze and pressed his lips together in a smile. "But I do not think that we have reason to fear Callum Baine."

It was all she wanted and more.

"Thank you," she whispered.

He puckered his brows. "For what?"

"For helping me across the courtyard. For tucking a rug over my knees. For talking to me." Frida leaned forward and placed a hand over her brother's. "Were you always secretly this nice, Jonah? Or has something happened to you since you came to stay with us at Ember Hall?"

A most familiar scowl flickered for a moment over Jonah's sensitive features before he gave her fingers an answering squeeze.

"Thank you, sister, for that timely reminder of how you and Tristan have always looked down upon me."

"We have not," she declared hotly.

"Nay, not only you and Tristan. Isabella too. She could scarce conceal her impatience to be rid of me."

"Isabella thinks only of making a suitable match before the winter sets in."

"Our little sister Esme has no affection for me either." He met her eyes as if challenging her to deny it.

Frida put her head to one side. "Jonah, I had no idea you cared so." She took a firmer hold of his hands, leaning closer to the warm glow of the fire. "Our sister Esme has her head in the clouds, while Isabella rarely lifts her gaze beyond the looking glass." She saw a smile trembling at his lips. "You know it is true."

"I know it." Jonah's gaze grew reflective. "Truly, Frida, I should not admit this. But seeing as we are exchanging views…" His voice trailed off.

"Go on," she encouraged him.

"'Tis a terrible thing for me to say. But when your ankle shattered and you could only walk with a limp, I thought this might prove a common bond between us."

Frida opened and closed her mouth, unable to think of an appropriate response. "I do not allow my limp to define me."

Jonah released her fingers so that he might spread his arms before him. "Nor I."

"'Tis true," she allowed. "You are an excellent horseman and highly skilled with a sword." She drummed her fingers on the arm of her chair, thinking it through. "May I tell you what I really think?"

Jonah drained his goblet of wine and placed it down on the table. "I am ready."

She chose her words carefully. "Tristan and I perchance were at fault for treating you differently, Jonah. You were born afflicted and have overcome it. That is a mighty achievement that I well know requires patience and resilience. Not just once, but every day." She sipped at her wine, remembering a plucky young boy determined to follow herself and Tristan around the fields of Wolvesley. They wanted to be free of the whining youngster who only slowed them down.

But is that not true of all siblings?

"I know what you call me," he said quietly.

Frida felt her cheeks growing hotter; not from the fire but the sharp prick of her conscience.

"The Scowler." He pressed his lips together before relaxing into a smile. "Mayhap I deserve the moniker. I certainly did naught to dispel it." He placed his elbow on the arm of the chair and rested his head against his hand. "I only wanted you to notice me."

"Oh, Jonah," she repeated, catching his eye. "We noticed you."

They both laughed, the slight tension between them evaporating like woodsmoke.

"Our family is full of strong-headed individuals," he mused. "The only one amongst us who has any amount of patience is Mirrie."

"And Mother," she added quickly.

"Aye, Mother has the patience of a saint."

"And Mirrie is kind and compassionate." She thought of her friend's gentle brown eyes.

"Whereas we de Nevilles are always running to the next thing before we have finished the first." Jonah squeezed her hand again. "And 'tis hard to run when you have a twisted foot."

"Or a shattered ankle," she agreed. "Are you saying that we should slow down?"

"Slow down, look about us, appreciate what we have." He sighed. "I have been doing that more since coming to Ember Hall. Dwelling more on gratitude than on envy."

She allowed a moment to pass. "You are envious of Tristan?"

He sat back in his chair so his face was half hidden from her. "'Tis not easy to be the brother of Tristan de Neville. Nor the son of Angus de Neville."

"You share many of their qualities," she demurred.

"And you, sister? Do you pretend that it is easy to be the older sibling of Isabella? The one they call the Rose of England?"

His words pierced her, even as a denial rose to her lips. From childhood, Isabella had been hailed as a great beauty. Four years older, with hair not quite so thick, skin not quite so flawless and a smile not quite so enchanting, Frida had always felt plain by her younger sister's side.

She bit down on her lip before releasing her discomfiture in a chuckle. "I do pretend, aye. But you are right, 'tis not always easy."

Jonah also chuckled. "There we are then. Allies at last."

"Allies." She lifted her goblet in a silent toast. "Tell me, why did we not have this conversation years ago?"

Jonah leaned forward with his elbows on his knees. His gaze rested on the glowing fire. "'Tis sometimes hard to hear the truth of your heart amidst the mighty clamour of Wolvesley Castle."

"Amen to that." She took her final mouthful of wine, savouring the richness of it and allowing Jonah's insight to ripple through her.

She had heard the truth of her heart.

She had acknowledged—to herself and to Mirrie—that her heart beat for Callum.

Mayhap that was why she had been so quick to distrust him. The very second her eyes alighted on those weapons, she had believed the worst of him.

Old habits die hard. And Frida had been barricading her heart for many winters now.

Was it time for a change?

CHAPTER TWELVE

THERE WAS SOMETHING *different about the light this morn*, Callum thought. For one, there was too much of it. For two, the hue was overly bright.

Still fuddled with sleep, Callum lay on his pallet, listening to the snuffling of Arlo's steady breathing, and waited for his mind to make sense of it all.

The cold was another thing. Bitter and biting on his face, e'en as his body was warm beneath a heavy rug. Callum watched his breath plume into the chill air and the answer slowly slid into his mind.

Snow.

Noiselessly, he rose out of bed and padded on stockinged feet over to the gable end of the barn. There, he bent his knees and fixed his gaze on the gap between two wooden slats in the roof. He could see little, but there was no hint of green outside.

Everything was white.

Grunting softly, Callum returned to his pallet, pulled on his leather boots and wrapped his heavy cloak about his shoulders. He was possessed of a desire to breathe this fresh, clean air and consider what it meant.

Leaving his men sleeping, he quietly opened the wooden door and slipped out into the biting cold. Flaming wall torches illuminated a world made different. Soft snow crunched beneath his boots as he carefully ascended the narrow stone staircase.

I must remember to clear these treads, he noted. Once the snow turned to ice, they would become treacherous.

At the bottom of the steps, he paused, reluctant to mar with his footprints the shimmering expanse of white spreading all around. The first rays of sunrise were just appearing, casting a beautiful rosy hue over the pristine snow that lay thickly over everything. For a moment, Callum was filled with wonder, like a child at yuletide. He wrapped his arms about his chest, pushing his hands beneath the folds of his cloak, and breathed it all in.

Yesterday in the chapel, he had asked the Almighty for a sign.

And this sign felt fairly conclusive.

Callum would not be leaving Ember Hall. Not today, nor on the morrow.

He pressed his lips together, unable to deny a thrill of relief that the decision had been taken out of his hands.

Aye, he was playing with fire still. Especially after that kiss.

A kiss that had seared itself into his very soul. Never would he forget how Frida's lips had felt against his, the sweetness of her breath or the softness of her body. Her gasp of pleasure that had all but robbed him of reason. But could he e'er allow it to happen again, given the layers of complexity that existed between them?

Callum ground his teeth together, his breath hanging in the air like steam from a dragon.

A movement from above caught his attention and he reached for the hilt of his sword, cursing silently when it was not there.

"'Tis only I," said a familiar voice, the words all but swallowed up by the muffling snow.

Callum relaxed his stance. "Andrew."

His friend made halting progress down the snowy steps and came to stand by his side. He smelled of hay and sleep, and his uncombed red hair hung in fiery tousles.

"Snow," Andrew declared, putting his hands on his hips and gazing about.

"Aye."

Andrew's blue eyes caught him in a trap. "It will make travelling hard."

"Well-nigh impossible." Callum leaned back on his heals. "More is still to come, if I am not mistaken."

"So we are to stay longer?" Andrew kept his voice low. Aware, as Callum was aware, of the sleeping guards nearby. And the guards on the wall who must be due to return soon.

"We have no choice, friend."

"I see that." Andrew nodded his head. He wore no cloak, but did not betray any discomfort from the cold.

"I am sorry for it." Callum was driven to frankness. "This mission has turned out very different to the one we anticipated."

Andrew grunted, his breath steaming before him. "That is what oft happens in this life."

"Aye," Callum said again, wishing suddenly that he might unburden himself.

Andrew was one of his oldest friends. And Callum had betrayed him almost as much as he had betrayed Frida. He had lied to them both; was lying to them still. Two people whom he valued above all others.

Regret swirled in his gut.

Andrew turned and clapped a big hand on Callum's shoulder, all but knocking him sideways. "Ye didnae summon the snow, man."

A smile tugged at his lips as he recovered his balance. "True enough."

"And I have stayed in worse places than this." The big highlander nodded ruminatively, his bushy eyebrows disappearing into his thatch of hair. "This stint ye arranged for us, as labourers?" He let out a bark of laughter, silencing Callum's denial. "It has done me good to spend time working the land. A break, ye might say, from constant battling and plotting and bloodshed."

"I think Arlo might see it differently." Callum's heart twisted as he recalled the moment the lad had fallen with a dagger between his shoulder blades.

"Ach, the lad is recovering now. And he could ha' been more

grievous injured had Gregor gotten his way." Andrew nodded in the direction of the guards' quarters. "The four of us against the lot of them."

"Aye." Callum rubbed his arms against the cold. "It would not have gone well for us."

"I'll no say I'll no be glad to be back home." Andrew lowered his voice. "But this is a reminder, ain't it, of what we're fighting for?"

Callum raised his eyebrows questioningly.

"Peace. A quiet life. Chance to till the land and reap what ye sow."

Callum's heart twisted again, but he couldn't allow his friend to see how his words affected him. He would trade all he had for the chance of a quiet, peaceful life with Frida.

Instead he cleared his throat. "You're mighty poetic this morn, Andrew."

"'Tis the snow. It has sent me soft in the head."

Callum guffawed, scooping up a handful of soft snow and tossing it in Andrew's direction. It landed squarely on the back of his head, white melting into fiery red. Callum realised that dawn had broken as they were speaking. The sky was bright with pink and orange rays, dazzling against the expanse of snow.

"Are ye starting something, man?" Andrew's eyes gleamed provocatively.

"Nay, I am finishing it." Callum went to scoop up another handful of snow, but the muffled squeak of boots trampling through snow halted his movements. The guards were returning from their nighttime shift.

As one, the two Scotsmen straightened up, arms hanging limply by their sides. They nodded silently to the line of uniformed guards, some of whom returned the gesture as they climbed the steps to their adjacent sleeping quarters.

"'Tis a good job we finished the barn roof yesterday," Andrew said quietly.

Callum nodded, his eyes widening as he realised what this

meant.

"The animals are still out in the fields." He spun around, his cloak flaring about his ankles. "I must go to fetch them in."

Andrew did not question him. "I shall come with ye."

Callum clapped him on the shoulder. "I thank you for the offer, Andrew. But one of us should stay here until Arlo wakes. He is not yet well enough to fend for himself, especially in these temperatures."

"Ye will go out alone?" Andrew's eyebrows once again disappeared into his thatch of hair.

"'Tis not too deep, yet." Callum demonstrated this by stepping further out into the courtyard. The snow came no further than midway up the feet of his leather boots. He shaded his eyes and looked to the west. "But see those clouds on the horizon? I'll wager they will bring us more snow before noon."

Andrew gazed at him, ruminatively. "I am not going to pester ye for the chance to trudge out in the snow and bring in another man's livestock."

"Another *woman's* livestock," Callum corrected, before he could think better of it.

"I begin to see how it is now." Andrew guffawed. "Ye have a soft spot for yon Frida de Neville."

Callum bit back the denial that had sprung to his lips. He must take care not to draw suspicion by seeming too sensitive on the topic.

"She is a fine woman," he said instead.

"Aye. Wi' a brother who would run ye through with his sword before thinking twice."

Callum looked again to the west, pretending to monitor the clouds as he schooled his face into neutrality.

"I will go now and get the job done."

"And I shall go back to the warm." Andrew jerked his head towards their loft. "Once Arlo is settled, shall I come and find ye?"

"Aye." Callum was grateful for the support. "Do that."

"And later we will raise a toast to yer lassie." Andrew waggled his eyebrows.

"We might raise a toast to each other." Callum grasped his friend's forearm. "I am right glad you're here, Andrew."

He meant it. Amidst the unrelenting turmoil of his thoughts, Andrew's steady good humour was a tonic.

A cold gust of wind hit him full in the face as he turned the corner away from the barns. He hadn't realised just how much shelter the courtyard provided. Callum had to pause for a moment, capturing both his balance and his resolve. The outlook here was bleak, with wind whipping up the snow and sending it spiralling into the freezing air. Tiny shards of ice rained down onto the hood of his cloak. He took a deep breath and strode onward, barely recognising the landmarks that had grown passingly familiar over the past few days.

A blackbird took flight into the pale sky, causing a wedge of snow to fall heavily from the branch it had been perching upon. There was no sign of the chickens, usually to be found scratching in the dirt. They would all be safe and warm in the henhouse.

Mayhap all living creatures were safe and warm within Ember Hall; bar Callum, intent on his mad quest.

He half smiled at the fancy, before realising he was wrong. Ahead of him, through the swirls of snow, he could make out another figure battling up the slight hill.

A slight figure, head bowed low against the wind, walking with a limp.

Frida.

Callum could hardly believe it. Within moments he experienced a whirlwind of emotions. Admiration for her pluck went into battle with a swell of anger at her foolish disregard for her own safety. He wanted to shout at her to go back inside, but knew she would not listen. And anyway, the wind would snap up his words and carry them away before she had chance to hear them.

There was nothing for it but to increase his stride, gradually closing the distance between them.

"Frida," he shouted into the cold.

She stopped her halting progress, her cloak flying up as she turned to face him. Snow stung his eyes as the wind burned his cheeks, but he continued without pausing until they were mere steps apart.

Frida was breathing hard, her cheeks red with cold and effort. Ice crystals had formed on the top of her hood.

"Callum," she said, as if she was greeting him across a banqueting hall.

"What are you doing out here?" He was breathless, and the question came out more harshly than he intended.

"I am out for a stroll." Her voice dripped with sarcasm.

"You should not be out in this cold." He stamped his feet, to bring feeling back to his toes.

She gave a little shake of her head. "Go inside, Sir Callum, if the weather bothers you so."

He could scarce believe it as she turned from him. "Frida," he shouted again, stumbling in the snow as he raced to catch up with her.

This time her blue eyes blazed as she spun around. "What?"

"'Tis dangerous out here."

"Dangerous for our livestock. You know as well as I do that they will die unless I take them to shelter."

"That is why I am here." He spluttered as the wind took his breath.

"I see." She pursed her lips. "Then you can help me."

"I can manage alone."

"They are my animals, Callum." She turned once again, but this time the demands on her ankle were too great and she stumbled. At the last moment, Callum saved her from a tumble into the snow.

He knew again the rush of feeling as he held her close, even though many folds of rough, half-sodden material separated them, even though the wind whipped around them still and Frida was looking at him with something like vexation burning in her eyes.

He could see how much this meant to her.

"You are a stubborn woman, Frida de Neville."

"It has been said before."

"And no doubt will be again." He helped her upright. "You will allow me to help you?"

She nodded once. "If you promise to make no more protests about me staying out in the cold."

"Not another word." He paused, glancing upwards in surprise. "The wind has dropped."

They were no longer buffeted by strong, freezing gusts. Instead the white world around them stood still and strangely silent, as if waiting for something.

"That is good." Frida sniffed and pulled her cloak more tightly about her.

"Aye." At the moment, it certainly seemed better than the alternative. But Callum was not convinced all was well. The grey clouds hovering overhead promised more snow about them. "Where are we headed?" He knew the cattle were kept in a field to the left, nearest the path to the village, whereas the sheep grazed the land approaching the cliffs.

"One of our tenant farmers brought in the cattle he tends yesterday. He is a country man and must have smelled the snow before it fell." Frida threw him a smile. "'Tis the sheep I am most worried about."

Callum bowed his head. "Then let us put your worries to rest." He ducked his head to better meet her eye. "Can I take your arm, milady?"

"Are you fretting about me falling again?"

"Not at all," he lied. Without waiting for permission, he took her gloved hand and tucked it inside his elbow. "'Tis a handy excuse for me to walk close beside you, that is all."

"I will accept that," Frida replied, primly. But she leaned her weight against him as they trudged forwards.

Callum felt that as an honour. *There are not many people,* he mused, *that brave Frida would allow herself to lean on.*

But no sooner had this thought formed, than another occurred to him.

Frida would not lean on me if she knew the truth of my identity, and the real reason I first came to Ember Hall.

But now was not the time to dwell on such matters. The most important thing was to rescue the sheep and see Frida safely home.

The sheep field was bathed in a dim yellow light when they finally crested the hill. Trees reached their snowy branches into the cold air and the wind had died to a mere whisper.

"There they are." Frida pointed to a huddle of shapes beside what could only be a snow-covered stone wall.

The sheep had black faces, which helped them stand out against the snow. Otherwise, their task would have been impossible.

"There is a hut to our right," she continued. "We must first fetch the crooks so we can better steer the sheep down the hill."

"Pray, lead the way, milady."

He followed her steady footsteps to the small wooden hut with a perfect blanket of snow covering the roof. Frida unfastened the door and they both stepped inside, grateful for shelter. Callum looked about him at a tidy shepherd's store, furnished simply and sparsely. A row of curved crooks had been propped against the far wall.

Frida held one out towards him and as Callum took it from her, his fingers brushed against hers, unleashing a wave of feeling which coursed all the way up his arm.

"Frida," he said again, softly this time.

When she turned her eyes upon him, he could see they reflected his desire.

She feels it too, this connection between us.

Of course she must, for why else would they have shared such a powerful kiss?

Callum swallowed, newly aware of their close proximity.

Of the unlikelihood of us being disturbed.

He reached out a hand and touched her cold cheek. "About yesterday," he tried.

She leaned into his palm, just for a moment, before turning her face away. "Let us not talk of that now."

The rejection stung, although he forced a genial smile. "Of course."

Her gaze snagged his. "Later," she whispered. "When the sheep are safe."

And his heart soared again.

"Later." He nodded, grasping the crook and following her back out of the hut, the snow crunching beneath his feet.

But what will I say, later, he demanded of himself as Frida fastened the door.

Will I declare the truth of my heart? That I'm falling in love with her?

For that was at the root of it all. This was no mere passing fancy for a pretty young woman. *I love Frida de Neville.*

A sharp breeze lifted his cloak away from his body, bringing the cold sting of reason to his racing thoughts.

Nay, he could not declare it. He had no business doing so. For he was still a spy for Robert the Bruce.

The enemy of her family.

CHAPTER THIRTEEN

F RIDA WAS ALMOST glad to be back outside, where the redness in her cheeks could be explained by the biting cold. She took a deep breath, filling her lungs with icy air and quelling the flickering sparks of desire that had ignited inside her belly.

Only momentarily though. For when she turned her head, there he was beside her. Handsome as ever, with his deep blue cloak swirling in the wind. The set of his strong shoulders promised her safety and protection, but the passion in his eyes declared something else entirely.

Something that made her pulse pick up speed.

But she should not think of such things now. She had plunged out into the snowy morn with the sole aim of bringing their flock of sheep to safety, and the animals were still out there.

"Ready?" Callum asked.

She nodded and they set off towards the sheep, booted feet sinking into the snow. It was hard work and she could not deny her relief that he had come to help. She would have managed alone, but it was nice to have support.

Her eyes flickered over to him as they approached the huddle of sheep. He strode confidently, lifting his crook and making encouraging noises in his deep ringing voice. The animals scattered at first, before settling into a group and plunging forwards down the hill. She raised her own crook to keep them pointed in the right direction, joining her voice with Callum's in perfect synchronicity. It was as if they had done this a dozen times. As if he was no knight, but a son of the land. And she, no daughter of an earl, but a farmer's wife.

Frida smiled at the fancy as they trudged downward, sliding a little in the snow. Ever since her fall form the horse, icy conditions made her anxious. She couldn't bear the sensation of her feet slipping, her body moving in a way she couldn't control. But the snow had not frozen and Callum's comforting presence helped calm her fears. Time passed and they reached the barn without incident, the sheep baaing to one another once they tunnelled inside and smelled the hay waiting in the manger.

Frida and Callum stood together in the doorway, blinking in the shadows after the dazzling light of sunshine on snow.

"They are safe," Frida declared, smiling at the scene. Her body was warm after their exertions and she felt almost giddy with the improbable success of her mission. If either Jonah or Mirrie had seen her leaving the hall at first light, they would have certainly tried to stop her. Mayhap Jonah would have even barred her way. Frida folded her arms and leaned against the wooden doorframe, allowing the tension to lift from her shoulders. Her friend and brother would have been right to doubt her ability to handle the task all on her own. She had entertained doubts herself, especially when the barrelling winds all but forced her back into the courtyard. But she had come to Ember Hall determined to prove that a woman could be as capable as any man. She could work the land, care for the animals, make the estate a success.

She had promised her father and she had promised herself.

Her gaze switched to Callum who had walked over to the sheep, checking that each of them was well. He put his hands on his hips as his dark eyes roved over the woolly creatures from top to bottom.

He is a good man, she thought.

Her fears over the hidden stash of weapons evaporated into the cold air as Callum lifted one of this year's lambs closer to the manger. Jonah was right. It had been naïve of her to expect that a knight would willingly sleep unarmed in a strange place.

"I count forty-four." Callum's deep voice broke into her thoughts.

Blinking, she met his dark gaze. "Forty-four?"

He nodded. "Is that right?"

Frida felt a clutch of fear. "Nay, I am sure we have forty-five."

She stumbled closer to the feeding sheep and began counting them herself, struggling sometimes to differentiate between the white wriggling bodies.

"Forty-four," declared Callum, once again.

"Aye." She nodded, swallowing as she realised what this meant. "We must have left one in the pasture."

Callum sighed. She knew, before he spoke, what he was about to say.

"I will go back," she blurted, before he could begin. Her ankle throbbed in protest but she ignored the pain.

"Nay, Frida." His hand on her arm would be something between a comfort and a temptation in other circumstances. "'Tis too much risk for just one sheep."

"That one sheep deserves my protection as much as any other."

He shook his head slowly. "Look." He pointed behind her, through the open doorway. "It has started snowing again."

She didn't even glance around. "Then I had better hurry."

His eyebrows lifted. "It would not be wise."

But Frida had been checking and re-checking the lines of sheep in front of her and now she was even more determined. "I know which one is missing. 'Tis one of this year's lambs. One with a torn ear. She is Mirrie's favourite."

Callum pressed his lips together. "Then I will go myself and find it."

She couldn't allow that.

"I will re-trace our steps." Frida turned as quickly as she could decently manage and plunged back out into the cold. Instantly she realised that much had changed during their short sojourn in the barn. Thick flakes of snow fell relentlessly, covering her hood and eyelashes within moments. Their footsteps from earlier were still recognisable, but only just. The pervading white of the snow did not just lay at their boots, it was all around them. Up and down, left and right.

"This is madness, Frida."

Callum was at her side, speaking with a force she had not heard from him before.

She shrugged. Perchance it was.

But she had come this far and she would not give up now.

Without so much as a glance in his direction, Frida stepped forward, willing her ankle to support her. It stayed strong, for now at least, although every stride through the snow was an effort. Before she had reached the end of the courtyard, her chest heaved and her lungs burned. Turning the corner into the blast of wind seemed like madness indeed, but turning back would be an admission of weakness that she was not prepared to make.

She would never admit it, but she experienced a rush of relief when she realised he was following her. His face was set, his lips compressed into a grim line, but he was close behind.

And she was grateful.

In this formation, they struggled onward. There was a slight incline which usually did not bother her much, but now felt like the highest of mountains. At last, they reached the plateau and she paused for breath with her hands on her knees. Callum came beside her, still silent and cross.

Resolved to ignore his steely disapproval, Frida glanced about to get her bearings. Everything looked the same in the snow. The fields and trees and low stone walls which she knew so well were cloaked in an undiscriminating blanket of white. But after a few seconds of squinting, she made out the shape of the shepherd's hut and even the water trough where the sheep had been gathered. Chances were, the missing sheep was still somewhere nearby.

Gripped with resolution, she strode forwards without thinking. She had forgotten the steep drop of the ground just here, and the fact the water spilled over from the trough and turned to ice once the temperatures dropped. This ice remained, even beneath the thick covering of snow, and once Frida's bad ankle started sliding, she could not stop herself from falling.

She landed with a bump, but not before fear had stolen her dignity and forced her to shriek out loud. Hot tears squeezed from her eyes, not because she was hurt but because the sensation of slipping out of control brought back painful memories from that dreadful day when her ankle shattered and her life changed forever.

Callum loomed above her, concern flashing in his dark eyes.

"Frida."

One word, which from his lips had the power to be her undoing.

But she did not want to be undone.

"I am fine." She struggled upwards, ignoring the hot ache of her ankle and a stabbing pain where she had twisted her lower back.

He paid her no heed, gripping her beneath the shoulders with strong hands and hauling her upright. Frida wavered in the snow, unwilling to catch her balance by leaning against him.

And so, instead of sobbing with cold and pain and effort, she got angry.

"I can manage, thank you," she spat.

Callum released his hold and she managed to shift her weight to her good ankle just in time to prevent another tumble into the deepening snow.

"Forgive me." His voice was dry.

The only thing that was.

Frida's racing mind took stock of their situation. Her cloak was all but soaked through. A numbing cold had taken hold in her feet and hands, and despite the adrenaline coursing through her body, she was shivering violently.

But the lamb, the one that Mirrie had laughingly named Gertrude, was still out there, somewhere.

Frida pushed herself forwards, thinking for one moment that she could make out a dash of black against the all-pervading white, but it must have been mere fancy on her part.

"Frida, this is madness," roared Callum, his words reaching her on a gust of wind. She turned to face him, surprised to see his coal-black curls and deep blue cloak all turned to white. "We must get inside."

He was right, part of her registered, though another part wished to keep searching. The wind barrelled into them again, making Frida lean down into the slope of the hill to withstand the gusts. For the first time, it occurred to her that the simplest thing might be to just lay down. The soft blanket of snow looked inviting. She could sink into it and rest, just for a moment.

But here was Callum, his face twisted up with something like anger. "Walk," he demanded, all but pushing her forwards.

"Do not presume to order me about." She drew herself up, every inch her father's daughter, despite her sodden clothing and aching limbs.

His answer was a bark of laughter. "I am trying to save your life."

"I do not need your help."

Even as the denial left her lips, she knew it was untrue. She had pushed herself too far in conditions that were too dangerous. She knew it, and Callum knew it.

Summoning every last drop of her strength, she wrenched one foot free of snow and placed it in front of her. All she had to do was repeat this process until she reached the shepherd's hut, looming atop the hill she had so recently tumbled down.

"Stay clear of the ice," Callum shouted.

She did not have the breath to vocalise her instinctive, angry response. Perchance that was a good thing. Beneath Frida's wounded pride was a growing recognition that, without Callum, she may indeed come to harm. When she felt his hand on her back, steadying her, helping her, she did not allow herself to flinch away.

Slowly, laboriously, they managed the ascent. Callum went ahead of her to unfasten the door of the hut and haul it open. Despite herself, Frida was glad, for all feeling had left her fingers and she did not think she could have managed it.

Silently, he stood back to let her pass inside. It was such a relief to be inside, away from the falling snow and gusting wind, that Frida felt she may weep.

"Take off your cloak," he ordered.

Her first instinct was to argue, but dimly she recalled the sense of his instruction. It was dark inside the hut, with snow piling up against the window and blocking out the one source of light. With fumbling fingers, she attempted to untie her laces whilst Callum strode over to the narrow store cupboard.

She couldn't manage it and a wave of frustration almost brought her to tears. Callum was busying himself at the low wooden table, so he didn't see her wobbling lip. Finally, a flare of light indicated he had found a tinder box and lit a taper. She breathed in the sharp scent with relief.

But her relief turned to embarrassment when he came over to her and untied the laces of her cloak in one quick movement. Her heavy cloak slumped to the floor and Callum handed her a coarse blanket.

"Dry yourself."

His orders were delivered in the tone of a man to servant, and Frida bristled.

"I know well enough what to do," she snapped, pulling the blanket over her shoulders. "I am not a child in need of constant instruction."

He regarded her for a moment in the flickering candlelight, the shadows jumping between them.

"Very well," he said.

Before Frida could react, Callum had walked over to the narrow door and disappeared out into the snow. She gazed at the spot with disbelief.

He had left her.

Her heart thudded with a mixture of adrenaline and disappointment. *What should I do now?* she wondered, before shaking the thought away and gathering herself up.

She must dry her hair, which was sending cold drips of melted snow down her neck and back. She must find out how many more candles were inside the cupboard. Mayhap she could even make a fire. She must somehow get herself warm and wait out the storm.

I do not need a man. Not even one called Callum Baine.

The hut smelled musty and the acrid smoke from the tallow candle made her eyes water, but Frida told herself this was comforting. Better by far than the disorienting torrent of white snow and icy wind outside.

A torrent which Callum was battling against right now.

So be it. He had left their shelter of his own volition. Perchance he was even now back at Ember Hall, warming his hands by a roaring fire. She pursed her lips at the thought, still unable to believe that he had left her here, alone.

She had told him that she did not need his help. But that didn't mean she didn't *want* his help.

They were two different things, she realised, as she rubbed at her hair. And perchance she should have been more gracious towards him.

When she saw him next, she must thank him.

A commotion by the door made her startle. Callum barrelled through, looking like some great half-frozen man made of snow. In his arms he carried a small, bleating bundle.

"Gertrude!" Frida exclaimed, rushing forwards to take the lamb from him and wrap her in the blanket.

"Rub her all over," Callum ordered. "She's half frozen."

Frida did as she was told, but her hands were still clumsy with cold. Callum came to stand by her side and help. This time, she didn't push him away with either words or actions. She simply looked up and whispered, "Thank you."

"I heard her bleating as we reached the hut." The lamb relaxed against his broad chest, closing her liquid eyes as Callum vigorously rubbed her with the blanket.

"You went out to get her?" Relief sank through Frida like a gulp of warmed wine.

He nodded and a clump of snow fell from his hood onto the wooden floor.

"You must take off your wet things," Frida declared. It was her turn to issue the instructions.

Callum gave her a wry smile. "Then I would be standing before you wearing very little."

She turned away so he would not see her blush. "Just your cloak then." She bustled over to the open cupboard where she had already spied the frayed edges of a second rough blanket. "Here." She tossed it to him and he caught it neatly with one hand.

"Here you go, little one." He bent his knees and released the lamb to the ground, where it proceeded to snuffle around and explore.

"You're a good man," Frida said, suddenly.

He paused in the act of wrapping himself in the blanket. Their eyes met and the moment stretched between them.

"I do remember you," she added, the words coming in a rush. "From Wolvesley."

"You do?" His voice was faint with surprise.

"Aye." She was determined to confess it all. "I knew you from the moment you arrived here. I had never forgotten you." Her words reverberated around the thin walls of the wooden hut.

Callum stilled again. "Nor I you," he said, throatily. His tousled hair was dripping with melted snow but he hardly seemed to notice. "Why did you pretend otherwise?"

"'Tis difficult to explain." Frida paused, uncertain how to express the truth of her heart that she had kept barricaded for so long. "That morning, when I fell." Their gazes locked together and she could not look away. "I should not have ridden out in those conditions. My horse was young and unsteady. But I did it anyway. Because I was trying to impress you."

There, she had said it. The foolish, painful truth.

Callum opened and closed his mouth. "I was already impressed."

"You shouldn't have been," Frida relied steadily, resolved to say it all. "I was a careless child. My attention was on you, not my young horse. That's why he fell. That's why I hit my head and shattered my ankle."

She stood taller and prouder now that she had declared herself. Callum looked like a man frozen by shock. His dark eyes bore into her but his body never moved. It was almost as if he had stopped breathing altogether.

She plunged on, the words falling more freely from her lips as if she had broken through the barricades. "I was ashamed. I thought I had to live my life along different rules as some kind of punishment, to ensure I was ne'er so foolish again. But then you came back to me and everything changed."

Without giving herself chance to pause and reconsider, Frida walked forwards and lifted her lips to his.

CHAPTER FOURTEEN

I**T TOOK LITTLE** more than a second for Callum to truly understand what his body so readily accepted: Frida de Neville was standing in his arms and kissing him.

And nothing in his whole life leading up to that moment had ever felt so good.

He wrapped his arms around her, pulling her closer and claiming her mouth with his own. Her lips were warm and soft; the lavender fragrance of her damp hair overwhelmed the bitter scent of the sputtering tallow candles.

"Frida," he said, cupping her cheeks and gazing down into her blue eyes.

I remember you, she had said. *I've never forgotten you.*

The deep connection he had always felt, shimmering between them, was real. He hadn't imagined it. Nor was it one-sided fancy on his part. His heart filled with happiness even as desire, profound and primitive, stirred his blood.

"Callum."

On her lips, his name was a caress. It hadn't been spoken so tenderly since his mother's untimely death.

He ran his hands through her hair, then traced the path of her arms from shoulder to wrist, all while his need for her grew stronger. She was all he had ever dreamed of. Standing in the small hut whilst outside the wind howled and the snow cascaded down, Callum couldn't recall the worries and concerns that had made him fret so. Or rather, he could recall them; 'twould be hard to forget his father's allegiance to Robert the Bruce and Callum's own orders to take down Tristan de Neville. But right now, none of that mattered.

All that mattered was Frida. Standing in his embrace. Where she belonged.

"I have…" he began, then floundered. "I have ne'er stopped thinking about you," he managed. "You have been in my heart these last years."

A painful part of his heart, until now.

She smiled and it was as if the sun shone down upon him in a blessing.

"Then kiss me again," she whispered.

Her invitation unleashed the fires inside him and this time his kiss was not gentle. Nor did he stop his hands from roaming where they longed to be—at first, up and down her slender spine; within moments, skimming sideways over her ribcage to brush against the swell of her breasts. She gasped and he took the opportunity to deepen his kiss, probing her mouth with his tongue, scarcely able to restrain his reaction when she responded with equal desire.

It would be the easiest, most natural thing in the world to unfasten her bodice and trail his lips along her collar bone and beyond. It took every ounce of self-restraint not to lay her down atop a blanket and introduce her to the pleasures of human flesh, claiming her as his very own in the process.

But he would not.

Trembling with repressed desire, he broke off their kiss, his face still hovering inches from hers. Confusion clouded her eyes.

"You are beautiful," he whispered.

She smiled at him again, tentatively this time. "Then why did you stop?"

He groaned and hauled her against him, wrapping her in his arms and holding on tight. "I would have no regrets between us."

Her breath was hot against his neck. "You would regret continuing to kiss me?"

"Never. But kissing you more would lead to other things. And those, we might regret come the morn." He took a deep breath and spoke quickly. "Frida, you don't know how I have dreamed of this moment. But ne'er in my dreams did we come together in a cramped hut, both nearly numb with cold."

"Where then?"

She was teasing him, he realised, with a jolt that was half pleasure and half surprise. "In a comfortable bed beside a roaring fire, where I might remove your silken gown with exquisite slowness and kiss every inch of your beautiful body," he replied without hesitating.

She lifted her head to look at him, her lips and her eyes dark with wanting. "That was what you dreamed?"

He chuckled. "That and more."

"Show me."

His heart threatened to jump outside of his rib cage. "I cannot." He cleared his throat, the unreality of the situation helping him to form his next words without pause. "Not until we were husband and wife."

A beat passed. "Is that what you want?" Despite the momentousness of the question, her voice was steady.

Callum could only answer with the truth. "That is what I have wanted since I first set eyes upon you in the banqueting hall of Wolvesley Castle." His hands started on a journey all of their own, sweeping down to span her waist as he summoned up the cherished memories. "You wore a gown of emerald green and your hair shone more golden than the sun."

She made a half-strangled sound. "My golden hair is a thing of the past."

"Now your hair shines silver like the stars," he said softly.

"I am not the same person I was." She rested her palms on his chest. "I am much changed."

"As am I," he intoned, pushing away the sharp-edged, bloodied images of the siege of Kielder Castle that had left scars on his very soul. Shrugging off the guilt that followed him everywhere like a faithful hound. All that mattered now was Frida. Not yesterday, not tomorrow. Just this present moment.

She stepped away and disappointment stabbed him in the heart. But she went only to light a second candle, casting a new glow of golden light into the hut.

"I have learned that life is full of twists and turns," she said softly. "The future is not always what we expect it to be. And not so long ago, my friend Mirrie told me I should fight for my happiness."

He reached out and took her hands. "Is that what you are doing now?"

"Nay, at least I hope fighting is not required." A smile danced across her lips. "But I am certainly not going to turn away from happiness."

He drew her towards him, his fingers tracing over her cheeks and down. "Do I make you happy?"

"Aye." She nodded simply.

"Perchance we could make each other happy."

He closed his mind to thoughts of family allegiance and treachery. With Frida by his side, anything would be possible.

She nodded again. "I think we might."

He had waited long enough. He would give her pleasure, even if his own must still be denied. He kissed her—first her lips, then her neck, then her throat. His hands roamed over her bodice until only a cotton shift lay between his warm fingers and Frida's small, perfect breasts. He nudged it downwards until the rosy bud of her nipple sprang free. With a deep sigh, he closed his lips around it.

Frida shifted in his arms making small moans of pleasure that unravelled the last of his restraint. With one hand, he held her waist and with the other, he reached beneath the hem of her skirts, travelling up over her stockings until he reached the heavenly softness of her upper thighs.

Here he paused. Lifting his face from her breasts, he shifted his gaze to her eyes, which were closed with pleasure, and her lips, which were parted as if waiting to meet his.

He dropped butterfly kisses onto the corner of her mouth as his gentle fingers found her curls. She moaned into his mouth, pulling him closer and eradicating any doubt that she wanted this as much as he did.

"Frida." He whispered her name softly as he slid a finger inside her, holding her steady as the first waves of pleasure took her.

"Oh," she gasped, sinking against him.

He took her weight easily, watching her face to see what touch pleased her the most. He stroked and cajoled until she tipped over the edge with a deep groan of release.

And then it was over and she was flushed and warm in his arms. He kissed her forehead as her breathing slowly returned to normal and her heart ceased to hammer beneath her shift.

"Beautiful," he repeated, still quite unable to believe what had happened.

Her eyes flickered open and held him transfixed in pools of blue. "I did not know it could be like that."

He reached for the blanket, tucking it around her shoulders against the cold. "That is only the beginning," he promised, guiding her over to a chair where he took a seat and pulled her onto his knee.

She smoothed her hands through his tangled hair before cupping his stubbled cheeks with her palms.

"The beginning of our future?" she whispered. "Together?"

"Together," he confirmed, interlinking his fingers with her. "We will make it happen, you and I."

She rested her head against his chest and Callum felt himself grow warm and relaxed, despite the hardness of the chair. For the first time, he could glimpse a future where he would be happy.

I will make it happen, he swore to himself, before letting his eyelids droop.

They dozed in the candlelight, tucked under the blanket, together.

CALLUM SHOULD NOT have allowed himself to fall asleep. He cursed out loud when he awoke some hours later to find the sun already set and the light all but disappeared from the day.

Frida was equally dismayed; her blue eyes were wide with shock as she stood by his side and they looked out at the darkening afternoon. The snow lay thick and unspoilt all around them. Slow flakes still drifted down, but the storm had lost its conviction. An hour earlier, they would have made the journey back with ease. But now, the snow was not the only danger—if they ventured out, they would have darkness to contend with, too.

"Mayhap, if we move quickly?" she suggested.

"Nay," Callum responded, before pressing his lips together and softening his response. "I do not think it would be wise," he amended. Frida was not one of his men and he should not address her as such. But after so many years barking orders—and receiving the like from his father—it had become something of a reflex.

Her shoulders sagged. "They will be worried, back at the hall."

"I know it." He took her hand and led her back to the relative warmth of the hut. "But in the morn, we can return and show them that we are safe and well. That *you* are safe and well," he corrected himself with a smile. "But if we set out now and fall into a snowdrift or wander of course, mayhap they will not find our frozen bodies until the first thaw."

"That is a terrible image." She closed her eyes against it.

"We have light." He was rummaging in the store cupboard and had found enough candles to last them until dawn. "But nothing to eat."

"I am not hungry." But Frida's audibly rumbling stomach contradicted her claim.

It was a hard, cold night that they spent together in the shepherd's hut. Not at all the start to this new stage of their romance that Callum would have wished for. He spread one blanket on the floor and both Frida and the lamb snuggled up together, beneath the second. There was scarce room for his long limbs in the cramped space, but he laid down as best he could and held Frida until she fell asleep. Then, moving with great care, he stretched himself up and spent the greater part of the night sitting on the uncomfortable chair.

The temptation to see all of this as a warning sign from above grew strong within him. One moment of passion they had shared, and already Lady Frida de Neville was reduced to sleeping in a shepherd's hut, hungry and cold, her lovely hair spread thickly over the dusty floor. But Callum was still light-headed with joy over Frida's admission of feeling for him. For now, he was buoyed up with hope for the future.

Well-used to the anxious wait of the hours before a battle, he steeled himself not to think too much during the night. Wonderings never spiralled in a positive direction while darkness prevailed and the body shivered with cold. He knew this of old. So as the owls hooted outside, he gazed at the soft outline of Frida's sleeping face and let a smile play about his lips.

Sometime before dawn, he fell asleep with his head and arms on the table. Waking with a stiff neck and sore back, he had to blink before his eyes adjusted to the bright shaft of light streaming in at the open door. The air smelled fresh and clean.

"Good morning," Frida said softly. With the lamb in her arms and the golden light behind her, she was a vision.

Callum sat up in the chair, wincing as his cramped muscles came back to life. "Good morning." His mouth was as dry as sawdust. What he wouldn't give for a skin of good wine.

"The snow has stopped. We can go home."

Her simple statement pierced him. Frida looked only to return to the house she loved with the man for whom she had proclaimed affection. The path forward seemed clear to her. But

Callum's deception meant that his way forward was paved with sharp rocks and treacherous drops, however much he might wish it otherwise. All at once, he longed for bitter winds and biting hail. Anything that might keep them here and prolong this beautiful privacy, just for them. But he forced his chapped lips to smile as he stood and rotated his shoulders.

"Did you sleep well?"

"Aye, well enough." She bent to lower the lamb to the floor. "I melted some snow for Gertrude to drink. But she has had no food inside her."

He frowned as he puzzled this out, then noticed the candle moved to the floor of the hut, beside a rough wooden bowl which contained a thin covering of water.

"Ingenious." He smiled at her again and then frowned. "For how long was I asleep?"

She inclined her head, her blue eyes dancing. "I can't tell, I'm sure. But I can tell you that you snored."

Her laugh brought fresh joy to his heart and he laughed along with her. "Never," he denied strongly.

Frida met his gaze impishly. "Is this the life I have to look forward to? A man who snores louder than a hound?"

Callum's worries floated away. He was light with happiness. "I hope so." He caught one of her hands and brought it to his lips.

She pretended to consider it. "We will have to sleep in separate chambers."

"Never," he said again, drawing her towards him. "Though mayhap I should refrain in the future from sleeping upright in a chair."

"Ah, so if you are laying down, you will sleep quietly?"

"As quiet as a lamb," he promised, indicating the snuffling young sheep who seemed about to curl up again on the blanket.

"That is good news indeed."

He dropped a careful kiss onto her forehead, conscious of his stale breath and the sharp growth of stubble on his cheeks. "We should make haste, before all of the county is sent out to search for you."

"Mirrie will know I am with you and that I am safe," Frida declared, but she walked over to where they had laid out their cloaks and picked one up. "Still damp." She wrinkled her nose.

"I am sorry."

"For what?" Her brow lifted in confusion.

"For the difficult start to our days together." He took his cloak from her. "Cold and damp and hungry," he added ruefully.

She laid a hand on his, her touch bringing him more comfort than she knew. "There will be better days, brighter days."

"Aye." He wanted to profess his love for her. E'en to formally ask for her hand in marriage. Callum had known since the first time he set eyes on Frida de Neville that she was the woman for him—however many obstacles lay in his path. But when he wanted to swear his devotion, the words dried up on his tongue. How could he promise her a future whilst she believed him a true Englishman?

Whilst my father and my lord wait for me to assassinate Frida's brother?

All he could do was squeeze her fingers in a show of affection as the cold light of day brought these complications into terrible focus.

It mattered not how strong the innate connection might be; they could not begin a life together based on lies.

He would have to tell her the truth, however hard that might be.

The realisation brought a flood of relief, for this at last was a way forward and Callum had never shied away from a challenge. But first they must return to the hall, to a warm fire and freshly-baked bread from the kitchen. His stomach rumbled at the prospect and Frida smilingly flung her cloak about her shoulders.

"Let us depart."

At first, they walked hand in hand, but their progress was slow and arduous, especially as Callum also carried Gertrude, tucked under one arm. The snow was deep and their boots sank on every step, but the sun shone brightly and icicles twinkled from the trees. Even a Scotsman could not deny the beauty of this English morn. All around them, the hills and valleys were blanketed in white. It was a world transformed and anything seemed possible.

The downhill slope was easier. Frida walked ahead, glancing back occasionally with a smile more dazzling than the reflected sunlight. Callum's worries circled and swooped like the birds flying in the blue sky above them, but he took courage from Frida's evident happiness.

Once they had eaten and Frida had warmed herself by the fire, he would tell her all of his tale. There would be no more lies. No more half-truths.

But a strange sight greeted them as they turned the corner to the main gates. The snow coming up from the village was not smooth and sparkling, but trampled and run through with mud and dirt, as if many men and horses had passed through. Frida turned towards him, a frown flickering across her brow.

"It looks like we have visitors."

"Aye," Callum agreed reflexively, his heart already sinking.

Whoever these visitors were, they were unlikely to bring good news.

They followed the rutted path through the gates, the uni-formed guards standing aside to let them pass with a respectful nod to the lady of the house. Callum walked behind her, unable to shake the feeling that he was already a condemned man. Was it his imagination, or did the guards avoid his gaze e'en more so than usual?

Moments earlier, he had contemplated a roaring fire and the comfort of food and drink. Now he glanced towards the barn where Arlo and Andrew had been sleeping, wondering if they were safe.

Are they still alive?

He thought of the daggers secreted beneath his pallet. So out of reach he may as well have given them over to Frida. Then he scolded himself for such drama. What was he anticipating? That the Earl of Wolvesley had ridden out to arrest him?

All was quiet as they passed through the outer courtyard. Callum felt his legs become more and more leaden with every step closer to the hall. Frida, in contrast, walked steadily, despite her ankle. Her head was high, her expression curious. No fears besieged her.

But even Frida's step faltered as they turned the corner and encountered two lines of armed and mounted men, swords glinting in the sunlight, horses' ears pricked towards them.

Frida put a hand to her heart. Callum wanted to go to her, so she might lean against him, but he felt frozen to the spot.

"What is this?" she asked.

The central horseman urged his horse forwards and removed his helm. All of Callum's fears solidified as he recognised the flaxen curls and handsome features of Tristan de Neville.

But Tristan did not spare Callum so much as a glance. His gaze was fully on his sister as he gestured his men forwards.

"Seize the Scot," Tristan ordered.

CHAPTER FIFTEEN

THE TWO SIBLINGS faced one another across the great hall while Frida fought to keep her spiralling emotions in check. When she had awoken that morn, she had thought herself a woman in love. Now she was a woman under siege, and from her own brother at that. A fire flickered in the grate but she had no desire to move closer to its blaze, nor to hold her damp cloak to the warmth. Her hunger and thirst were forgotten as well.

Tristan had all the height and bearing of their father; the same thatch of thick blond hair, which curled just above his powerful shoulders, and the same piercing blue eyes. Even his sworn enemy would call him handsome. But it wasn't just good looks that drew people to the future Earl of Wolvesley; energy and charisma radiated from him. His bright smile was contagious; his determination to succeed was a key component in cementing his mighty reputation.

Little more than a year separated their births, and Frida had always thought that she would trust her brother with her life. Now she wanted to grab him by the shoulders and shake him. She was no longer cold from her night in the shepherd's hut; her whole being burned to be heard.

"It is no crime to be of Scottish descent," she stated into the vast room, which was empty but for the two of them. Jonah was keeping his distance, though she had no doubt he would be listening nearby. Mirrie, who hated conflict, had melted away to the kitchens.

Tristan eyed a tapestried chair and she thought for a moment that he might go and sit down. He had, after all, endured an arduous ride from Wolvesley in challenging conditions. But the revered knight of the realm merely folded his arms across his chest and sighed. "Mayhap not. But it is suspicious indeed to tell false tales about one's descent."

Aye, she could not deny the truth of that. And the question of *why* tore up her insides. Frida felt like a little ship tossed this way and that in mighty waves. She could not search for all the answers at once. She must deal with the most pressing issue first. And that was undoubtedly the fact that the man she loved had been dragged away by armed soldiers and locked in the cellar by her brother.

The two men he'd travelled with, Arlo and Andrew, had been flung in there alongside him. For safety, Tristan had said.

"You knew Callum at Lindum," she tried again. Trying to make sense of it as much as anything else. "You invited him to Wolvesley."

A frown flickered across his brow. "I scarcely knew him at Lindum. And 'twas one of my instructors who pressed me to invite Baine for the yuletide celebrations." His blue eyes narrowed. "That means Scottish treachery is embedded even within our most heralded institutions."

Frida could not be less interested. "He and his men have been useful here." She opened her arms, thinking of Callum helping her to bring in the fruit harvest and ploughing through the snow to rescue one lost lamb. "They fixed the barn roof, chopped firewood, helped with the animals. One of them lies injured, e'en now."

Tristan let out a short bark of laughter. "I know all about that particular incident. But, sister, pray, may I take refreshment before we talk further? My throat is parched." He looked about as if hoping Mirrie might magically materialise with a tray.

After all, Mirrie habitually anticipated Tristan's every whim and wish. But not today.

Today, pure-hearted Mirrie would be almost as bewildered by this turn of events as Frida.

Frida fought off an urge to refuse. She wanted answers more than he wanted wine. But he was, after all, her brother. This was his ancestral home. And he had ridden here with some misguided notion of securing her safety. Furthermore, she knew of old that there was no sense trying to reason with Tristan when he was hungry.

"I will ring for refreshments," she said, stepping forward to pull at the bell rope. "Sit down," she added, somewhat begrudgingly.

Tristan did so, stretching out his long legs and rotating his muscular shoulders. "You look in need of rest and refreshment yourself," he observed. "And perchance a dry change of clothes?"

He was right. Her dress and cloak were both crumpled and damp, but she couldn't bear to retire to her chamber with so many questions left unanswered. She made an impatient gesture. "Later."

"I do not want you to catch a chill."

She shook her head at him. "You sound just like Mother."

He leaned forwards. "And you are acting most out of character. Why so much concern for the Scot?"

Because I love him.

She could not say that. Certainly not now. Instead, she perched on the edge of the adjacent chair and made an effort to steady her breathing. "Because he has been nothing but kind to me."

Tristan let out another bark of laughter. "Sister, he came here to kill me."

She could not believe it. *Would not* believe it. Her hair swung over her shoulders as she shook her head violently. "Nay."

"Aye," he corrected, firmly.

"You were not even here."

He drummed his fingers against the arm of the chair. "And

that proved to be the first obstacle in his path."

They both fell silent as Jennifer carried in the heavy tray and settled it carefully upon a low wooden table. Frida nodded her thanks and the serving girl curtsied respectfully before scurrying away.

Tristan fell upon the food like a man who was starving. He had always had a big appetite. She watched as his white teeth tore into the freshly baked bread and felt her own stirrings of hunger fade away.

It was unlikely that Callum would be enjoying food and drink down in the cold, dark cellar.

She cleared her throat. "Since arriving here, your friend Callum Baine has saved both the fruit harvest and our first flock of sheep. Why would he act in such a way if he intended harm to our family? Why would he not simply seek you elsewhere?"

Callum took a deep swig of watered wine. "I do not know. That is what I need to ask him."

She ground her teeth with frustration. "But what makes you think he came here to kill you?" The words formed with difficulty and suddenly the reality of what she was saying—of what Tristan was accusing Callum of—settled within her.

Tristan had his faults, and as his older sister who had grown up beside him, Frida would happily list them to anyone prepared to listen. But he was no fool.

"Why do you think that?" she whispered.

"Because his accomplice told me everything." Tristan placed his goblet on the table and turned to face her. "Allow me to ask *you* a question."

Pulse pounding, she nodded her assent.

"Why did Baine tell you he was here?"

She struggled to remember; it all seemed so long ago. So irrelevant, given everything that had happened since. "He told me you sent him," she muttered, her lips grown dry and her throat constricted with tension.

It must have been a lie.

Tristan held her gaze. "I knew that, of course, for Jonah sent me a letter detailing everything." He shrugged. "But I wanted you to realise that he was deceiving you from the start."

Frida couldn't bear it. Hot tears sprang to her eyes, and she looked down at her hands, clenched tightly in her lap, so that Tristan wouldn't see her distress.

His tone softened as he continued. "As soon as I received Jonah's letter, I knew that both of you were in danger." Frida shook her head, still not prepared to accept this, but Tristan spoke on. "Mayhap if the snow had not come, things would have played out differently. Baine is a clever man. A charming man." Frida felt the full force of her brother's gaze resting upon her and realised that he was offering her something of an excuse.

"*Aye,*" she could say, "*he conned us most cleverly. That is why I so readily fell into his trap. Thank goodness you arrived in time to show me the truth.*"

But she could not be grateful. She had believed Callum because she loved him. Loved him still. Could not accept his deceit.

"Because of the snow we had to take shelter in the forest. And there, we met Gregor."

Now her eyes flew to his. She remembered the tall, angry man who had thrown the dagger at Arlo. "Gregor?"

Tristan nodded. "The man had the nerve to try and steal food from our camp fire. Yet he lacked the finesse to do so without being caught. We showed him leniency, at first. I would not see a man starve in the snow. *Eat with us,* we told him. And he did," Tristan snorted. "Right until the moment he tried to stab me in the back."

Frida's hands covered her face.

"Then the man spoke most freely and his Scots brogue became clear. He told us everything. How Callum Baine took his orders from Robert the Bruce himself. How they had ridden here with the express purpose of assassinating me." Tristan tore off another hunk of bread and sat back in his chair. "Clearly my absence from Ember Hall spoiled their plans. The information passed up country must have been false. A mix-up between myself and Jonah, perchance." His lips twitched. "Mayhap I should be grateful for Scottish incompetence."

Frida felt as if she might be sick. Only the fact that there was nothing in her stomach kept her from retching. "He has shown us nothing but kindness," she whispered. But in her mind's eye, she saw the stash of gleaming weapons beneath Callum's pallet in the hayloft, and she grew close to weeping once more.

"That may be so, sister. But we do not know what he was planning to do next." Tristan chewed ruminatively and washed it down with another mouthful of wine. "Or rather we do know, but not the detail of it."

"Nay." Frida shook her head. She could not accept this; Tristan must have made some mistake. "Gregor was angry with Callum when he left. 'Tis clear to me that he must have lied."

A log spat in the fire as if to accentuate her distress, but Tristan remained unruffled.

"Callum's father is Rory Baine."

Tristan announced this as if the name might mean something, but Frida shrugged her shoulders, still focused on holding back the tears that threatened to expose her love for Callum.

Sir Callum Baine, the knight that had trained alongside my brother.
Not Callum Baine, the Scot in league against my brother.

The two could not be one and the same person. She wrung her hands in anguish.

"He is a mighty Scottish clansman. A faithful follower of Robert the Bruce."

She scrabbled to make sense of it. "Then how did Callum come to be at Lindum? Why does he speak with an English accent?" Her voice rose triumphantly. "What are his connections to Egremont House?"

"I do not know every inch of his life story." Tristan pressed his lips together. "You can ask him these questions yourself, if you wish."

"I do." She nodded vehemently. She would believe nothing

until she had heard it from Callum's own lips.

He inclined his head. "Very well. After I have rested a while, I will interrogate the prisoner myself. You can come in once my men have softened him up."

Frida's blood ran cold. "Nay." She rose up from her chair, ignoring the stab of complaint from her ankle. "You will not hurt him."

But Tristan's eyes were hard. "This man lied to you whilst plotting to kill me. You cannot expect leniency?"

Her legs threatened to give way beneath her and she was forced to lean on the arm of his chair for support. Coming closer to her brother, she saw again the determined set of his jaw and the anger flickering in his blue eyes. "I expect you to give him a fair trial."

He held her gaze. "I will give him a trial, aye. In front of witnesses at that. But no one threatens the de Neville family and gets away with it."

CHAPTER SIXTEEN

I SHOULD HAVE *been more prepared for this.*

Callum's eyes had grown accustomed to the dark of the cellar and he could discern the outline of both Arlo and Andrew nearby. Arlo was laying on his side, his lean body occasionally shuddering with cold. Andrew sat beside him, head down. The only sound was their laboured breathing and the occasional dripping of melting snow outside.

Callum wanted to reach out to both his friends and apologise, but his hands and feet were bound and his mouth gagged. He could neither move nor talk, and the twitching and grunting he *could* accomplish would achieve nothing. All he had were his endless thoughts of self-recrimination, which whirled around like the branches of a sapling tree in a strong wind.

I should not have put Arlo and Andrew at risk.

I should not have lied to Frida.

I should not have allowed this to happen.

But despite the direness of their circumstances, he could not berate himself for staying too long at Ember Hall. These last days with Frida had been the most precious of his life. He only wished he had found a way to send his men away before the three of them were discovered to be traitors.

Again, he concluded that he should have known something like this would happen. The de Neville family were among the wealthiest and most powerful in England. Tristan had spies and allies everywhere; he was not a man to cross.

Callum shuffled on his backside until he could lean against the rough stone wall, relieving some of the ache across his shoulders. Cold had settled deep into his bones from a combination of damp clothing and the chill of the small, underground chamber. At least the air was fresh. It seemed nothing had been stored down here for some time. A faint shaft of light filtered through the gap in the double doors above them, through which they had all been unceremoniously shoved some time earlier. He had lost all sense of how long they had been down here, but the unchanging light told him it was still the same day.

The same day which had dawned with such hope and promise. With Frida by his side. With him daring to dream of a future.

Callum shook the memories away. Dreams had no place here. Survival had become his aim, for his men if not for himself.

Footsteps above his head broke through his reverie and had him sitting up straighter. Whatever happened next, he willed it would happen to him and not faithful Andrew nor young Arlo. There was a creak as the horizontal doors were wrenched open, and a flood of sunlight blinded him for a long moment. The next thing he knew, hands were grasping his upper arms and he was yanked up the wooden stairs to ground level, his shins banging painfully against every step. He tried to reach Andrew's eye, to signal to him that he would do all he could to keep him and Arlo safe. But his long-time friend and comrade did not so much as turn his head in Callum's direction.

Outside, the world was still impossibly white and soft with snow. His damp breeches became soaked through as his captors dragged him across the courtyard. Callum turned his head from right to left, looking for Mirrie or Jonah, for any ally who might show by their expression what awaited him. But the usually bustling yard was deserted.

He was glad that he did not see Frida. He could not bear the idea of her witnessing his shame.

He winced at the painful banging of stone against the front of his calves as they ascended the steps to the front door. Then they were through into the blissful warmth of the great hall, where a fire crackled in the grate and the scent of lavender from the rushes soothed his senses.

This was where he had imagined telling Frida the truth.

Now it was where he would face the wrath of Tristan de Neville. Callum could see him standing to one side of the fire, deliberately looking away as if the sight of Callum was something low and degrading.

Just behind him stood Frida.

Callum's heart somersaulted and dived. The mere sight of her reminded him of all he wanted to live for. His captors threw him onto the floor like yesterday's rubbish and he lay still, unable to right himself with his wrists so tightly tied behind his back. No matter, he would remain here, unresisting, until they gave him chance to speak. They would have to remove his gag for that. From the corner of his eye, he spied black leather boots walking towards him. And then the pain began.

First it was a kick to his side that had him writhing in agony. Almost immediately afterwards, a kick to his head made his vision blur. Every bit of him became a target for what must be several men, all seemingly determined to kick him to his death. Callum struggled for breath, turning his head towards the floor in an effort to protect his face. What madness was this? Soldiers gathering en masse to strike a man who was both bound and gagged? His blood raged at the injustice as the blows rained down. Then he remembered who his assailants were.

The English.

Men who thought nothing of kicking a man while he was down. Nor of killing innocent women and children in the storming of a castle.

I should expect nothing less.

He would bear it bravely, quietly at least, for he would not give them the satisfaction of seeing him wince, much less sob or beg for mercy.

Nor would he show weakness in front of Frida.

When he was beginning to think he would die right here on the floor of the great hall, the kicking ceased. Through a haze of pain, he heard the trample of footsteps moving away from him, into the entrance hall and out of the door. He heard sobbing and worried for a moment that it was his own. Then he realised the truth was even worse.

It was Frida.

She came to him with cool hands and a tender touch, urging him to sit up, steadying him when the room started to spin. Her blue eyes were red with sorrow and he could not bring himself to meet her gaze.

"I will remove this gag," she stated, in the direction of her brother.

Tristan had taken a seat in one of the tapestried chairs which usually sat before the fire. At the moment, they had both been shoved backwards. Callum now slumped in their usual place, unable to take any comfort from the warmth of the fire.

Tristan watched on idly, as if only mildly diverted by the evening's entertainment. He inclined his head, blond like his sister had once been, although Tristan was a bigger-boned, bigger proportioned member of the de Neville family. He resembled his father, Callum recalled. A giant of a man.

"As you wish," he said.

If Callum had the power of speech, he would have said no. No to Frida removing the one thing that guaranteed his silence. For silence was far preferable to the admission of deceit that Tristan was surely about to extract from him. But it was still a relief to have the cloth pulled free from his mouth and feel closer to human again.

"I'm sorry," were the first words he said, aimed at Frida, who winced almost as if he had struck her.

She turned away from him and rose slowly to her feet, her ankle clearly paining her as she staggered back to her brother.

Tristan's gaze was as cold as the cellar floor.

"Callum Baine?"

Callum ran his tongue against his teeth, checking all were still present. His body felt bruised and raw, but he had taken many a battering before, and he could tell that this was no worse than what he'd previously endured. He would survive.

He kept his answer brief. Tristan knew who he was well enough. "Aye."

"Callum Baine, fellow of Lindum, knight of the realm. Or Callum Baine, Scottish rebel, servant of Robert the Bruce?"

Tristan's voice was low and mocking. Deliberately so, no doubt, as to provoke a reaction in Callum. A reaction that was even now brewing inside his belly. Callum raised his bloodshot eyes to the handsome man, so impeccably attired in spotless breeches and a dark green tunic shot through with gold thread. He had once counted this man amongst his friends; had risked his own safety to spare his life. But Tristan's finely-drawn face showed no recognition of their past friendship. He was every inch the English lord, looking down at a Scot with derision.

Callum wanted to spit at his leather boots, but he would not be uncouth before Frida. Instead he forced his chapped lips into a smile. "Take your pick."

Tristan threw him half a smile in return. "A faithless man, then? A man who will fight for whichever side is winning?"

"Nay, never that." Callum's blood boiled, even as he told himself that Tristan was doing his best to provoke him.

"What then?" Tristan leaned forward, his hands clasped on his knees, looking for all the world as if he was interested in the state of Callum's soul. "My sister here thinks I should show mercy to you and your men. Whereas I am minded to string you all up." He shrugged lightly, as if he didn't care very much either way. "This is your chance to speak, Callum Baine."

I will plead for the life of my men.

"What do you want to know?" His voice came out as a growl. A growl which made Frida press the heels of her hands to her eyes.

Callum looked away from the woman he loved. If he had one wish, he would not use it for his freedom. He would use it to send Frida far from this conversation.

She stood restlessly behind Tristan's chair, sometimes turning as if she would walk from the room, other times looking for all the world as if she might drop to her knees and release Callum's bonds. Her eyes were titchy and her movements as jumpy as a young colt.

Callum's heart ached for her.

But the ache in his heart was accompanied by stabbing pains in his ribs and lower back, constant reminders of the beating he had endured at her brother's command.

Tristan put his head to one side, as if considering the question. "Do not make the mistake of thinking I don't already know every part of your sorry tale," he answered softly.

"What can I add to it then?" For the sake of his men, Callum chased the sneer from his face.

"That is my question to you, Callum Baine. I once thought you a man of wit and learning. Was I wrong about that as well?"

Callum kept his temper in check as his mind attempted to process the facts. Tristan had come to Ember Hall with an army of soldiers. He had acted swiftly and decisively. The actions of a man who already knew he had been crossed.

But Callum had not so much as raised a hand against the de Nevilles or their property. Neither had his men. This must surely count in his favour?

He cleared his throat, closing his eyes as the great hall lurched to the left. If only his hands were not so tightly bound behind him, he might at least find his balance.

"You know then that I came to Ember Hall with orders to kill the lord."

Frida's sharp gasp of shock was almost his undoing, but Callum kept his gaze trained on Tristan.

He nodded, his blond head all but haloed by candlelight. "I do."

"And you know that I was never informed as to the identity of this lord? That as soon as I arrived here and recognised Lady Frida, everything changed?"

Tristan tapped the arm of his chair with his index finger. "Why then did you keep a stash of weapons beneath your bed?"

Callum's heart sank, but he did not allow his reaction to show on his face. He had guessed that their loft would be searched.

"No man likes to be defenceless."

"Especially when he is planning an assassination." It was a statement, not a question.

Frida's sob was audible. This time, Tristan turned to her with a mixture of concern and impatience flashing across his blue eyes. "Sister, you do not have to stay."

Frida gazed bleakly back at him. "I want to."

He inclined his head. "Then come and sit beside me. Do not scurry about in the shadows like a serving maid."

Callum could not help his gaze fixing on Frida, silently begging her to go elsewhere, but she did not so much glance in his direction as she carefully sank down into the tapestried chair.

Tristan snapped his attention back to Callum. "You were anticipating my arrival and planning an assassination, yes?"

Was I?

Callum fought to keep his breathing steady.

"My assassination," Tristan added, as if helpfully.

"It was not as simple as that," Callum managed. Wherever he looked, he could not escape the stunned expression on Frida's face. It would be branded across his memory forever.

"Why else did you stay here for so long? Three warriors, four warriors," Tristan corrected himself. "Laying down their weapons and tilling the land. *English* land," he emphasised.

Four warriors.

Callum exhaled, realising that Gregor had most likely had a hand in furnishing Tristan with what he saw as the truth.

"Speak, man," Tristan exploded. The first sign that he was not calmly in control.

"Methinks my long stay here is evidence against your claim. If my intention had always been to assassinate you, de Neville, believe me, you would already be dead." At Frida's gasp of anguish, he softened his voice. "In truth, I have enjoyed tilling your English land. Ember Hall has given me a sense of peace I have long been lacking."

Now Frida's eyes met his and their gazes locked as lovers. Despite everything, Callum felt that all things may yet be well. With this woman beside him, he might e'en be King of England.

But 'twas not his place to tell Tristan de Neville of an understanding between he, Callum Baine, and Lady Frida de Neville. Those words would have to come from Frida's lips.

Tristan's face betrayed no surprise at Callum's words. "Peace, eh? Is that right?"

"Aye." Callum drew himself up as best he could on the hard floor. "I brought in the harvest, chopped the firewood and rescued the sheep when the snow came early." His heart beat painfully in his chest as he recalled how recently he and Frida had embraced in the shepherd's hut. "My men fixed the barn roof—in good time, I might add."

"All of this I know." Tristan sprang from his chair so quickly that Callum could not help rearing backwards in surprise. In less than a second, Tristan was beside him on the floor, pressing the sharp edge of a blade against his neck. "I also know that while you split my sister's firewood, you waited patiently for my arrival so that you might run me through with a blade, much like this one."

Callum wanted to shake his head, but to do so would exert pressure on the blade that was already digging into his bruised flesh.

"'Tis not the case," he managed to gasp.

"Tristan, stop." Frida rose to her feet and stretched out shaking arms in entreaty.

"'Tis exactly the case," Tristan spat. "I ask again, man, why else would you stay here so long?"

Because I love your sister!

The words were forming on his tongue when Tristan pressed his head closer to Callum's, the hatred in his blue eyes all too visible. "I will tell you why, shall I?" He grabbed a fistful of Callum's hair, forcing his head back with the blade still held firmly against his neck. "'Tis because you are a Scottish coward, like all of your kin who lie and creep around and kill."

Callum let out a roar of pure outrage. "'Tis not the Scots who are cowards."

Tristan's voice was a low, menacing hum in his ear. "I have seen for myself the true calibre of those who follow the Bruce."

He had seen for himself.

With dreadful clarity, Callum recalled his conversation with Jonah in the solar just days prior. When Jonah told him that Tristan had been in Scotland at the time of the siege on Kielder Castle, his family home.

I have to know the truth.

"Were you in the highlands this summer?" He wanted to look Tristan full in the eye, but could not manage it with the knife at his throat.

"I am the one asking questions." Tristan gripped his fistful of hair more tightly, but Callum was beyond caring.

"At Kielder Castle." His stare locked onto his captor. "Did you give the order?"

Tristan paused. For a moment all they could hear was the crackle of logs in the fire and Frida's broken sobbing.

"You are asking if I ordered the siege of Kielder Castle?" Tristan's voice was unreadable. If he knew what Kielder Castle was to Callum, he gave no sign of it.

"Aye."

"I do not deny it."

Anger blurred both his vision and his senses. Consumed with lust for revenge, he twisted out of Tristan's hands, away from the knife, and headbutted him full in the groin.

Tristan swore as he went down, giving Callum enough time to somehow get to his knees, his movement made possible by sheer force of will. He would not lay on the floor and wriggle like a worm before his aggressor. He would face him with all the height he could muster.

"'Tis you English who creep around and kill, not caring how much innocent blood you spill in your endless greed."

Tristan was still holding the knife, and within moments he would recover enough to wield it, but Callum no longer cared. In his mind's eye he saw the fallen bodies of Arlo's parents, together with the young and old of his highland village.

Tristan had been there, perpetuating violence against peaceful people.

He spat on the floor, pleased to see the spittle land close to Tristan's hand.

The future Earl of Wolvesley rose to his feet, looking down upon Callum as if he were a small thing, worthy of naught but disgust.

"I shall kill you," he said, calmly.

"Do want you want," Callum roared back. "What is more Scottish blood on your filthy hands?"

At the last moment, Callum had one thought. *Frida*. But already Tristan's long legs were striding towards him. There was a massive blow from above. Then the world turned black.

CHAPTER SEVENTEEN

S OME HOURS LATER, Frida stood in the dying light of the day in the deserted western corner of the courtyard, beside the old bakehouse. Behind that locked wooden door lay Callum. Though in what state, she hardly dared imagine. She had packed her basket with herbs and salves to treat a variety of ailments, unable to rest without at least alleviating some discomfort for the man she loved.

Aye. Still loved, despite all she had learned. So Callum had ridden to Ember Hall intent on killing an English lord. What did that matter, when to him the lord was nameless?

When he had learned who he faced, he had lowered his weapons. Surrendered some, hidden some. So be it. The important thing was he had not inflicted any harm on anyone.

Nay, the truly important thing was that he made her heart soar and dance. That his arms felt like home. That she still dreamed of a future with him.

But was it doomed to be an impossible dream?

Sniffing away her tears, Frida motioned to the guard to stand aside. Thankfully, he did not question her authority, despite Tristan's arrival.

She rapped on the door to give Callum fair warning, and then pushed it open. It took a second for her eyes to adjust to the late-afternoon gloom. Weak light filtered in through the shutters, illuminating a large, rectangular room with an earth floor. It was

185

empty of everything save a rug, a candle and Callum.

Callum.

Just the sight of him soothed her troubled soul, e'en though he was bloodied and bound. His brown eyes opened wider when she lowered her hood and he recognised her face.

"Frida," he said, his voice thick with pain. "You came."

"Of course I came." She hurried forwards, the healer in her troubled by the deep gash at the side of his head which she had seen inflicted by her own brother's boot. "How do you feel?"

"I'm grand." His answer was swift, accompanied by the smallest smile.

She tutted, hiding the wave of relief that threatened to take strength from her limbs. He had recognised her, so his sight was not compromised. And he had joked, so his reasoning must be intact.

"Let me light the candle." She fished in her basket for a tinderbox.

He cleared his throat. "I would prefer it if you didn't."

She paused in surprise, one hand still in her basket. "How so?"

His brown eyes held her gaze, like she was the prisoner instead of him. "For one, I would not have you see me like this. For another, I know you are a skilled healer. But on this occasion, there would be no point to your ministrations when I shall be dead long before any remedy could have time enough to heal me."

She choked back a sob. "Don't say that."

"Frida." His voice was as soft as honey. "I am glad in my heart to see you. But I am guessing your brother does not know you are here?"

Frustration rippled down her spine. "I do not need his permission to go where I please. I am mistress at Ember Hall."

"Aye, and a right good one at that. But your brother Tristan intends to kill me on the morrow, whether you are mistress here or not."

The last of her strength deserted her and Frida found herself on the earth floor beside him, curling her body against the hardness of his chest. His hands were still bound so he could not reach to hold her, but he lowered his head until his chin rested upon her hair.

"Do not speak like that," she whispered, "I cannot bear it."

"'Tis the truth." Came his reply. "And there is no escaping it."

"Nay." She shook her head vigorously, breathing him in. But his usual scent was obscured by blood and cold. "I will speak to Tristan in the morn. I will reason with him."

His warm breath against her scalp offered scant comfort. "You have already tried your hardest. Already done more than I deserve."

"I shall set you free." She sat upright, her eyes gazing into his. "Right now, I shall cut your bonds and you shall go free."

For a moment, hope flickered across his face, but then a sad smile took its place. "You must not. For your own sake and for the sake of my love for you, you must not."

Tears stung her eyes and she reached out to grasp his hand, entwining her fingers with his, despite the cloth that bound his hands uncomfortably behind his back.

"How so?"

Callum gave her fingers one last squeeze and then released them. "Because your brother has stated that he was responsible for the razing of my ancestral home in Scotland." She frowned her incomprehension and he continued, his voice rough with emotion. "My father is the laird of Kielder Castle. I fought on the battlements during the siege and saw women and children slaughtered as they ran for their freedom."

"Nay," she gasped.

"If you let me go free, I will take my revenge upon Tristan de Neville for what he has done." He looked her fully in the face, ensuring his meaning was clear. "I will kill him, the first opportunity I get."

Frida reared backwards in distress. "You cannot make such threats." She scrambled to her feet, heart pounding beneath her cloak. "He is my brother." She clenched and unclenched her hands, hoping desperately that she might have misunderstood.

"Aye. And you are the woman I would lay down my life for. Which is why I beg of you, leave me now."

There was no ambiguity here.

"Then there is no hope for us," she whispered, the words burning her throat.

"None," Callum agreed, already turning his face away from her. "I know you to be a merciful woman. Please leave and do not come back. The sight of you causes more pain than I can endure."

Part of Frida wanted to argue, but a larger part still reeled from Callum's declaration of violent intent towards her brother. She had heard with her own ears Tristan admitting to ordering the siege on Kielder Castle, though she hadn't known in that moment what Kielder Castle meant to Callum.

Forsooth, just one day ago she had thought him a true-blooded Englishman.

Stifling her sobs, she walked unsteadily from the dim room, scarcely remembering to acknowledge the guard when he bowed. The door slammed shut behind her and the guard shot the bolt home.

She would never see Callum again.

FRIDA KEPT A tight hold of her composure until she was safely inside her bedchamber, then she sank down onto her mattress and let her tears flow unchecked. She didn't know how much time had passed when Mirrie tentatively opened the door, her face creased up with compassion for her friend.

"Oh Frida," she said simply, walking towards her with her arms outstretched.

Frida had no words. She rested her head on Mirrie's shoulder and continued to sob.

"You could go and see him," Mirrie suggested quietly, smoothing Frida's hair away from her eyes.

"I already did."

"In the cellar?" Mirrie's eyebrows shot up in surprise.

"In the bakehouse." Frida straightened up and dabbed at her eyes with a handkerchief. "It's where I had the guards take him after Tristan stormed out, leaving him unconscious on the floor."

"Tristan is all of a dither," Mirrie said, conversationally. "I sat with him at dinner, but he hardly ate a thing."

Frida shook her head, unwilling to speak of her brother. She was still unable to unsee the moment when he aimed that final kick at Callum's head. But she noted Mirrie's best blue dress and the way she had pinned back her wayward curls with extra care, and she hoped that Tristan would not break Mirrie's heart as well as her own.

"I forgot to come down." Frida crumpled the sodden handkerchief in her hand. "I did not mean to…" she paused. *What did I not mean to do?*

She had been about to say that she had not meant to make matters worse. But the man she loved was about to be executed by her own brother. How could missing a meal make that any worse?

Mirrie could read the secrets of her heart like an open book.

"Tristan knows you are upset."

Frida lifted her eyes to meet Mirrie's. "Does he know why?"

"I don't think so," Mirrie whispered. She reached out and grasped Frida's hand. "What are you going to do?"

"I don't believe there's anything I can do," Frida answered numbly.

Mirrie's light brown curls danced in the candlelight as she shook her head. "There is always something."

"Not this time."

"Frida." Mirrie's reprimand was as sharp as a slap in the face. "If Tristan kills Callum, you will never recover from it. Nor will you ever forgive him."

Frida tried to swallow the lump that was forming in her throat. She could not deny the truth of Mirrie's words, but they changed nothing.

"If I set Callum free, he will take his revenge on Tristan."

Now Mirrie's eyes grew wide with fear. "For what?"

"For razing his ancestral home, killing unarmed women and children in the process."

"Egremont House?"

"A place called Kielder Castle." Frida sniffed again. "In Scotland."

"Oh." Mirrie sat back on the bed and digested this for a moment. Shadows flickered across her face from the spluttering candle, making her expression hard to read. After a while, she walked across the room to light a fresh candle, commenting carefully, "that doesn't sound like something Tristan would do."

Frida could not spare a thought for this. "Who knows what men might do when their blood is up in battle?"

"But still," Mirrie persisted. She came to sit beside Frida again, taking hold of her hands. "Are you sure there is no mistake?"

Frida shook her head. "I was witness to the interrogation." She held up her hand when Mirrie went to speak again. "I cannot say more on this."

"Of course." Mirrie was contrite. "Forgive me."

"There is naught to forgive. But you are right. I will ne'er forgive my brother after he draws his sword against Callum." Her throat closed against her saying anything further.

"And that is a rift that will destroy the de Nevilles," Mirrie prophesied gravely.

Frida nodded, her heart heavy. "You are right."

"You must ensure it does not happen." Mirrie was insistent once again.

"How can I do that?" Frida opened her arms. "Tell me how, and I will do it."

Mirrie jumped up from the bed and began pacing up and

down the chamber, her goat-skin slippers making no sound against the heavy rugs. "There is no bargaining with Tristan." She flung out her hand, dismissing the idea. "Your only hope is to persuade Callum to leave Ember Hall and never come back." She spun around to the window, as if the twinkling stars still visible through the shutters might provide an answer. "Callum will not gain entry at Wolvesley," she said emphatically. "The only danger to Tristan is here and now."

Frida wished she could share in Mirrie's determination, but despair had already made a home in her heart. "Or the next time Tristan rides out with the hunt or journeys some place on the road." She pressed her lips together. "Callum has told me he will kill Tristan, the first opportunity he gets."

"Then you must hold his retaliation in check by balancing it against something he holds dear."

"There is nothing." She choked on a sob.

"Oh yes there is." Mirrie's eyes glittered with triumph. "You can bargain for Tristan's life with the lives of Callum's men."

CHAPTER EIGHTEEN

FRIDA'S HEART BEAT so quickly she thought it might bring armed guards running to the western corner of the courtyard. There were no wall torches to illuminate the way here, only the dimming light from several flaming sconces still visible at the front of the house, and the vast moon above. It was a clear and still night, full of stars. The thaw had set in during the afternoon and much of the snow had melted away into puddles, but those puddles were solidifying into ice on the paved paths and Frida had to pick her way carefully. For many reasons, she could not afford a fall now.

The guard was sitting in a hard chair outside the locked door of the old bakehouse, a torch flickering above his head. He had fallen asleep on duty, his mouth open and his head tilted back. As the first notes of his rippling snores reached her, Frida had started in fright. Then she realised what the source of the noise was and she smiled.

This would make her task easier.

Although she could not rely on a man's natural sleep being deep enough to suit her purpose this night.

Adrenaline kept her body warm, even as her breath steamed in the freezing air. Frida took a moment to settle her hood and smooth down her cloak; one hand gripping an ornate goblet taken from the great hall. She stepped forward with renewed determination, her wooden pattens ringing on the stone flags beneath her.

"Good evening," she sang out.

The guard bolted upright, one hand instinctively going to the hilt of his sword. "Who goes there?"

"'Tis I, Lady Frida." She kept her voice deliberately light.

"Lady Frida." He lumbered to his feet and gave an awkward bow, his limbs still heavy with sleep. "I was merely resting," he added, his eyes darting sideways as he realised the gravity of his error.

Frida pulled her lips into a smile. "Pray, do not be alarmed on my account."

"Milady."

"Sit," she urged. "I have brought you this." She pressed the goblet towards him, swirling the liquid gently so the fragrant aroma of mulled spices would reach his nose.

The guard swallowed, clearly discomfited. The guards were not permitted to drink on duty. Frida knew this as well as he did. But she also knew how hard it would be for him to refuse an order from a member of the de Neville family.

"Warmed wine," she added. "To chase away the chill of the night."

"'Tis kind of you, milady," he stammered. He took the goblet from her but lowered it.

Frida's heart plunged. The man was about to resist. If he refused to drink the wine, her plan must be aborted and she had no other.

She could not fail.

Before he could find the words to refuse her, she sashayed forwards and placed her own hands over his. She felt rather than heard his sharp intake of breath.

"Drink," she urged again, her blue eyes boring into his. "Take comfort, rest a while. All will be well."

As if hypnotised, the man put his lips to the goblet and drank deeply.

"Very good," she encouraged him, pushing on the goblet to

tip it higher and ensure he finished every last drop.

It was done. Now all she had to do was wait until the sedative took effect. Frida nodded regally and took her leave as if nothing untoward had taken place. As she stepped away, she heard the creak of the wooden chair as the guard sank back down. She slipped around the corner and stood patiently, until his rippling snores once again ripped through the night air.

Frida exhaled heavily, almost dropping the goblet in her relief.

The guard would sleep deeply now, without wakening, but she still had no time to lose. Walking as quickly as she dared, Frida returned to the door of the bakehouse and wrestled with the bolt until it finally sprang free. She cautiously pushed open the door and stepped inside.

"Callum?" she whispered.

Torchlight filtered in through the shutters, but made little impact in the far corners of the room. For a terrible moment, Frida feared she was too late—that Callum had gone, Tristan having already taken him. But then her ears tuned in to his light breathing and she finally discerned his outline. He was not taking his rest, sitting on the floor or laying on the rug. He was standing in the corner, every muscle in his body braced for attack.

She pursed her lips, going straight to the basket which she'd abandoned in here earlier, and fetching out the tinderbox. Without looking behind her, she struck the flame and lit the candle before returning to her basket and fetching out a small dagger. After a moment's thought, she went back to the half-open door and pulled it closed.

Only then did she turn to face Callum.

"Frida," he said softly, shaking his head. "I told you not to return."

She tested the sharpness of the blade on the ball of her thumb. "And I am more accustomed to giving orders than taking them."

But despite the bravado in her voice, her nerves jangled. For even with his hands and feet bound, Callum was every inch the warrior. The candlelight illuminated the powerful bulk of his shoulders and the determined set of his jaw. This was a man determined to kill her brother if he had the chance.

And she was about to set him free.

She paused for a moment, noting the matted blood on one side of his head and the way he stood, favouring his right side. She could not let him leave without giving some attention to his wounds.

"I am here to make a deal with you."

She saw surprise wash over his face. "Go on."

Frida wanted to walk closer, e'en to stand on her tiptoes and kiss his stubbled face. But this was the most important conversation she would ever have. She must do her best to keep her voice free of emotion.

To act like a man, speaking with authority as he negotiated before a battle. Looking to spare bloodshed.

She lifted her chin. "I cannot stand by and see you executed by my own brother."

"You have no choice." Callum's voice was harsh.

"We always have choices," she echoed Mirrie's sentiment from earlier, appreciating the full truth of it. "I am here to set you free."

Callum let out an anguished sound. "Then I will hunt Tristan down and you will come to hate me."

"Nay," she interrupted him quickly, "you will not. You will leave Ember Hall and never return." She swallowed down her pain at the thought. "Not unless you wish to cause the execution of your men, Andrew and Arlo."

He blanched as if she had struck him. "Andrew and Arlo."

"Aye." She nodded once. "If you harm Tristan in any way, I will have them both killed."

Callum's brown eyes bore into her soul. "You could not do such a thing, Frida," he said softly. "You are no killer."

His words reverberated around the empty room like the

tolling of a bell. With a growing sense of dread, Frida realised that he was right.

I am no killer.

But without the lives of Arlo and Andrew to use as leverage, her plan had no foundations.

She swallowed, keeping her back ramrod straight. "I will do what I have to do, like we all must, in these turbulent times." The candlelight flickered as if doubting her sincerity.

Callum shook his head. "You know in your heart that you cannot bring harm to anyone. I watched you nurse Arlo back to health. Do you truly expect me to believe that you could give the order for a blade such as that to slit his throat?" His eyes flickered towards the dagger she still held.

Frida's breathing faltered as her imagination played out such a scene. She saw Arlo's trusting face turned towards her, his young eyes filled with a mixture of fear and hope.

Her stomach rolled with nausea. But the face she showed Callum was devoid of all feeling.

"I expect you to believe it," she said calmly, drawing strength from the full range of emotions she felt as a daughter, a sister, a *woman.* "I expect you to believe that I would do whatever it took to ensure the safety of my beloved brother." She paused, giving her claim extra weight. "To keep my family complete."

A beat passed. Callum's face was in shadow and she could not properly read his expression, but she sensed that her words had landed.

"Very well." His voice was tight. "I believe it."

She did not give voice to her relief. Instead, she walked steadily over to him and indicated with a nod of her head that he should turn away. When his all-too-distracting eyes were fixed on the plastered wall, she began to cut through the bindings on his wrists. As she worked, she was overly aware of his height and width, of the lines of muscle over his back and the sinewy strength of his calves.

Aye, this man would be a threat to her brother for as long as they both lived. Tristan was a skilled knight, but Callum was a warrior in his own right. Either one of them might kill the other in any number of scenarios, meeting in a battlefield far from here, months or even years in the future. Frida could not do anything about that. All she could manage was the here and now.

Her Sight, which once might have shown her every outcome and how to avoid it, was gone.

She stifled a sob as her blade cut through the last of the rope and Callum gave a slight moan of relief, flexing his wrists and clasping his hands together.

"Will you sit while I free your ankles?" She kept her voice expressionless.

Callum hesitated and she thought he would refuse, but then he sank gracefully to the floor and stretched out his long legs before him. In the dim light, she saw him wince and she remembered her earlier intention to check his wounds.

Frida got to her knees and started to work on the second binding. This one was looser than the first, freed no doubt in the beating Callum had received earlier. She closed her mind to thoughts of this. All that mattered was that he left Ember Hall before dawn.

This time it was Frida that exclaimed out loud when the blade sliced through the rope. Callum rotated his ankles but otherwise stayed still. She could feel his eyes fixed on her, burning the back of her neck.

"Thank you," he said. "I should have said it before."

"'Tis nothing." Her reply was automatic. She rose awkwardly to her feet and fetched her basket, bringing the candle closer and setting it on the floor by Callum's feet. "Wait while I check your ankle." Carefully, she removed his boot, rolled his breeches up over his bulging calf and probed all around his ankle joint. His flesh was hot to the touch. "I do not believe it is broken," she declared. "I shall pack it with dried comfrey to bring down the swelling."

She half expected a protest, but his response was soft. "Thank you."

She worked quickly, tying a clean bandage around his foot and ankle and replacing his boot. All the while, he stayed still and quiet, his eyes burning into her.

She could not avoid his gaze as she turned to face him, and her breath vanished from her lungs as their eyes met in the candlelight. Callum's stance was passive, but his expression blazed with feeling.

Feelings that she shared—but that she dared not release from the barricades of her heart.

"Are you injured elsewhere?" she asked, forcing the words out. "Aside from your head?"

He shook his head slowly.

"I should have brought warm water," she said almost to herself, leaning forward to examine the wound.

"Leave it," he said throatily.

"I cannot."

"The bleeding has stopped. 'Tis naught but a scratch."

"A scratch that felled you, knocking you into unconsciousness."

"Aye." He caught hold of her hand, their fingers entwining as if they had minds of their own. "Your brother knows how to land a kick."

His voice was light but the memory was still too sharp-edged and terrible for her to raise a smile. She looked down at their joined hands and tears filled her eyes.

The only way through this was as a healer.

"Infection may set in. The cut should be cleaned and covered in honey."

"Nay, Frida." Now his fingers travelled along the inside of her wrist, sending shivers of anticipation down her spine. "You would not send me out into the night with my head dripping with honey, would you?"

This time, she smiled. "Mayhap you are right."

"I *am* right." He drew her closer, so she was sitting within the circle of his embrace. It was the most natural thing in the world to rest her cheek against the sold warmth of his chest and close her eyes.

"Where will you go?"

"I cannot tell you." His reply was instantaneous. When she pulled pack to gaze at him questioningly, his eyes were soft. "You don't think this question will be asked of you, come the morn? You don't think your brother will know if you are keeping this information from him?"

Tears leaked from her eyes. "Again, you are right."

"I wish it were not so."

"There is nothing to be gained in wishing for the impossible." She knew this of old.

"You have given me back my life. I am forever in your debt." He pulled her hands over his chest. "You will live forever in my heart."

Before she could think of a response, he had risen to his feet.

He was about to leave and suddenly, she could not bear it.

"Wait," she commanded, scrabbling upwards, ungainly and awkward after spending so long on the hard earth floor.

Again, she anticipated resistance, but Callum turned towards her almost eagerly.

"What is it?"

"One last kiss," she dared to say, walking towards him across the empty room. "One last kiss to remember you by."

He seized her like a drowning man offered a lifeline. His hands were at once around her waist and in her hair, gathering her close. Their lips joined together hungrily, melding as one in a kiss that increased in intensity with every heartbeat. This would be the last time she stood in Callum's arms, the last time she tasted him, the last time his hands caressed her body; Frida could not bear to step away.

Instead, she pulled him closer, gasping as his stubble rasped the tender flesh of her neck while kissing him back with an urgency she had never before experienced.

"Frida," he said, simply.

And she understood what he meant.

"Yes," she said, shaking with passion and her own daring. She tugged on his hand, trying to lead him towards the rug.

He stood unmoving. "We should not."

She rested her palms at either side of his face, tilting her head back so she could gaze into his eyes. "I would have you, once, before you leave forever. I will be yours forever in my heart. Let me be yours just this once, in the flesh."

Her words seemed to free him of doubt. Now it was Callum who led Frida over to the woollen rug, which he spread out on the earth floor before laying her gently upon it.

"I love you," he said, his face hovering over hers.

"I love you, too." The words were easy to say, because they were true.

He dipped his head and claimed her lips, softly now, as if they had all the time in the world. His expert hands made light work of the fastenings of her dress while she pulled at his tunic until, at last, her palms encountered the hard plane of muscles over his stomach. Her traitorous mind recalled Callum's words the last time they had embraced with such passion. When he said they would not come together without a comfortable bed and a roaring fire.

Without being husband and wife.

For a moment, grief lodged in her throat and threatened to overwhelm her. Callum immediately noticed that something was wrong.

"What is it?"

"Ignore me," she half sobbed.

He stretched out beside her, washed golden by the candle-light. "I cannot ignore you, Frida." His finger traced the line of her cheek. "Not at any time, but least of all now."

She rose up on her elbow to look at him fully. "I only wish we had more time."

But as she gazed down at the warrior beneath her, his tunic

untied to reveal the scars and sinews of his powerful shoulders, another feeling overcame her. This time, it was she who lowered her head to drop a kiss on his waiting lips, her hands that pushed aside fabric to explore warm and willing flesh. His body was long and taut with muscle, so different from hers. She pressed her lips to the hollows of his clavicle whilst her palms slid down until they encountered the part of him that was most swollen with need. His breath came in a gasp and she tightened her fingers around him, revelling for a moment in the feeling of power this gave her.

By now she was clothed in only her shift, a thin cotton thing that did nothing to lessen the thrill of feeling the heat from Callum's body. He unfastened the laces to free her small breasts, kissing and caressing until she moaned with desire. Then he rolled them both, until she laid back on the rough woollen rug with him positioned above her. When his warm hand stroked her inner thigh and found her curls, she moaned again, knowing this was exactly what she'd been yearning for. As he slid a finger inside her, she thought she might implode from the sharp, exquisite pleasure of it.

But that was nothing to when he entered her fully. At first, she knew a stab of pain, but Callum stilled above her until her body relaxed around him. Then came a feeling totally different to anything she had known before. They were as one, and she felt complete as never before. He rocked slowly, filling her up, introducing waves of sensation that robbed her of all notions of time and place. There was only Callum. Only now. She clung to him as the tension built inside her, not understanding where it would lead her, only knowing that she wanted more. When he took her over the edge, she wrapped her legs around his back and dug her fingernails into his shoulders, pulling him as deeply into her as he could possibly be.

He said her name, his lips pressed against her neck as his body tensed one final time. Then it was over and they clung to one another as their breathing and pulse rate slowed.

She rested her head against his chest, slotting against him as if she was home. But reality was already asserting itself and Frida's face soon grew wet with tears.

Callum gently stroked them away with his thumbs. "Did I hurt you?" His voice was rough with concern.

"Nay." She shook her head. "All that pains me is the knowledge that you must leave me." She wanted to bury her face in his shoulders and hide from the truth, but they both knew that in a few hours, dawn would break and it would be too late for him to make his escape.

"I must leave," he stated bleakly, echoing her thoughts. "I do not think I can do it."

"You must," she whispered, furious at the very notion of anything else. "Before the guard awakens."

His face was drawn as he leaned in for one last kiss. "I will ne'er forget you, Frida de Neville."

"Nor I you." She pulled away before emotions could get the better of her again, knowing it would be selfish to sob and force words of comfort from him.

Any comfort there was, they had already taken.

He rose onto his knees as he fastened his tunic. "Will you go first, Frida?"

Still laying on the rug, she shook her head. "I will stay and watch you go."

He dropped down, one hand on either side of her. "That I cannot do. I will not walk away from this place knowing you are here, on your own, in the dark. You must return safe to your bedchamber in the hall. Only then will I go."

"'Tis misplaced chivalry, Callum. I am the mistress here. I am in no danger."

She expected a speech about danger lurking around every corner. But he only traced a finger over her lips. "Do this one last thing for me, please."

How could she refuse him? E'en though it would break her heart to be the one to walk away.

She pushed herself up onto her elbow, hating to leave the

warmth of the rug. "How will you get past the guards on the gate?" Fresh worry forced her voice to wobble. She had thought that drugging the guard would be the greatest challenge, but now she saw that many obstacles lay in Callum's path to freedom.

"Do not fret about that. Come the morn, you will rise from your bed and I will be gone." His eyes were molten in the candlelight.

"That in itself is enough for me to fret over." She forced herself to be brisk as she pulled back on her crumpled dress. Callum's gentle hands soothed her trembling as he moved aside her hair to secure the fastenings.

"I cannot think of you worrying. Promise me that you will find a way to be happy."

"I will try," she lied, forcing a smile to her lips as she turned to face him. "Go well, Callum."

It was woefully little to say, when her heart burst with so much more. But words of fondness and farewell had already been spoken between them. She could not bear to utter them again.

If she said goodbye, her heart might splinter entirely.

He pulled her to him for an embrace that was short and tight.

"God's blessing be upon you, Frida, for the rest of your days."

She blinked at his unanticipated spirituality, but Callum was already turning away from her. With a surge of sorrow, she understood that their time together had come to an end.

This was the moment she must leave.

And although every fibre of her being resisted, Frida forced her feet to carry her out of the bakehouse, past the sleeping guard and through the icy paths of the courtyard. Her breath plumed before her and the cold wrapped fingers of steel about her body, but Frida did not care.

It was her heart that was cold now—and it would remain so forevermore.

CHAPTER NINETEEN

Despite his bold words to Frida, Callum had no real idea how he might leave Ember Hall without being caught. Much less, where he would go afterwards. Home was the obvious choice. But it was a long ride back over the border, and he dare not steal a horse from the stables. With Frida gone and all prospects of their shared future gone with her, he had to dig deep beneath the pain and weariness that filled him to find the drive to escape.

But Callum was a warrior, well used to summoning steely resilience in times of need. Yet this time he was not galvanised by the bloody memories of Kielder Castle, nor by the hope of a better life waiting just around the corner. It was only a deep-seated desire to survive that made him find the strength to flee from the bakehouse, noting the icy paths and the freezing temperatures that would surely prove his undoing. Tristan's sword might even be a preferable death, he thought grimly, gathering his cloak around him. But he had told Frida he would be gone from this place by dawn. And he could still see the pain in her eyes when she spoke of her brother's intentions. It would devastate her if she had to witness his execution.

This, at least, he would do for her.

The guard still snored at his post. Callum thought briefly that he might take the wall torch for purposes of heat and light. Then he lowered his hands, shaking his head at his lunacy. What better way to illuminate his escape than to carry a flaming torch through the dark night? The bang on his head had mayhap done worse damage than he had thought. With every jolting step, his vision blurred. He must make it beyond the boundary walls of Ember Hall before losing consciousness.

Perhaps once he was away, he would find the comfort of a roaring fire and a warm bed, he thought, moving stealthily forwards. He had no coin for an inn, but a man could dream.

He reached the outer edge of the courtyard without incident, cloaked in darkness and keeping close to the walls of the outbuildings as shelter from the wind. He did not need to watch the main gates for long to realise that he would never make it through. Tristan had ordered the guard be doubled. Flaming torches illuminated at least a dozen men atop the fortified wall. All of them upright and alert.

He shook his aching head and slunk back into the shadows. His only option was to take the eastern gate. But that did not lead to the road and the possibility of a fast escape—only to rolling fields and rearing cliffs. Progress would be slow over such terrain in these conditions. But he would have kept his promise to Frida. Right now, Callum couldn't think much beyond that.

Taking in a gulp of cold air in the hope it might steady his thoughts, Callum turned around and retraced his steps until he reached the barn. Here he had to close his mind to memories of the day he and Frida had rescued the flock of sheep. He also pushed away the temptation to sneak inside, amidst the straw and animal warmth, to rest his aching limbs.

Nay, warmth and rest were not on offer for him this cold night. But one thing he could take to ease his journey was the shepherd's crook which Frida had abandoned by the barn wall. Callum closed his fingers over the smooth handle, thinking of Frida's slender hand gripping the very same wood. He flinched as an icy gust of wind whistled through his damp cloak, adding to the myriad pains racing up and down his bruised body. He must keep going else his very bones may freeze.

Made reckless by cold and circumstance, Callum strode directly across the courtyard, his eyes trained on the orange glow of the brazier by which the lone guard of the eastern gate would be keeping warm. The crook made it easier to walk on his bad ankle. Perchance he would make it, after all—but only if the guard was not very diligent. There were no buildings or trees to cloak his progress. Nor was it possible to proceed quietly when his boots alternately slid on ice or crunched through snow. Speed and surprise were his only allies. Together with the shepherd's crook, which delivered a clean blow directly across the back of the guard's head when Callum was able to sneak up behind him.

Callum knew a flicker of guilt as the man slumped on the slushy ground. But the brazier was close enough to stop him from freezing to death. And he would be found soon enough when the watch changed, surely.

Without looking back, Callum strode through the arched gate, his boots plunging into snow. He trudged onwards, listening out for the crashing of waves which would give some signal as to the proximity of the cliff edge. All he could hear was the howling wind and the occasional screech of an owl. At any moment, he feared he might slip and plunge over the edge of the white world to his death on the shingle beach far below, but there was no alternative but to persevere.

I am brought low, he thought, his habitual strength and fortitude much diminished by the beating he had endured. It was near enough three days since he had tasted food, and it took every ounce of energy to place one foot in front of another and carry on up the hill. When he walked bodily into something cold, hard and tall, it was almost a relief to have the excuse to stop.

His heart raced as he waited for a blow from an opponent, but everything around him remained still and calm. Even the wind had eased a little. Greatly daring, Callum reached out again, running his hands over a rough level surface.

Granite stone.

He blinked to better focus his vision, leaning back to take in the outline of a large, rectangular stone jutting out of the earth to the height of his shoulders.

What monolith was this? His racing mind recalled his mother's tales of witchcraft and superstition in these parts, but he was too tired to be much afraid. When the moon slid out from behind a cloud, he made out an oddly-shaped circle of similarly shaped stones. He rested his arms and forehead against the cold granite as he caught his breath.

If this was a place where witches met and cast their magic, then so be it. They could do with him what they wanted. 'Twould be a more interesting fate, at least, than the one awaiting him at the point of Tristan's sword.

Slumped against the stone, Callum felt the last reserves of his strength drain away. He was chilled to the bone, bruised, battered and bereft of hope. He turned his head to the side, wishing for a glimpse of Ember Hall, where Frida slept safely in her bed. Only then did he realise the enormity of his error.

His footsteps were clearly visible in the snow.

Footsteps that would lead Tristan's men, e'en Tristan himself, directly from the felled guard to Callum's current position. It did not matter if he found the strength to run or the luck to stay from the edge of the cliff—they would find him. If he wished to live, he would need to take action—erase the footsteps, lead a false trail, do something to protect himself. But he could not find the energy to move at all.

He had no strength left. And his luck had clearly run out.

Callum allowed his knees to buckle and he sank to the cold, slushy ground thinking that at least he had kept his word to Frida.

Much good it would do him.

WHEN FRIDA CREPT back inside the hall, she did not think she would sleep. How could she, when her mind still raced with all that had passed? When her body still hummed from his touch and her heart grieved his departure?

She was weighed down by such grief as she was sure would never leave her. But she could bear it better by far than the overwhelming despair of seeing her lover executed by her brother.

Frida crawled beneath her covers, still dressed, and pulled the blanket over her head. She could not allow those terrible thoughts to stay inside her mind, for they would drive her to a form of insanity. She had done all she could.

And she had known what it was to be loved. By a man she loved in return.

Holding onto that, she drifted into a deep, dreamless sleep.

Mirrie woke her soon after dawn. Frida opened her gritty eyes to find her friend kneeling beside her bed, shaking her urgently.

"You must get up," she was saying, her hand gripping Frida's shoulder.

Frida blinked. Her bedchamber was still half in shadows, for the sun was not fully up. Pale pinkish light was all that filtered through the shutters.

"You must prepare your story," Mirrie urged. "Tristan is already up and raging. If he sees you like this, he will know."

She struggled to sit up. "Know what?"

"That you were the one to free the prisoner," Mirrie whispered.

The memory flooded back to her. Last night, she had cut Callum's bonds and urged him to leave Ember Hall. And now, she must face Tristan's inevitable outrage over the loss of his prisoner.

Tristan would be determined to find him.

Frida must put him off the scent.

Fully awake now, she flung back her covers. "Help me to dress," she gasped. "I must change into something clean."

"And dry," supplied Mirrie, already rooting through the

wooden chest at the foot of Frida's bed.

"Aye." Frida made no attempt to argue, standing passively as Mirrie wrestled her damp and crumpled gown away from her.

"Oh." Mirrie paused, her arms full of fabric.

"What is it?"

Mirrie pursed her lips, perchance hiding a smile. "Your shift tells a tale."

Frida's cheeks grew pink at the memory of what had happened whilst she was wearing her shift. "'Tis not a tale for anyone's ears but your own."

"But of course." Mirrie helped her out of it and passed her a clean one from the trunk. "A tale for us to discuss in full another morn; one that is not so fraught."

Frida nodded as she pulled the cotton shift over her head. "I will tell you all that has passed." She paused to grip Mirrie's hands. "'Twill be a relief to confide in someone." But as she spoke, tears pricked at the corner of her eyes and she had to turn away.

"I have brought a basin of warmed water, so you can wash." Ever practical, Mirrie gave her a moment of peace, bending to gather up all of Frida's discarded clothing. "I will put these with mine, to go to the laundry. I'll return to dress your hair."

Frida sniffed her thanks and splashed water on her face until all traces of her tears had gone. She stepped into the plain grey gown of stiffened wool that Mirrie had picked out for her. It would be warm, at least, on a day that promised little comfort or cheer. She glanced towards the shutters, wanting to look out and scan the horizon for any remaining sign of Callum, but there was no time.

A faint knock at the door heralded Mirrie's return. She sat Frida on the bed and tugged at her tousled hair with a comb, apologising breathlessly when Frida failed to hide her winces.

"Tristan cannot see you so dishevelled."

White-lipped, Frida nodded her agreement. She was relieved when Mirrie declared herself done. Her hair was plaited neatly.

Her dress was presentable. This was all that mattered.

"Where is Tristan now?" she asked, rising up from the mattress.

"I last saw him pacing the length of the great hall." Mirrie paused. "There is still no sign of Jonah. Methinks he has gone into hiding into all of this is over."

Frida grimaced. "Jonah had better stay in hiding. All of *this* is his doing." At Mirrie's look of confusion, she added, "Jonah caused all of this upset by writing to Tristan in the first place."

"Ah." Understanding dawned upon Mirrie's brow. "Remember, Frida. They are both your brothers and they love you."

Frida shook her head fiercely. "I do not know the man Tristan has become. The brother I knew would not order a castle razed to the ground, nor the slaughter of innocent women and children."

Mirrie held up her hand. "Bide on that, Frida, prithee. Ask Tristan yourself about the siege of Kielder Castle."

"Aye," she grunted, smoothing down her skirts as she prepared to leave her chamber. "Believe me, I shall."

Tristan had dark circles around his eyes and his thick hair had been tamed by neither comb nor water. Frida thought that she had never seen her handsome brother so dishevelled.

He paced up and down the great hall like a man possessed; his progress monitored carefully by the hounds stretched out by the fire. Frida had thought she might aim for nonchalance, but as soon as Tristan saw her, he strode across the room and grasped her by the shoulders. His forceful gaze could have pierced a path through stone.

"Did you set him free?" he demanded.

Shocked, Frida could only summon her resolve and meet his glare with one equally passionate. "What if I did?"

The sound coming out of Tristan's mouth could only be described as a growl. "Then you are a traitor to your family."

"Nay." She wrestled herself away from his hold. "I am not the one who should wrestle with my conscience."

The two siblings stood feet apart, both pairs of blue eyes blazing. Tristan's hands clenched into fists, but Frida was certain he would not raise them against her.

"I have no time for riddles, sister. I ask you again. Did you set him free?"

Frida reminded herself that the important thing was to buy Callum enough time to run far from Ember Hall. She made a show of skirting around Tristan and lowering herself gracefully into a chair by the fire. "Why would I do that?"

Tristan sighed, looking momentarily defeated.

It was not a look Frida had ever seen on her brother before. Nor, despite everything, was it one she enjoyed.

"Because when the three of us were in here last..." He paused, indicating the stretch of floor where Callum had lain. "Your sympathies were not with me."

Frida felt her throat constrict. "That is not entirely true," she whispered.

Tristan turned anguished eyes towards her. "Always it has been you and me against the world, Frida. You have always stood in my corner, always backed me. And I have always tried to do the same for you."

She nodded slowly, unable to deny it. Tristan's unwavering support had gone a long way towards convincing their parents that she and Mirrie should be allowed to set up home in Ember Hall.

"Until now," he added. "You look at me and you think of the Scot. Can you deny it?"

Indignation rose within her. "Nay, I cannot deny it. And nor should I have to."

"You *were* the one to set him free." His voice rose, but whether in triumph or disbelief, Frida could not say.

She jumped up from the chair and regretted it as her ankle threatened to give way beneath her. "I was. I freely admit it." She clung onto the back of the chair for support. "I would set him free a hundred times over so he might escape death by your sword."

"And so you spared him—the man who came here with orders to kill me?" Tristan folded his arms, a pulse flickering at his jaw.

Frida didn't allow herself to feel so much as a pang of guilt. "The man whose home you destroyed, whose people you slaughtered for no higher purpose than your own bloodlust."

Tristan reeled backwards as if she had struck him. "You speak of the siege of Kielder Castle? This is what Mirrie was asking of me yesterday." He spun around as if looking for their friend, but Mirrie was wisely keeping out of sight.

Frida nodded, not trusting herself to speak.

Tristan dragged a hand through his hair. "I played no part in the siege of Kielder Castle." His voice was quiet.

A beat passed while Frida tried to make sense of this. "But you said…" She waved her hands towards the fire, recalling the scene with Callum. "You said that you gave the order."

Tristan shook his head, his lips pressed together into a thin line. "I did not."

Adrenaline drained away and left her weak. "I was here. I heard you say it."

"Then you remember incorrectly." Tristan sighed deeply. "What I said was, *I don't deny it.*"

Frida felt suddenly as if they were back in the school room, squabbling over the fairest allocation of honey cakes. "That is the same thing."

"God's bones, Frida, it is not," he exploded. "I didn't bring Callum here to talk of Kielder Castle. I wanted to find out what he was doing here, at Ember Hall, with *you.*" He put his hands to his knees as if the outburst had exhausted him. "My real business north of the border was strictly confidential, not to be shared with anyone—least of all a Scot."

Looking at him stirred sisterly concern within her in spite of everything. Frida found herself wondering when he had last slept. But she chased the thought away. She could hardly process what he was telling her. "You were not involved in the siege?"

"Not in any way—not in its planning or its execution. I assure you, no siege under my command would involve such senseless slaughter. Difficult decisions must oft times be made in battle, but there is no justification for the killing of the unarmed and innocent." Tristan raised his hands, his face an unhealthy pale colour. "Sister, do not tell me that you set Callum free on the strength of that suspicion?"

She must sit back down before she fell on the floor. Frida tried to speak but no sound came out.

My brother is innocent. He was still the hero she had always believed him to be.

But Callum, the man she loved, would never know that.

"He said he would kill you," she whispered.

"Aye. And likely he will, now that he has his freedom."

She shook her head. "We will hold his men hostage."

Callum gave a mirthless bark of laughter. "And you think that will stop a man like Callum Baine? Nay," he answered his own question. "Our only recourse is to find him now and bring him back."

Leaving Frida slumped on the chair, Tristan strode outside to put his plans into action.

WHEN CALLUM NEXT opened his eyes, the rosy rays of dawn had transformed the horizon into a vivid blaze of pink. The darkness had been banished, along with the icy grip of snow, for the rising sun was causing a thaw all around him. Snow dripped from the tops of the standing stones and birds sang from the trees. He had woken to a different world. One filled with light and colour...and hope.

Callum's whole body protested as he tried to stand. He rested his weight upon the wet stone until he found his balance. Hunger clawed at him, but more pressing was his thirst. He scooped up a handful of melting snow and sucked it from his fingers. Glancing back towards Ember Hall, he saw smoke rising from the chimneys. The household would be up; his escape might already be known.

And yet the terrors of the night had receded. Already, the thaw had made the outline of his footprints more difficult to discern in the snow. Within another hour, he fancied they would be gone.

Perchance his luck was changing.

Callum fixed his gaze on the distant hills and started walking.

CHAPTER TWENTY

WEIGHED DOWN WITH regret and worry, Frida found the day passed with painful slowness. To stay out of the way of Tristan's men, she confined herself to the hall. And never had the large, comfortable rooms seemed so restrictive. She found no comfort in the sweeping views of moorland and paddocks, for everywhere she looked she hoped for a glimpse of Callum—and hoped to never see him again.

Hoped to see him so that she might know he was safe, but knew that if she *could* see him, he was in grave danger of being spotted by Tristan or his guards.

She shook her head and closed her eyes, sending up prayer after prayer that the man she loved would be kept safe.

Frida had taken refuge in the solar when Mirrie finally found her. A fire crackled cosily in the grate and the wooden panels on the walls reflected the golden glow of firelight. But none of this was enough to settle Frida's agitation. She jumped at every footstep and would take nothing to eat.

"I am not hungry," she insisted, when Mirrie pointedly positioned a platter of bread and cheese within easy reach.

Mirrie raised her eyebrows but said nothing. "May I sit with you?"

Frida barely looked up from her pacing between the door and the window. "You may sit wherever you wish," she replied.

"And will you join me?"

Frida wrung her hands together. "Nay. I cannot rest. I cannot be still."

"Your exhaustion will not help Callum's cause." Mirrie broke off a piece of cheese and chewed slowly, her hazel eyes fixed on her friend.

Frida did not dignify this with a response. "I might kill my brother, when he finally returns," she blurted out.

Mirrie nodded. "I daresay he deserves it."

"Forsooth, he deserves stringing up on the walls." Frida gesticulated violently in the direction of the main gate. "If he had only told the truth from the beginning, all of this could have been avoided. He's entirely to blame."

Mirrie tore at the bread, releasing the pungent aroma into the small room and making Frida's stomach rumble. "Jonah too, I guess?"

"How do you mean?" Frida folded her arms lest she snatch the bread out of her friend's hands.

"This is at least partially Jonah's fault. If he hadn't written to Tristan, none of this would have happened. You said it yourself."

Frida snapped her fingers. "Aye, you're right. Both Jonah and Tristan are to blame." She paused in front of the low wooden table. "Mayhap I will take some of that bread."

Mirrie nodded, shuffling up on the couch to make room for her. Frida intended to take only the smallest heel of bread, but once she had tasted it, she wanted more. Soon she was breaking off a hunk of cheese as well.

"You don't need to look so pleased with yourself," she said crossly, once she had swallowed. "I was always going to eat at some point."

Mirrie folded her hands in her lap. "Of course."

"It's Callum's fault as well," Frida went on, returning to their prior conversation as she brushed at the crumbs on her grey skirt.

"Callum's fault?" Mirrie's face was without expression.

"I am no fool, Mirrie. I know this situation is of Callum's own making. He should have told me the truth about who he was and why he came here. God's bones, we shared enough together." Tears stung at her eyes again.

"But Callum did not trust you. And Jonah did not trust Callum. And Tristan did not trust either you or Callum." Mirrie stretched her legs. "And so, here we are."

"In a mess forged by pride and anger." Frida gazed in the direction of the fire, the orange flames made blurry by salty tears.

"But thanks to your courage, Callum is free. He has every chance of escaping Tristan's retribution. And then who knows what the future may bring."

Mirrie reached out for her hand and Frida willingly gave it to her, even as she shook her head to refute her words. "I place no hope in the future. Callum is a Scot. I am a de Neville. Nothing can bridge that gap."

Mirrie squeezed her fingers in sympathy, but before she could say more, footsteps beyond the solar had Frida leaping out of her seat.

Has Tristan returned?

Frida thought her heart might jump out of her chest, but when the door finally opened, it was Agnes who appeared. The cook bobbed into a small curtsy.

"Beg pardon, milady. Miss Mirrie."

Frida turned around to hide her distress and Mirrie waved Agnes forward.

"Come in, Agnes. You know we don't stand on ceremony here."

"I don't like to interrupt. But I need to know how many to cook for tonight." Agnes pulled at her sleeves, nervously. "We were not expecting such an influx of guests."

Frida felt a jolt of shame. She had neglected her duties around the hall in these last days, and it had never even occurred to her that the servants might struggle to accommodate the newly arrived Wolvesley army.

"Do what you can with what we have, Agnes," she said. "Mayhap a soup or a stew that can be reheated? We know not what time the men will return, but we must feed all who serve us."

Agnes did not look convinced. "For the family too? E'en Lord Tristan?"

"Lord Tristan will eat what the rest of us eat," Frida replied swiftly. "If he doesn't like it, he can go back to Wolvesley Castle."

The cook hid her shocked expression by bobbing her head in acknowledgment. "Very good milady."

Mirrie and Frida exchanged a look as she left.

"Methinks Agnes does not share your poor opinion of your brother," Mirrie commented mildly. "She would prefer to serve him some special dish rather than see him supping stew."

Frida allowed herself to smile. "Tristan charms e'en the birds from the trees." She rubbed at her arms, crossly. "I oft think I am the only one immune."

"I would not say that," Mirrie replied.

Frida snorted. "Do not try to tell me that you are immune to my brother's smile."

Mirrie's cheeks flushed pink but she shook her head steadily. "I was thinking of Jonah."

"Ah yes. Well then, you are right." Frida grasped Mirrie's wrist. "I am sorry for teasing you."

Mirrie's expression softened. "I was glad to see you light-hearted for a moment."

Frida let out a deep sigh and sank back onto the settle. Aye, for a moment she had put her worries behind her. But now they were back with a vengeance. Her head throbbed and her stomach churned with nerves.

"Just think," Mirrie continued. "'Twas not more than a sennight since that you vowed to live a life free of men."

Frida covered her face with her hands. "I do not think I can speak of this now."

"I only meant it as an example of how things can change." Mirrie's voice was gentle. "We know not what the future holds. We may think we do, but surprises wait at every turn."

Frida rested her elbow on the arm of the settle, but did not lower her hand. "I cannot deny the truth of your words. But nor can I find the strength to hope just now."

"All I ask is that you do not close yourself off from what the future could hold." Mirrie rubbed her back comfortingly. "Hope may yet come and find you."

They sat in companionable silence for a while, the only sound being the occasional hiss from the fire and footsteps coming from the kitchen. Frida's distress began to subside, replaced with fatigue and even a flicker of suspicion that Mirrie might be right.

Who knows what the future may hold?

If Callum had got clean away, as she hoped with every fibre of her being, then all of this furore would die down soon enough. Tristan would return to Wolvesley. Frida and Mirrie would return to their chores. Who was to say that Callum would not one day return to Ember Hall?

He knows well enough where to find me.

All she had to do was stay here and wait.

The heavy tramp of booted footsteps jolted her from her reverie. This time there was no doubting Tristan's quick, intentional tread. He flung open the door of the solar and stood for a moment, framed by the archway. His golden hair, curling just above his shoulders, was streaked with sweat. His emerald green tunic was creased and shadows smudged his eyes, but even when fatigued and foiled, Tristan de Neville continued to exude a charismatic energy that filled the room.

"We did not find him," he said.

His words brought Frida a sharp rush of relief.

Mirrie rose to her feet. "Come and sit down," she urged. "I will fetch you some wine."

Tristan shook his head. "I will take refreshment in the great hall, not here."

Mirrie looked nonplussed. "As you wish." Her hazel gaze swung to Frida. "We can all go and sit by the fire there."

"Nay." Tristan's voice was emphatic. "I will not sit and sup with my sister, pretending that all is well between us." Mirrie flinched, as if she was the one bearing the brunt of his anger. Tristan looked fleetingly contrite, but then he steeled his expression into granite again. "'Tis your doing, Frida, that near twenty of Wolvesley's best men were forced to spend fruitless hours searching the lands surrounding Ember Hall for a man who had already fled."

She shook her head, bristling with emotion. "'Twas not my doing, Tristan. I did not give that order."

"You set him free." His voice rose. "A treacherous Scot who brought violence to your door."

This time she could not contain her anger. "Callum brought no violence to my door, brother. The beatings and threats only began when you arrived here."

Tristan stepped forward menacingly but Frida held his gaze, refusing to be cowed.

"Enough," Mirrie stepped between them, her arms out-stretched entreatingly.

"You are right, Mirrie, enough." Tristan's voice was calm although he still glowered at Frida. "This experiment of you both living at Ember Hall has conclusively failed. You must return to Wolvesley."

Frida's blood roared in her ears. "You cannot make us do that. You have no authority here, Tristan."

Tristan smiled thinly. "Mayhap not, but our father does. It's your choice, Frida. Either you return to Wolvesley voluntarily, or I will send a message to our parents to inform them of recent events." He smiled, evidently pleased with her stricken expression as realisation sliced through her. "Then you will have to return to Wolvesley, at the earl's command."

CHAPTER TWENTY-ONE

A S THE DAY wore on, Callum saw more patches of sludgy green emerge from beneath their blanket of early snow. The northern borderlands were waking up from icy slumber, with birds beginning to sing their plaintive winter songs. Gradually, the landscape was changing from unending white to a patchwork quilt of wooded copses amidst rolling moorland.

His healthier, stronger self would take pleasure from this evidence of renewal. But Callum was weak, his body racked with pain. 'Twas naught he had not experienced before, but coupled with gnawing hunger and an enduring feeling of faintness from the blow to his head, he was uncharacteristically despondent. And the melting snow caused patches of mud which slowed him further.

Where am I even going?

He couldn't answer the most basic question of all. He simply put one foot in front of another in an effort to increase the distance between himself and Ember Hall.

At first, Callum had thought he would head for home. But where was home? Kielder Castle had always held that name, but even when it was whole and sound, it had provided little in the way of calm and comfort, presided over, as it was, by Rory Baine, the most bloodthirsty and embittered clansmen the highlands had known for many a year.

And now... Did what little remained of the once proud

stronghold still count as home? E'en though most of the friends he'd known there were either dead, fled or held captive?

Callum stopped, hands on hips, watching the rare sight of a graceful herd of roe deer picking their way through the trees. Their long legs found easy purchase along the rutted tacks, liquid brown eyes glancing around in a constant hunt for predators. It was a wonder they had not kicked up their heels and bolted over the moors at the first sight of him.

Once the last deer had disappeared, Callum resumed his wanderings. Mayhap he should become a creature of the woodland, laying his head wherever he found himself that night? But that would be folly at this time of year, with winter creeping ever closer.

Mayhap Egremont House then. His mother's family home. The place he had spent his childhood and grown to a man.

Aye, that was the home where he had last been happy and carefree. But for all he knew, the house had been bordered up since his mother's death and his father's return to Scotland.

Callum scratched at his growth of beard, trying to remember. Had his father said that Egremont House would be let to some kinsman of his mother's? His memories skittered just out of reach. And thinking caused waves of pain to ripple through his temples.

Callum would simply walk. He was heading north, in the direction of both Scotland and Egremont House. If he reached either, it would be a miracle.

He came out of a wooded valley to be greeted by a scene of destruction. A small village had once stood by a crossroads. His tired eyes counted the remains of a dozen dwellings. What looked like a church. All of them ruined now, broken beams blackened by fire. Doors hanging loose on hinges, roofs gaping open to the sky.

Sickened, Callum resumed his aimless journey. It mattered not, he realised, whether it was the Scots or the English who had razed that village. Blood had been spilled either way. Acts of violence had led these humble villagers to ruin.

His feet dragged behind him now. He was so weary, it was an effort to keep his eyes open. If only he had a little ale to soothe his thirst.

The sharp howl of a wolf chased away all thoughts of ale. He stopped still, hoping the chilling sound had come from some dark hole in his imagination, but the howl came again. High and mournful, it cut through the cold air and caused all the hairs on Callum's neck to stand on end.

Slowly, he raised his eyes. Sure enough, there was the animal, standing atop a small incline just ahead of him. Tall and lean, the wolf had gleaming amber eyes which were fixed on Callum.

Any wolf venturing out in the light of day must be hungry indeed.

Callum assessed his options. He had not the strength to run. Nor had he a blade with which to defend himself. He could no more climb a tree than he could take flight into the sky. Dimly, he wondered if the ruined village might still contain some tool or weapon he could use against a wolf, but it was close behind him. It could easily catch him before he reached the first crumbling walls.

His heart thudded against his ribs. Of all possible endings, Callum had never imagined his last moments would be spent facing a wolf.

He was a trained knight, a feared warrior, but now he had become no more than prey. His lips twisted into a smile as he considered the irony.

The wolf had not moved, but neither had it shifted its focus from Callum's face.

Callum swallowed, knowing that animals could sense fear. 'Twas lucky then that he was too fatigued to feel much of anything.

He took a hesitant step forward, then another. If he ran away, the wolf would give chase. If he walked to meet it, the wolf might observe his height and strength and reconsider attacking him.

As he grew closer, Callum thought with relief that the animal may not be a wolf after all. It seemed not quite tall enough. And it stood all alone whereas wolves traditionally hunted in packs.

He could not prevail against a pack of wolves, but if this turned out to be merely a lone hound, then that was a different proposition.

Callum straightened his back, drawing himself up to his full height. If only he had a stick to wave. His eyes skittered left and right, looking for a fallen branch.

The hound/wolf pricked his ears. Was he about to bound forward? A thrill of fear chased down Callum's spine. Then something hit his head, his knees buckled and he slumped down onto the rutted track, slushy earth filling his nostrils.

WHEN HE AWOKE some hours later, it was to the sound of domesticity. Logs crackling in a fire, someone stirring a cooking pot, the ladle scraping against the sides of the pan. He heard a woman's voice and tried to decipher the words, but he was too far away to make them out.

Callum half expected to find his wrists and ankles once against bound, but when he cautiously stretched out his fingers and wiggled his toes, he realised this was not the case. Nor was he housed in some dark cellar. On the contrary, he was laid on a soft straw mattress with warm rugs heaped atop him. Cautiously, he turned his head to take in more of his surroundings. A small shuttered window to his left allowed bars of fading sunlight into a square chamber holding little more than a bed and a wooden trunk. He sat up, wincing at the pain in his head. Tentative probing revealed that the head wound Tristan had given him had been bandaged and, going by the sharp aroma emanating from the rough cloth, it had first been packed with mint.

His fingers encountered a new, painful swelling at the other side of his head. This was where he had been struck after seeing the wolf.

He scanned the chamber once more, looking for any sign of the fierce beast, but there was none. His eyes were gritty and his tongue felt stuck to the roof of his mouth with thirst. Fighting a wave of dizziness, Callum lowered his feet to the floor. He must discover where he was and why he had been brought here.

Two steps took him to the door and he opened it cautiously. Immediately, the smells of cooking enveloped him. Herbs, roasted meat, woodsmoke from the fire. His belly rumbled and he stepped back into the shadows of the chamber, not wanting to be spotted so soon.

But it was too late, for the grey-haired woman stood by the cooking pot called over to him without altering her position.

"Come, Callum. Let us make ourselves known to one another."

The voice was high and quavering, as if the woman was unused to conversation.

How does she know my name?

Callum squared his shoulders and stepped into the outer room. The first thing his eyes alighted on was the hound he had mistaken for a wolf, stretched out by the fire. Callum paused, but the hound merely opened one eye and wagged his tail lazily against the hard floor.

"That's just Gil. He won't hurt you." The woman bent low and tasted something off the ladle. Smacking her lips together, she walked over to a narrow cabinet and fetched out two roughly hewn wooden bowls. "Come," she repeated.

Callum thought he may have willingly walked into hell itself if it smelled as good as this. He limped forwards, aiming for a rickety wooden chair pulled as far away from the hound as possible.

"There's ale in the jug," the woman said. "Help yourself."

He did not need asking twice. His desperate gaze found the stone jug tucked into a crevice in the stone wall. Hands trembling with need, he poured a stream of thin brown ale into a small cup and drained it in one gulp.

Aye, this could all be a trap. The woman might be aiming to poison him. But he would not be long for this world without food and drink inside him regardless.

Besides, Callum thought it more likely that all this was a product of some fevered dream. His mind may be here, sipping ale in a cosy chamber, but his body was most likely laying in some forest ditch, or else being set upon by wolves.

He refilled the cup and drank again, before remembering his manners.

"Thank you."

The woman nodded, busy ladling out a delicious looking stew. "Sit," she instructed. "Eat this and then tell me if I am right."

He accepted the warm bowl and spooned up juicy meat before anyone could take it away from him. Flavour filled his mouth and he half closed his eyes, barely silencing a moan of pleasure. He swallowed another spoonful before wiping his lips with the back of his hand and raising his eyes to the woman.

She was small and wizened, mayhap with age. Her hair was long and grey, pinned loosely at the back of her head. She wore a plain woollen dress, ornamented with neither broaches nor ribbons. But her green eyes were bright as they followed his every move.

He cleared his throat "I should ask your name, dear lady, and thank you again for your kindness."

She shook her head. "Me first." She took a sharp intake of breath. "You *are* Callum, aren't you? Son of Elizabeth?"

It was so long since Callum had been called the son of anyone but Rory Baine that it took him several seconds to answer. "My mother's name was Elizabeth, aye."

She nodded, her eyes gleaming like a bird's. "Lady Elizabeth. I knew it, as soon as I saw you properly."

He lowered his spoon, his hunger momentarily forgotten. "You knew my mother?"

She nodded again. "And you too, Callum Baine, though you were still in short trousers when I left your mother's service." She sat up straighter on the settle. "Do you remember Alys, your mother's maid?"

"Alys." He rolled the name around in his mouth. It *did* sound familiar. He had a sense of small kindnesses, singing songs, honey cakes. "You served my mother at Egremont House?"

She looked pleased. "Indeed I did. And saddened I was to learn of her passing, God rest her soul." She made the sign of the cross over her chest and clasped her hands together as if in prayer.

Callum gave a small nod of thanks. "Alys," he said again, hoping to strengthen the memories. "And this is your home?"

"A small home but a happy one." She took a neat spoonful of soup.

"And this is your hound?" He nodded towards the dog.

Alys tightened her lips. "I'm sorry if Gil frightened you. But these are troubled lands and troubled times we are living in. I am an old woman living alone and must take whatever the good Lord provides me for my protection."

Callum finished the last of his stew. "And the lord gave you Gil?"

"When he was but a pup." Alys stroked the dog's head. "Gil keeps intruders away. When he howled, I knew someone was approaching. I'm only sorry I didn't recognise you straight away."

Callum's hand gravitated to the new lump on his head. "'Twas not your dog that inflicted harm on me," he said, wincing a little. "Did you see the man that struck me?"

Alys hid her smile. "'Twas no man, Callum. I swung the pan myself." She nodded towards the cooking pot, which had made the meal he had just eaten.

"You hit me?" His eyebrows shot up with such force that a new wave of dizziness came over him.

"We must err on the side of caution, Gil and I." Alys placed her spoon inside her bowl. "But as soon as I had a good look at your face, I saw the young boy who would hide behind his mother's skirts and steal honey cakes when he thought no one was looking." She smiled fondly. "So I brought you here to recover."

Callum took a breath. It was something of a relief to discover he was not obliged to hide away from any new knight or warrior.

"You brought me all the way in here, from all the way out there?" He indicated the shuttered window, through which narrow glimpses of the farm track could be seen.

Alys inclined her head. "I tend my own garden and manage my own firewood. I am stronger than I look. Though I am afraid your cloak is torn in many places and near good for nothing by now. I used it as a stretcher to drag you on."

Callum opened his mouth to say it was nothing, but then shut it again with the words unsaid. He had grown up with cloaks aplenty, but right now he had naught but the clothes on his back and the loss of his good cloak would be keenly felt.

Still, without food and drink, perchance he would not have lived through many more days. With or without his good cloak.

He glanced down at his heavily crumpled tunic, then reached up to scratch at his many days' growth of beard.

"Forgive me, I have not bathed nor changed my clothes in many days."

Alys nodded. "Come the morn when the sun has regained some warmth, we can see to all of that. For now, Callum, take your rest. Then mayhap you can tell me who or what you are running from?"

HE REFUSED TO take her bed, but the settle proved far more comfortable than the hard floors he had been obliged to lay upon these last days. Callum slept deeply by the dying embers of the fire, the only disturbance being occasional snores from Gil the dog. When he awoke, the small house was bright with sunlight and Gil was nowhere to be seen.

Callum laid still for a moment, making a mental inventory of his injuries. His ankle still throbbed, though less insistently now. The rest of him was recovering. For certain, nothing was broken. Even his head seemed clearer. He could swivel his neck and look about him without any dizziness or nausea.

I will live.

Though what he might achieve with the life left to him, he could not yet imagine.

A murmur of conversation reached him through the open doorway. Callum stood and stretched his arms over his head, his fingertips brushing against the rafters of the roof. He could make out the chirping tone of Alys, and the other speaker seemed to be a young boy. Outside, the air smelled sweet, washed clean by the melted snow. Alys turned a smiling face in Callum's direction and then bade farewell to the boy, pressing something into his hand first.

"For your troubles," she said. "God bless you, Matthew."

"God bless you, Missus Alys," the boy replied in a high piping voice. Then he set off running down the narrow path as fast as his little legs would carry him.

Callum rotated his shoulders, pleased to feel his body coming back to something approaching its usual strength.

"Who was that?" he asked, as Alys stepped back inside.

"The gardener's grandson from Egremont House. I worked with his father for many years. Now he sends the lad to check on me and bring me treats along with bits of news." She lifted a small wicker basket, from which came a most entrancing aroma of freshly-baked bread. "Today we have a gift of food from the kitchens; much appreciated if little needed." She sniffed. "I try not to take offence at the implication that I cannot fend for myself."

"'Tis human kindness," Callum commented, reaching to relieve her of the basket and place it carefully on the scrubbed table.

"Aye, and human need for connection which I value just as

high." Alys pulled a shawl about her shoulders, her eyes dancing. "You cannot imagine what news Matthew brought with him this morn."

"I cannot." Callum could think of little save the bread in the basket.

Alys smiled as if divining his thoughts. "Let us sit together and break our fast, then I will tell you what I have learned."

This time Alys perched on the wooden chair and Callum returned to the settle. The fire had been restocked with logs and was blazing merrily. Gil trotted in and took his usual place with a deep sigh of contentment. For a long while, all was well. Callum filled his mouth with soft, sweet-tasting bread, washed it down with another cup of ale. When Alys produced a small package of nuts and berries from the bottom of the basket, Callum closed his eyes at the explosion of flavour against his tongue. He had tasted naught like this for many days.

"There is better colour in your cheeks," Alys commented.

"I am better by far," Callum declared, brushing crumbs from his tunic. "Well enough to deliver to you the explanation you are owed."

She held up her hand. "Let me tell you this first of all. Matthew brought news from o'er the border."

Callum could not help his spine instinctively stiffening. "From Scotland?" Alys nodded and his mind immediately conjured images of battles and bloodshed. "God's bones, what has happened there now?"

"'Tis good news." The old woman's green eyes danced. "Your man, Robert the Bruce, has been recognised as king of an independent Scotland."

Her words echoed in his mind without him grasping their meaning. "An independent Scotland?" Just the idea would be heresy in some households, although it was the very thing that his father lived for. "By whom?"

"By the pope himself," Alys breathed.

Callum leaned back on the settle, looking at her curiously.

"Are you a Scot, Alys?"

"Nay." Wisps of grey hair escaped their pins as she shook her head. "I am a true-blooded English woman, the same as your mother."

"But I am not," he interjected.

"You are Scottish on your father's side, English on your mother's," Alys said, as if this fact had not haunted so many of his days. "So that means you are both English and Scottish yourself. To that end, I am sure this news has special significance for you, Callum dear."

Callum took another mouthful of ale. His father indeed would be celebrating hard, amongst the ruins of Kielder Castle. "How does this bear special import for me?" He sighed. "I do not see it, myself."

"Is it not another step towards peace?" she suggested gently.

"I have abandoned all hopes of peace," he replied, his tone almost savage. He bowed his head at the shocked expression on Alys's face. "Forgive my anger. But I have watched friends and family on both sides of the border come to harm. I am a man of faith, but I do not see what words the Pope can say that will remedy such decades of animosity."

A shadow crossed over her face. "There has been much bloodshed."

"Aye." He placed down the empty cup, his fingers shaking. "And whilst there is such hatred and mistrust on both sides, I do not think there can e'er be peace between England and Scotland."

Alys nodded. "There are people working actively for peace," she whispered, looking over her shoulder as if fearful of being overheard. "One man in particular. A brave man in whom I place all my hopes for a peaceful future."

"What man?" He looked at her curiously.

"I should not say." She pressed her lips together, as if keeping the words inside. "Tell me your tale, Callum. What turn of events brought you to my door in such a sorry state?"

He smiled grimly. "'Tis the oldest, sorriest tale of all."

"Love?" she whispered, tilting her lined face upwards.

"Love." His throat closed over the word and he cleared his throat roughly. "I am in love with an English woman, even though I was tasked by the Bruce to move against her family."

A moment passed. Gil raised his head, ears pricked, as if aware something momentous had been said. Callum knew his words were shocking, but he was determined to tell no more lies about his true identity.

"You work for the Bruce?" Alys sat on the very edge of her chair as if she might fly away.

"My father insists upon it."

"Aye, he was always a man of strong emotion." Alys leaned back, though her eyes remained wary.

"I have been sent on two commissions by the Bruce. I have failed them both." Callum rubbed at his beard distractedly. "I will not be welcomed back at my father's house. Although little of my father's house remains. It was razed by the English at midsummer."

Razed by Tristan de Neville, he thought but did not say.

Alys bit down on her lip. "'Tis a sorry tale indeed, Callum. I am saddened by your troubles. Your poor mother would be beside herself with grief for it all."

He nodded, unwilling to invite more self-pity.

"But what of this English woman? Does she know you love her?"

He nodded, thinking of their last embrace. "She knows it."

"And does she love you in return?"

A small smile broke through. "I believe she does."

"Then naught should stand in your way." Alys folded her hands together as if that was all there was to say.

Callum gazed into the orange flames of the fire, wishing they could burn away everything that made this situation so impossible. "We cannot have a future, because she is English and I am Scottish."

"Half Scottish," Alys corrected.

Callum shook his head. "'Tis all the same to them. They are one of England's most noble families."

Alys's green eyes caught him in a snare. "Which one?"

He sighed. "The woman I love is Frida de Neville." Her sharp exclamation of surprise almost silenced him, but he spoke on. "The man who ordered the destruction of my family home is her brother, Tristan de Neville."

A long moment passed between them. Callum thought he had said too much.

"You are wrong."

Of all things, this was not what he was expecting to hear. "I am not," he responded, steadily.

Alys shook her head, her gaze also fixed on the fire. "Callum, there is something you must know."

He forced a laugh, rubbing at his tired eyes. "Many things, I am sure."

"Nay." She fixed him once more with her impossibly bright eyes. "One thing of the greatest import." She took a breath. "The man who is working secretly for peace between England and Scotland is Lord Tristan de Neville."

CHAPTER TWENTY-TWO

CALLUM SAT AS still as stone, his meal entirely forgotten. For a long while, the only sound in the little cottage was the crackling of logs in the fire.

Greatly daring, Gil raised his great head and delicately lifted a heel of bread from the table. He chewed quietly, but the thumping of his tail against the floor slowly brought Callum back to his senses.

Tristan is secretly working for peace with Scotland.

Nay, that could not be.

Frida's brother had told him how he had given the order to raze Kielder Castle. Callum's blood pounded in his ears every time he recalled that conversation. And the beating that had gone along with it.

He cleared his throat, not wishing to contradict Alys who had treated him with such kindness, but knowing that he couldn't let her hold such a false belief.

He opened his mouth to speak but she got there before him.

"Do not tell me I am mistaken," she said, eyes gleaming.

Callum was nonplussed. He folded his hands in his lap and looked down upon them.

"'Tis a great secret," she added in a whisper. "I would not have told you had I not faith that you would keep it to yourself."

He shook his head. "I will not repeat it."

For I do not believe it.

Alys nodded, although she looked sad, as if she could see that he was unconvinced. "I will fetch a basin of water for you to wash. I can also clean your tunic, though I have naught for you to wear in its stead but a rug over your shoulders," she smiled impishly.

Callum stood, wincing only a little. "I will fetch the water," he decreed. He would not allow an old woman to fetch and carry for him.

Sometime later, he had splashed warmed water over his face and body, scrubbing dried blood from his neck and hair. In the dim light of the bedchamber, he saw the mottling of purple bruises stretch all about his body and again, and his pulse raced with the instinctive urge to take revenge on the man who had beaten him.

Still, it was a relief to scrub the memory of the cellar from his skin. He felt somewhat more himself, until the moment when Alys took up his tunic with nimble hands.

"There is no need to launder my clothes," he insisted, clad only in his hose. "I am not going before gentry." He intended it as a joke, but Alys was not amused.

"You are Lady Elizabeth's son," she insisted. "I always made sure her clothes were cared for. I cannot allow you to leave my house covered in blood and filth."

And she showed Callum the back of his tunic, which was indeed splattered with a combination of dark mud and red blood.

He inclined his head. "Thank you."

"Come and sit before the fire," she commanded. "You will catch a chill otherwise."

Meek as a child, Callum followed her through to the main room of the cottage and sank down upon the settle as Alys took a stiff brush and set about removing the worst of the stains from his tunic. He felt her eyes upon his body and sensed, rather than saw, her shock at his bruises.

She sat back on her haunches, her work forgotten. "Who did this to you?"

He would not upset her, but nor would he lie. "'Tis better I do not say."

Alys grunted, fetching a faded blanket from the cupboard and handing it to him. "The world would be a better place if more people gave honest answers to honest questions."

Callum shook out the blanket and draped it over his shoulders, grateful for the warmth. The room was not cold, but the chill of the last few days seemed to have settled deep into his bones. He leaned back on the settle, breathing in the smell of woodsmoke from the fire and the scent of fresh bread which still lingered in the air.

"Was it the de Nevilles who beat you?" she demanded. "Did the Earl of Wolvesley discover your feelings for his daughter?"

"Nay." He shook his head. "I have not seen the earl for two winters now."

Alys's eyes narrowed. "It was the de Nevilles. I see it in your eyes. Did Tristan find you together with his sister and take against you?" She pointed the dampened brush towards him and Callum thought that he had regarded the tips of swords with less trepidation.

"Tristan does not know of my feelings for Frida." It hurt to say those names out loud.

"But it was he that did this to you." She nodded sagely, preempting his denial. "God's bones, you must have angered him. Tristan is a man of honour. He does not chase violence."

Her words floored him. They were worlds away from the man who had beaten him so callously, and yet they evoked the young man he had known briefly at Wolvesley in that long-gone yuletide celebration when all things seemed possible.

They also hinted at a personal acquaintance between the old serving maid and the future Earl of Wolvesley. Was it possible her proclamation about Tristan working for peace was more than the misguided mutterings of local gossip?

Callum shifted uncomfortably under his blanket.

"Tristan discovered that I was at Ember Hall under false

pretences."

"Working for the Bruce?" Alys chipped in.

"Aye." He sighed. "With orders to assassinate Tristan himself. But Tristan was not in residence when I arrived," he went on hurriedly, seeing the shock in the older woman's face. "Forsooth, I did not even know the name of the man I was ordered to kill. 'Twas not until we arrived that I learned Ember Hall belonged to the de Nevilles." He looked down at his hands until his rising emotions were more under control. "I once counted Tristan as a friend. And as for his sister, she has held a special place in my heart these last years."

He spoke with frankness and honesty, because nothing else would explain his actions.

"You never raised your sword against him?"

"I could not have brought myself to do so, even if I had the opportunity."

Alys sighed and put down her brush. "'Tis a tangled mess you have woven for yourself. But Tristan allowed you to go free. That means he must have forgiven you."

"Nay. Tristan planned to kill me. His sister set me free." He could not help a tremble in his voice as he recalled Frida's bravery.

Alys put her hands to either side of her face, her eyes wide. "But I am a sworn ally of Tristan de Neville."

Numbly, Callum rose from the settle. He took the blanket from his shoulders and folded it. "Then I shall leave. I would not put you in a difficult position."

"Sit down," she flapped her hand at him. "You are Lady Elizabeth's son. I watched you grow. I will not watch you leave my house with a head wound still vulnerable to infection and naught to cover yourself with."

Awkwardly, Callum did as she asked. He could not, after all, stride out into the day bare-chested. He watched as she finished working on his tunic then laid it before the fire to dry. Hundreds of questions chased around his head and in the end, he could not keep himself from asking one of them.

"How came you to be an ally of Tristan de Neville?" His voice rose with curiosity.

Alys turned to give him a thin-lipped smile. "You mean an old woman like me and a grand knight like him?"

Callum nodded. "Aye."

They both laughed, which helped ease the newly formed tension between them.

"I am not one to gossip." Alys reached out to pat Gil and the hound shifted so he could sit with his head in her lap. "But then, if I am able to mend this rift between you, it may keep one or both of you alive for longer. E'en open the door to a future between you and Frida de Neville."

"I am afraid that is impossible." Callum spoke softly but firmly. "Do not compromise yourself in hope of such a thing."

She fixed him with her all-seeing green gaze. "You truly love her?"

"I do."

"Then you could ne'er wreak harm on her brother. They are a close family."

He pressed his lips together, keeping words and emotions inside. "I did not lay so much as a finger upon him."

"'Tis all because of the position of my cottage." Alys spoke in little more than a whisper. "We are right close to the border, but few people ever find me unless they know where to look. I am away from the road, hidden amongst the trees. You will see for yourself when you leave."

Callum gave a little shake of his head. "I do not understand."

"Tristan himself came to see me more than two summers since. He was dressed in disguise. I thought him a beggar at first." She smiled at the memory. "But Gil trusted him, and that was enough for me. I allowed him inside and gave him a cup of ale. 'Twas then he removed his hood and I saw that thick golden hair of the de Nevilles. He told me he needed somewhere close to the border. A bolthole, he said. Somewhere he could hide, if needed.

He said it would be dangerous and I did not have to help him."

"Then why did you?" Callum's voice was gritty. Despite himself, he could well imagine the conversation. His mind's eye saw Tristan, mayhap sitting on this very settle, charming Alys into following his plan.

"Because there will be no peace for this land until England and Scotland lay down their weapons. If I can do even a little to achieve that, then I will die a contented woman."

Callum frowned. "And you truly believe that Tristan shares this goal?" Tristan himself had admitted to going into Scottish lands as an English warlord, baying for blood.

Yet now he examined that more closely, the picture did not ring true.

Tristan is a man of honour, Alys said.

That sounded more like the kind and upstanding youth which Callum had once known.

"I know it." She leaned closer towards him. "This summer last, Tristan went into Fort Dunkeld itself."

"Fort Dunkeld?" Callum raised his eyebrows, thinking of the mighty Scottish stronghold in the foot of the highlands, kept by the Bruce's kinsmen. "Why would he do that? Surely he would be torn limb from limb."

"Aye." Alys nodded sagely again. "That is what I said. But Tristan knew that some of the family shared his vision of peace. And he thought that if they worked together, they might achieve it."

Callum sat silently, digesting this.

Tristan de Neville, perchance the most well-recognised of all English knights, venturing deep into Scottish territory in a bid for peace.

"Did he take an army with him?"

"Of course not. How would that have worked to build trust? He went alone."

Alone.

"That is brave indeed," he muttered, unable to deny it.

Alys nodded emphatically. "Wait there." She got to her feet

with surprising grace for a woman of her years and disappeared into the bed chamber. Callum heard a scuffing sound, as if something was being dragged along the floor. When Alys reappeared, she held a gleaming sword in one hand and a fearful-looking dagger in the other.

Callum could not help jumping up from the settle in shock. "What are those?"

Alys shrugged. "Proof, for I can see that you doubt my tale." She swung the sword with apparent nonchalance. "Tristan leaves them here. In part for my protection. In part in case he needs them himself. See?" She held the hilt out towards Callum so he could see the emblem of the de Neville family inscribed into the metal.

He nodded, unable to formulate any response.

"Tristan is working for peace with Scotland," she insisted. "He did not order the destruction of your family home. He returned to me just as the leaves were turning and spoke with hope that his mission had been a success."

Callum sank back down, his knees weak. Slowly, Alys's story was beginning to make sense. Tristan de Neville had always been a man of honour. The idea that he had been responsible for the devastation of Kielder Castle had been put in Callum's head by Jonah's throwaway comment that his brother had been in Scotland this summer.

Working for peace, at Fort Dunkeld.

Callum's heart beat hollowly in his chest.

Then why would Tristan have claimed he was present for the siege at Kielder?

He did not, a voice spoke in his head. *He merely did not deny it.*

Callum thought he might be sick. His stomach churned as his mind raced around in endless circles.

Why would his orders have been to assassinate a man who was no threat to the Scots?

As soon as the question slid into his mind, Callum knew the answer. And this, more than anything else, proved to him the truth of Alys's words.

He thought of his father's endless bloodlust—of his father's friends and their deep-seated hatred of the English.

Some Scots do not want peace.

Forsooth, there were those on both sides of the border who would prolong this war indefinitely in the hope it might bring them land or power or glory—or simply the destruction of their hated foes, with little care for if the battle destroyed them as well.

And if Tristan de Neville was seen as a man who might bring an end to the violence, well, then he was a man who must be taken out of the picture.

Callum's blood ran cold as he realised the truth.

He had been ordered to assassinate Tristan precisely *because* he was working for peace between England and Scotland.

He raised stricken eyes to Alys. "I have allowed doubt and hatred into my heart," he intoned. "And it has killed off all hopes for the future."

CHAPTER TWENTY-THREE

Three days later

FRIDA AND TRISTAN had reached an uneasy truce, helped in part by Mirrie, who could not bear tension between two of the people she loved the most in the world. Loathe to cause her more distress, they had once again started to dine together in the evenings and talk with the civility expected of the eldest de Neville siblings.

Another factor in their rapprochement was Frida's quick thinking. She'd realised that, much as her father would be disappointed with her actions, he would be equally aggrieved to learn that his eldest son had linked their family name with the lawless slaughter of innocent women and children. She wrote as much in a scribbled note to Tristan, which she slid under his bedchamber door.

Her brother never openly acknowledged receiving her missive, but nor did he talk further about her returning to Wolvesley.

The snow had melted away entirely now, leaving the lands around Ember Hall to enjoy the last gasp of autumn. Mornings were white with frost but although many leaves had fallen, the woodlands still retained a hint of fiery colour. Frida loved this time of year, but every time she stopped to admire a display of flame-red holly berries, she thought of the men trapped in a dark cellar who could not enjoy it.

It did not take long for her to find a solution.

Jonah was the first to mention it.

"You have arranged for the prisoners to be moved," he commented as they broke their fast before a roaring fire in the great hall. The temperature at night had dropped heavily and the heat of the morning fire had yet to permeate the vast chamber. The two siblings had pulled their chairs as close to the hearth as they could manage, their knees all but knocking together.

Frida kept her response short. "Aye." She spread a cut of bread thickly with home-churned butter.

"Did Tristan give his approval?" His blue eyes watched her closely.

Frida did not look up from her trencher. "He did not need to. Tristan is not in charge here."

"I think he will have an opinion."

"He usually does." Frida raised her eyebrows and they chuckled together conspiratorially.

"I still say, take care, sister." Jonah's hand dropped to her wrist and held it for the smallest moment, whilst Frida all but froze with surprise at the unprompted show of affection. "I would not see you hurt," he added.

"The prisoners will not hurt me," she declared boldly.

But she was extra aware of her every move when she went to see them later. Following the paved path to the bakehouse, she pushed all thoughts of her last journey there out of her mind. She could not hope to converse with anyone if she was forever blinking tears from her eyes.

She missed Callum with a force that was almost painful and her only comfort was that it seemed he had got clean away from Ember Hall.

She nodded to the guard, one of her own men, who shot back the newly added bolts on the thick door and stood aside to let her pass.

Andrew and Arlo did not smell very sweet and both were disguised by a thick growth of beard. Their hair was mattered and their clothes dirty. Frida was concerned that infection may have set into Arlo's wound, even after her days of careful tending, but she could not discern the unhealthy tang of putrefaction amidst the general fug of unwashed bodies.

She stood before them, struggling to control her nerves. The prisoners were not bound and could come at her in a moment, but how would that serve them with an armed guard waiting at the door? Besides, the two men slumped together on the earth floor did not have a look of defiance about them. Their eyes, which previously had sparkled with life, had grown dull and listless.

She cleared her throat. "I asked for you to be moved here for the better light. I am only sorry it did not happen sooner."

Not so much as an expression crossed over their faces.

"You are being offered food and water, are you not?" she asked with sudden concern.

One of them, she thought it must be Andrew for the tinge of red in his dirty hair, nodded once.

"You can speak," she said abruptly. "I know that you kept silent before for fear of giving away your accent. But all of that is in the open now."

Andrew looked for a moment as if he might. Arlo only gazed at the floor.

Frida twisted her hands behind her back. It had been a mistake to come here. She had told herself that she wanted to make sure the prisoners were being afforded their basic dignities, but in reality, she had been driven by a more selfish goal.

Andrew and Arlo are my last link with Callum.

As if thinking his name had triggered a response. Andrew finally spoke up, his voice reedy with lack of use.

"Where is Callum?"

Her eyes opened wide. "You do not know?" At their blank looks, she cursed her stupidity. How could they know? It was unlikely the guards would share any gossip as they brought in their rations. She bit down on her lip, considering the best response. In the end, she settled for the truth. "He has escaped."

This got a reaction. Andrew lifted his head and smiled. Arlo looked as if he might weep with relief.

"You thought him dead?" she guessed.

"We feared the worst, aye," Andrew agreed. She heard immediately the Scottish brogue that the big warrior had masked all this time.

"I do not know what has happened to him since, but he left Ember Hall under his own volition." She turned her gaze to Arlo. "Is your shoulder healed?"

When he nodded mutely, she sighed in frustration.

"Does it pain you still?"

This time there was a pause, followed by a slight shake of his head.

Frida looked to Andrew for support, but the highlander only shrugged. "He talks to me still. You needn't fear the lad has lost his wits."

Frida thought that she should walk over to Arlo and inspect his wound for herself, but something held her back. Something that she was not proud of. Distaste of getting too close to the men who had not washed for many a day was part of it. Fear of provoking a physical attack was another.

She fought an urge to apologise for the rough treatment they had received from the guards and for taking away their liberty. Even now, she was still refusing them the right of fresh air and exercise.

But these men had come to Ember Hall intending her family harm. They had lived and worked here under false pretences. She could not forget that.

She gave her head a little shake. "I am sorry this has happened," she said. It was true enough. She wished it had all turned out differently.

Arlo spoke up, making her start with surprise. "Thank ye for bringing the news that Callum still lives."

She nodded. The emotion in the lad's blue eyes made her say more. "You were close to him? You have known him long?" Again, she cursed her foolishness. Surely they would sense her misguided need to hear more of her lover's past and would choose to ignore her.

But Arlo held her gaze without flinching. His lips trembled with sincerity. "He is like kin. The only kin I have left to me."

Andrew's voice was harsh. "Both Arlo's parents were cut down at the siege of Kielder Castle."

She could not help an instinctive gasp of horror, picturing the scene and Arlo's subsequent heartbreak. "I am sorry for your loss," she muttered, her words ineffective against a past containing so much bloodshed.

Andrew inclined his head. "War is war," he said, cryptically.

Frida nodded, not knowing quite what she was agreeing with. "Callum was your leader?" she suggested, hesitantly.

"On this quest, aye." Andrew looked away from her, as if embarrassed to talk of the planned assassination of her brother, but Frida realised after no more than a second that this was not so. The highlander was thinking only of Callum. "I also think of him as kin." His tone was gravelly now. "I have ridden out alongside him in many a battle. There is no man I would sooner have with me than Callum Baine."

Her heart lifted to hear her lover praised, despite the grim circumstances. She knew she should take her leave, but she could not bring herself to break off the conversation just yet. Mirrie's words, words that she had dismissed out of hand at the time, hovered in the stale air before her eyes.

Who knows what the future may bring?

"You would say he is a man of courage, then?" she ventured. "One that will ne'er give up on once he has set his heart on something?"

There was a long pause, during which she could hear only the pounding of her pulse in her ears. Andrew regarded her steadily, as if fully aware of her secret. 'Twas Arlo who broke the silence.

"Callum is a man who ne'er gives up on anything he wants," he declared, fervently.

Calum will not give up on me.

Frida had vowed to harden her heart to hopes of the future,

but in that moment, her hastily-erected barricades crumbled.

Callum will find a way to come back to me.

Before she could say more, Frida turned and walked briskly away from the prisoners, keeping her composure until she had turned the corner away from the guard. Then she leaned her back against the outer wall of the gatehouse and heaved a deep sigh, releasing her pent-up emotions. She flattened her palms against the stone wall, as if by sheer force of will she might travel back in time to the evening she had last seen Callum.

Not to do anything differently; just so she might gaze upon his face one more time.

She only became aware of Jonah when he cleared his throat and stepped into view.

"I did not mean to startle you," he said, pre-emptively.

"What are you doing here?" Frida put a hand to her heart, feeling it beat beneath the grey wool of her serviceable dress.

Jonah was dressed impeccably in the emerald-green colours of Wolvesley. His hair shone golden in the autumn sunlight. He resembled their older brother more than he would ever see.

"Waiting for you." He leaned forward and took her hand. "Come, we cannot talk here." He nodded sharply towards the bakehouse wall and Frida realised he did not want the prisoners to overhear them.

But Jonah did not lead her to the hall. Instead he took a roundabout path to the sheep barn. 'Twas one of the last places Frida would willingly go, for the painful reminders of that last, carefree day with Callum.

She frowned as they stepped into the hay-scented warmth. The sheep had not yet been returned to the fields, but Frida saw she must give the order for this to happen, else the flock would eat through their winter supplies before yuletide.

"What is it, Jonah?"

He held up his palms in a gesture of surrender. "I am learning to face my flaws, just as I know you have always wished."

Her frown deepened. "I am in no mood for puzzles."

"We all know 'tis my fault that Tristan came here. And therefore everything that took place after that can also be attributed to me." He gestured wildly to indicate Tristan's ferocious beating, Callum's escape and the arguments that had rippled through Ember Hall subsequently. "At the time, I hid away rather than meeting your wrath."

Frida rubbed at her arms, her body taken by a sudden shiver of premonition, despite the shelter of the barn. "Why would you fear my wrath?"

He threw her a smile. "Come now, sister, do not pretend that you are not in love with Callum. I know it. Mirrie knows it. The only person who hasn't realised is Tristan, but that is because our beloved brother is, as ever, consumed only with his own affairs and interests."

She held herself entirely still. "You know." Her heart sank as she realised the consequences.

"I believe it your secret. Your business. My lips are sealed." He grimaced as if unconvinced she would believe him. "You have my word."

Not so long ago, Jonah's word would have meant little to Frida. Now, however, she placed more faith in him. "Thank you." She hugged her arms about herself, wishing she had thought to bring a shawl.

He inclined his head. "I have not brought you here for thanks. I am afraid I have failed you, once again."

She saw she would have to drag this confession out of him. "How so?"

"I saw you go out to the bakehouse. I knew you would talk to the prisoners. I was curious and I followed you."

His clipped tone indicated there was more to come and Frida waited for it with bated breath.

"Tristan saw me leave the hall. He followed me."

Frida's pulse picked up speed. "You overheard us?" Her mind raced as she tried to remember the detail of their conversation.

He nodded, his face grim. "Aye. And a matter we hoped was

settled has now sprung back to life."

"Jonah, will you get to the point?" The words exploded from her.

"Tristan heard the prisoners declare that Callum is not a man to give up. It convinced him that he was right to suspect a retaliation against his person."

Frida shrugged. "What can he do but wait it out or leave?"

Jonah held her gaze, though she could see he would rather look anywhere but at her. "He is ordering that you return to Wolvesley, for your own protection."

FRIDA THOUGHT SHE had better face the situation head on, especially when she saw a troop of Tristan's men rounding up the saddle horses in the paddocks. She watched grimly until her own grey mare was haltered and led into the stables, then she spun on her heel and marched into the hall.

She found Tristan in the solar, standing by the mullioned window with his arms crossed over his chest. He had aged since he came to Ember Hall, his brow creased with worry and his blue gaze piercing rather than laughing as it used to be.

The events of the last days laid heavily upon him, and despite her grievances, she was sorry for it.

"Brother."

He nodded with no trace of a smile.

"You can stand your men down and release the horses. I will not return to Wolvesley."

He turned back to face the window, his shoulders set. "It is not safe for you here. The Scot will come looking for vengeance."

Frida took a deep, steadying breath. "Callum may return, aye. But not for the reason you think."

Still he did not move.

For the second time that morn, Frida had recourse only to the truth.

"He poses no danger to me. Nor to you, once he discovers you played no part in the siege of Kielder Castle." She stepped closer to Tristan, joining his vigil at the window. The courtyard was a hive of activity, with almost all of Tristan's soldiers engaged in readying horses for imminent departure. It was a far cry from the usual peace of Ember Hall. She glanced up to see his gaze fixed on the distant horizon. "Are you listening to me at all?"

For a dreadful moment she thought he would not answer.

"It is no surprise to me that you do not want to leave. I know how you love this place."

Her eyes filled with tears. "'Tis not only Ember Hall that I love."

This time she saw a flicker of confusion in his face. It was the prompt she needed to summon all her courage and continue. "I love Callum. And he loves me." She blinked away her tears. "That's why he'll return—and how I know he will never hurt me."

She had hoped for a smile or a softening of his expression, not the thin-lipped sneer she now received.

"Frida, I had thought you were wiser than this." His eye bore into hers. "Did the Scot seduce you?"

"'Twas not like that," she protested hotly. "I have loved Callum since he first came to Wolvesley." She lifted her chin to show she was not ashamed. "And as soon as he arrived here, I knew I loved him still."

Tristan gave a little shake of his head. A pulse flickered at his neck. "You think he loves you in return?"

"I know it."

"And I know that a man's love for his country will always come first."

"You are wrong." She rounded on him. "You speak as a man who has never been in love."

Her blow landed. She saw the minute changes in Tristan's expression as he considered the truth of her words.

Tristan dragged a hand through his hair. "Is that why you set him free?"

She nodded.

"I wish I had known that. It would have saved me a lot of grief."

At once, he was her brother and ally once again and her eyes filled with tears for a different reason.

"I should have told you."

He pursed his lips. "I understand why you did not. I was filled with rage. Rage at myself more than anyone, as I was responsible for bringing Callum into all our lives."

She put a hand on his shoulder and was relieved when he did not flinch away. "I know that you were trying to protect me."

He embraced her—the first real show of affection they had exchanged since Frida and Mirrie's departure from Wolvesley Castle. Frida rested her head on her brother's broad shoulder and thought that she should have been honest with him from the start.

We should all have been honest from the start.

He cleared his throat. "I am glad we are friends again. I have missed you."

"I have found peace and comfort in your absence," she replied airily.

He gave a snort of laughter and put his hands on her shoulders. Looking up at him, she was reminded how close he had become in height and bearing to their father.

Tristan's face twisted with regret. "I'm sorry, Frida. But this changes naught."

She felt as if he had reached into her chest and stopped her heart from beating. "How so?"

"Callum is a trained knight, a warrior. I know how his mind works. How his blood will burn to take revenge for the beating I gave him."

"Nay," she began, but he silenced her with a look.

"He will return with weapons and men, looking to retaliate.

Any love he feels for you will make his emotions run even stronger."

She tried to swallow but found her throat had gone dry. "You cannot order me from my own home."

He gripped her shoulders. "For your own safety, I must. You have to leave Ember Hall, today."

CHAPTER TWENTY-FOUR

ALYS HAD MADE it clear that she did not want him to do this. She had even gone so far as to beg him to reconsider. But Callum was adamant. Once he had set his mind upon something, nothing would dissuade him from the path.

With a sad shake of her head, Alys commented that he had been that way since childhood. More pointedly, she added that it was mayhap the only way in which he resembled his father. 'Twas a comment that gave Callum pause, but by then he had already secured the loan of a horse from the new tenants of Egremont House. His plan was set in motion.

The horse was dapple grey and had a long stride that ate up the miles between Alys's humble cottage and the mighty walls of Ember Hall. Before the weakening sun had started its afternoon descent, Callum found himself trotting up the path that led to the great outer gates. His heart quickened as he saw the guards gesticulating in his direction. He slowed the horse to a walk when one of them ran at full pelt down the narrow stone steps in the direction of the house.

Gone, no doubt, to summon his master.

So be it, thought Callum. The sooner the better to face the inevitable showdown.

The horse flicked his ears backwards, as if picking up on his unease. Callum reached down to pat his neck, speaking calm words of reassurance.

Words that he did not entirely believe.

He expected to meet with resistance at the gatehouse, re-membering how first Mirrie and then Frida had come out to meet him last time. But the guards swung open the gate and stood back to let him through without a murmur of dissent.

Callum would almost have preferred a confrontation. His heart hammered beneath the cloak of rough-spun wool that Alys had somehow procured for him and his horse skittered sideways, scattering chickens. As soon as they turned the corner to the courtyard, Callum got his wish.

Here was his opposition.

An impenetrable line of twenty armed men faced him, swords drawn. At the centre, standing slightly ahead of his army, stood Tristan.

Callum had ne'er been more aware of the differences be-tween them. Tristan's plate armour gleamed in the pale sunlight. His horse was one of the finest and largest in the land. Opposite him, Callum felt as ill-equipped for conflict as a farmer sat astride a plough horse. He would have pulled the animal to a halt, but the horse had ground to a stop anyway, snorting gently in growing distress.

He dropped the reins and held up both his bare palms. "I am unarmed."

Tristan gave a little shake of his head, as if this fact was of little consequence. "Turn around, Callum, and go back to where you came from."

Callum held his horse still with his calves. "I cannot. Not until I have said what I came to say." He scanned the courtyard, desperate for a glimpse of Frida.

"And I cannot grant you safe passage through de Neville property."

This was a standoff that could continue for some time, and Callum did not have the appetite for it. He swung one leg over his horse's hindquarters and dropped to the ground, his swift actions causing a couple of Tristan's soldiers to break ranks and step towards him, ready to strike. Tristan held them back with his arm half-outstretched.

Callum sank to his knees, right there on the damp earth, and bowed his head.

"I cast myself on your mercy. You can do with me what you will. I ask only two things in return." His heart pounded, knowing that he had placed himself in a position of extreme vulnerability. If Tristan came at him now, he would have no way to defend himself. He was relying entirely on the future earl's integrity.

Integrity which days earlier, Callum would have disputed the existence of.

The polished black boots, which he recalled striding towards him as he laid on the floor of the great hall, did not move.

"I will not show mercy to an enemy of my family," Tristan gritted out.

"That is your choice." Long seconds passed and Callum's hopes began to wane. There was no point in saying he was a long-admirer of the de Nevilles, nor that he would willingly lay down his life for Frida. Tristan would always see him as the man hired to assassinate him.

Tristan's command, when it finally came, was loud and clear. "Stand down."

Callum felt weak with relief as he heard the guards shuffling backwards and marching away. Now just one pair of boots stood before him.

"And you, stand up. I will not speak to a man prostrate on the ground before me."

Callum stood up, unsteadily. His body was healing, but his ease of movement had not yet returned.

"Thank you, Tristan," he said, with feeling.

"Do not presume to thank me." Tristan's face was white with anger. "Or to address me as if we are friends. You have seconds to tell me why you are here."

"I am here to apologise."

He knew a thrill of gratification when Tristan's jaw dropped.

But England's most renowned knight recovered quickly.

"You said you wanted two things from me. What are they?"

Callum longed to put a hand out to steady himself, but the only thing to lean on was his horse, who was so on edge he might well shy away from him.

"I ask that you release my men," he said, breathing hard.

"Impossible."

"And I ask that you convey a message to Frida." He swallowed down the swell of emotion caused by the feel of her name on his lips. "Unless, of course, you will allow me to speak to her myself."

Tristan laughed. "It is miracle enough that I allow you to stand here and speak to *me.*"

"I know it," Callum agreed, equably.

Tristan put his hands on his hips. "What is the message?"

"The same as I give to you. An apology."

Tristan breathed out heavily. "Your apology is worth nothing."

"I sincerely hope that is not the case." Callum straightened his shoulders, aware of the crucial importance of getting this right. "My apology is worth my life. I come before you unarmed, knowing you might well strike me down. But I was in the wrong, staying here, accepting hospitality, e'en pledging my troth to your sister." He noted Tristan's expression of surprise. "And when a man is in the wrong, he should confess it." Tristan looked as if he might interrupt, but Callum spoke on before he could do so. "There is no hope for peace in this land, if no man can admit when he is at fault."

Tristan's blue eyes widened. For a moment, they looked just like Frida's eyes. He lowered his sword and rested the tip on the ground, clasping his hands around the hilt.

"'No hope for peace in this land, if no man can admit when he is at fault,'" he repeated. "Do you truly believe that?"

"Aye." Callum nodded. "And peace is what I desire most of all."

"Peace between England and Scotland?"

Callum nodded once more.

Tristan sharpened his gaze. "Despite what happened to your ancestral home?"

"Revenge has to stop somewhere, else there will be naught left for any man to defend."

A smile flickered across Tristan's face, there and gone in an instant. But even when it had fled, there was a new warmth left behind. "I hear my own beliefs echoed here."

Callum nodded. "I know you were not responsible for the attack on Kielder Castle."

"I should ne'er have allowed you to believe I might have been."

The two men gazed levelly at one another. Greatly daring, Callum held out his hand. After no more than a moment's pause, Tristan grasped it.

"You have your wish, Callum. I forgive you. And I will release your men."

Relief made a smile stretch across his face. "Are they in good health?"

"Aye, they are well enough, as I understand it."

"And Frida?" Callum held his breath.

Tristan's gaze grew wary. "She is also in good health."

"Nay." Callum made an impatient gesture. "I mean, may I see her?"

Do I need Tristan's permission, he wondered.

Perchance not. But minutes earlier, Callum had feared Tristan might run him through with his sword. And if he was e'er to be his brother by marriage, Callum should not test his friendship so soon.

Tristan folded his arms, his face regretful. "Frida is not here."

Of all the words he could have said, Callum was not expecting that. "Not here," he echoed, stupidly.

"She returned to Wolvesley just this morn." Tristan grimaced. "But I will see that your message is conveyed to her."

Callum felt as if he might sink to the ground with disappointment. He had hardly dared hope that Tristan would accept his apology. Nor that he would allow his men to go free. That both of those things had been granted had bolstered his confidence that he might, this very day, gaze upon the face of the woman he loved.

"Mayhap I can go after her." He looked doubtfully at the dapple-grey horse. Would he carry him all the way to Wolvesley?

Would I e'en be welcomed there?

'Twas one thing to arrive unannounced at a small country manor, like Ember Hall. Quite another to attempt entry at one of England's mightiest fortresses. Especially when the earl may have been warned of Callum's treachery.

He forced such negativity from his mind. He must do whatever it took to reach Frida and hold her in his arms.

Tristan appeared to be looking at something over his shoulder, as if too embarrassed to meet his gaze. "'Tis a long ride to Wolvesley," he intoned. "And your man, Arlo, is not strong enough for it yet. But I will ask the kitchen to make provisions for your journey back across the border."

With that, Tristan de Neville strode away, leaving Callum alone in the courtyard.

He had achieved so much and also so little. He wanted to both punch the air with joy for the freedom of his friends, and also to growl with frustration. Giving in to a surge of weariness, he rested his arm on the horse's withers and leaned his head onto his palm. Another journey awaited him. Another long negotiation. Mayhap several.

Whatever it takes. He did not hear the light footsteps coming across the courtyard, nor see Frida's smiling face until it was inches from his.

"I am not at Wolvesley," she said, pressing her arms about him.

Callum's surprise rendered him momentarily speechless. He inhaled her lavender scent. "You are not a figment of my imagination?" He leaned back a little to take her in. Her blue eyes. Her emerald green gown. Her slender fingers, pale against the dark grey of his borrowed cloak.

"Nay, I am real enough."

"I got here in time," he said wonderingly, running a hand through her silvery waterfall of hair. "And your brother has forgiven me."

She put her head to one side, smiling impishly. "I heard also that you have forgiven my brother."

He gave a great, shuddering sigh of relief. "You were listening all the while?"

She nodded.

"But Tristan said…" He broke off, spinning around to see if Tristan could still be seen.

"I know what Tristan said." She tossed back her hair with a smile. "'Twas one of the first times in my life that my brother stood back and allowed me to make my own choices."

"He knew you were there?" Callum's heart was filling with joy.

"All the time."

"And he knows about us," he pressed, wanting to be sure.

Frida's lips curved into a smile. "I told him the truth about my feelings for you earlier today."

Callum grasped her hands, hardly daring to believe it. "We have his blessing?"

She moved into the circle of his arms. "I don't know about that, but he shook your hand, did he not?"

Callum opened his mouth to say more, but Frida put her fingers to his lips. "Allow me to ask a question."

"Anything." He held her tightly and thought he might never let her go.

"Can we stop talking about my brother?" she breathed. "And better yet, can you kiss me, please?"

CHAPTER TWENTY-FIVE

Four years later...

THE MOMENTS JUST before dawn always had a certain magic for Frida. A stillness, as if the world was holding its breath; a promise of renewal, a gift of hope.

The light was milky, making only the smallest impact on the darkness of the night. She could see enough to make out the faint path they were following up the grassy hill, Callum beside her. When he smiled down at her, she could see his white teeth gleaming.

"Nearly there," he said, holding out his hand so they could walk side-by-side along this final section. She entwined her fingers with his, relishing his warmth.

The tang of sea salt filled the fresh morning air, along with the rhythmic sound of waves crashing onto the small pebble beach far below them. To their left, this year's lambs began bleating for attention just as the first piping notes of the black-bird's song trilled from the trees.

Frida stopped. Not because the climb exhausted her, but because she wanted to take it all in. She sighed as the pinkish rays of sunrise appeared on the horizon.

"So beautiful."

Callum frowned. "Aren't we too late?"

Her husband had made the transition from warrior to gentleman farmer with ease. But even after four calm and contented years at Ember Hall, he had not yet shaken off his warrior's sense of urgency.

"The sun is not in a rush," she said with a smile.

They rounded the corner at the perfect moment to see the standing stones bathed in rosy light.

Nay, not "bathed." Rather, they blazed with the glory of the rising sun, as if Mother Nature had arranged the spectacle just for them. Light shimmered and danced on the horizon in celebration of this midsummer's day. Callum squeezed her hand, and she knew that he was equally awe-struck.

"So beautiful," he confirmed, dipping his head and pressing his lips to her forehead. "Almost as beautiful as you, dear wife."

Laughing, she pushed him away. "I have already borne you two children. You have no need to shower me with compliments."

He put his hands on his hips, unfazed. "I speak the truth as I see it."

"Aye. You always do." She took his arm and they walked closer to the circle of large, upright stones. She was flooded with gratitude, both for the beauty all around them and the news which had reached Ember Hall just yesterday. "Peace." She sank down onto the first, flattish stone and tilted her chin so her face was warmed by morning light. "Who would have thought it?"

He sat down beside her, curving his arm around her slender shoulders. Frida nestled closer, glad of his warmth and the comfort of his nearness.

"I, for one, have always dreamed of peace. Your brother, Tristan, for another." Callum gazed out at the horizon, unaware how the rosy dawn haloed him with light. Constant work in the fields had honed his warrior's physique even further and the muscles in his shoulders rippled beneath his tunic. Long days in the sun had brought golden highlights to his shock of dark hair, and the contented tumble of family life had chased away the lines of worry previously etched around his brown eyes.

"Aside from the two of you, I mean." She nudged him, laughing a little. "Not that I doubt the combined power of my husband and brother to bring the world to rights."

"I am glad to hear it." His stubbled chin nuzzled against her cheek. "But do not forget Alys. She risked everything to secure peace. Indeed, when she stayed with us last yuletide, I believe she prophesised this day would come."

Frida smiled at the memory. Alys had surprised them all with her appetite for feasting and celebration, delighting in the company of young children and regaling them with tales of Callum's boyhood antics. One evening, she had taken hold of Frida's hands and proclaimed that peace would be achieved before the next harvest.

"Indeed she did." Frida bit down on her lip, thoughtfully. "But I dare say not even Alys could have foreseen this particular outcome."

The message, inscribed by her father and carried north from Wolvesley by a pink-cheeked messenger-boy, had been brief. The earl's words had been few, but his relief had been evident in the flamboyant swirls of his elegantly-formed letters. England had renounced its age-old claim on Scotland on the coat-tails of an unanticipated military defeat which all but saw the young King Edward III captured.

It was not an outcome that anyone could have foreseen. But it was one which had filled their hearts with hope. Now, at last, they could sleep easily in their beds. Peace, finally, seemed within their grasp.

"We should send word to Alys," Frida thought aloud.

Callum smiled down at her. "I have already dispatched a messenger, though I have no doubt that Alys already knows. Most likely she will send some new information back to us."

"You are right." She reached to take her husband's hand. There was one issue, closer to home, which troubled her still. "Might you return to Kielder Castle now, to visit with your father?"

Callum's ancestral home had been slowly, painstakingly rebuilt over the years, but Frida had never met Rory Baine, the famed warlord of the highlands; her father-in-law. And though she knew that relations between father and son were strained, she could not imagine living her days as Callum did, without the warmth and blessing of her kin. When Callum wrote to tell him of their wedding, Rory's reply had been brief.

Your mother would have been proud.

The glare of the sun meant that she could not properly read his expression, but she felt him tense. "I do not think my father will welcome the peace."

"But he is still your father. Your family."

"My only kinsman," he finished for her.

She heard the catch in his voice and her heart squeezed in sympathy. At least both Andrew and Arlo had been present at their wedding, waiting until after the ceremony to journey back to the highlands. Since then, Andrew had written often, sharing more news of Kielder Castle than Callum ever received from the laird.

"Aye. Whilst you are surrounded by my kinsmen from dawn till dusk." She leaned her head on his shoulder, wanting to dispel the note of gloom. "We must flee the hall afore sunrise if we are to know a moment of peace."

He laughed quietly. "You know how I love being a part of your family. And I enjoy their frequent visits."

"Even Esme?" She raised her eyebrows in mock consternations. Frida's youngest sister had caused much excitement in the nursery last night, when she took it upon herself to teach her niece and nephew the makings of a new, raucous ballad she had learned at Wolvesley. After enduring hours of hand-clapping and whooping, Frida eventually intervened and carried her exhausted offspring to bed.

"She's a delight." Callum winked. "When is she leaving?"

Frida raised her palms to the sky. "When is *Jonah* leaving is more the question. All these years and he still hasn't learned how to wield a hoe."

"I take pleasure in his company," Callum told her, diplomatically. "We are a contented group, are we not?"

"We are, all except Mirrie." Frida sighed, smoothing back her hair which had been tousled by the breeze. "I fear that while I have found my happiness, she is still searching for her own."

Callum looked surprised. "She is always quick with a smile or a laugh. I did not guess she was unhappy."

Frida shrugged. "We came here, Mirrie and I, to lead a life free of men. I have rather reneged on the deal."

"Would you like me to leave?"

His sombre expression made her chuckle. "Nay, 'tis too late for that. I only wish Mirrie might know the same happiness that we share."

"Mayhap in the coming months, her luck might change." Callum looked about him with a smile playing across his full lips. "'Tis near enough four years since I last saw the sun rise around these stones, on the morn I fled from Ember Hall. I was half starved, bruised head to toe, and your brother was determined to kill me." He shook his head in wonderment. "I ne'er thought to see the day England would back away from Scotland. Nor did I dare to dream that I might marry Lady Frida de Neville."

He reached towards her and she leaned into his caress, taking comfort from the touch of his familiar, work-roughened hands. "You are saying that all things are possible?"

"If you follow your heart," he whispered.

She snuggled closer, so close she could hear the steady thumping of Callum's heart. With his arms around her, she was whole.

Frida stilled for a moment, allowing the realisation to ripple through her. She had once thought she would never be whole again, that the loss of her Sight meant the severing of her connection to the natural world, that she would be lost and alone for the rest of her days. But since she learned to unbarricade her heart, everything had changed. Day by day, her senses were attuning themselves to the spiritual more and more so that once again she felt part of the rich fabric of being—a tapestry which reached back into the past and forward into the future.

Now she knew that Callum spoke the truth.

Love had power beyond aught else. And all things were possible, if you followed your heart.

THE END

About the Author

Elizabeth grew up in a rambling old farmhouse high on the Yorkshire moors, where a sense of history was never far away. She studied English at university, specialising in mythology and folklore and often bemoaning the lack of sword-wielding heroines. After graduating, she spent several years moving between northern France, southern Germany and London, where she worked in travel publishing and PR.

She now lives a stone's throw from her childhood home, with her husband, children and a feisty black cat who enjoys interrupting her writing. She plots most of her novels while walking in the rugged Yorkshire countryside, finding endless inspiration in the rolling hills.